SHROUDED INSANITY

SHROUDED INSANITY

Jamian Snow

A BARTON BOOK

This is a work of fiction. The characters and events described in this book are imaginary and resemblance to actual persons living or dead is purely coincidental.

Correspondence to Author:
📖 Barton Press
P.O. Box 3201
Erie, PA 16508
jamian1@hotmail.com

Printed in the United States of America
10 9 8 7 6 5 4 3 2 1

Library of Congress Cataloging-in-Publication Data

Snow, Jamian
Shrouded Insanity / Jamian Snow
p.   cm.
ISBN 0-9742981-0-7 (Limited Edition)
I. Title

Book design by Ken LeClair

For Ed and Maria

My sincerest thanks to my wife, Michelle, my assistant, Seth, my children, Stephanie, Christopher, and Nicholas, and my friend, Lucille for their continued support and patience during this long, arduous journey through the Gordian maze of research and creation.

"God doesn't sleep, He only rests his eyes."
Katherine T. Mann

CHAPTER I

His head was a time-bomb, ticking, ready to explode at any moment. Between the high-pitched laughter and thunderous footsteps, which slammed the broken pavement, the cacophony ricocheted against the sides of his brain with a force greater than any previous episode. Pain wrenched his temples. This time, it appeared he would lose his battle to the teeming mass of pedestrians.

Overwhelmed with nausea, he pushed his way through the overcrowded marketplace, rushed up to a makeshift kiosk, and grabbed the wooden post, combating the chronic urge to heave. "No!" he cried aloud. "I won't allow this to happen!" Standing perfectly still, he drew in a deep breath and waited, praying that the mingled stenches of meat and fish, which poisoned the unseasonably warm June air, would diminish. But as fate would

1

have it, the odors lingered.

After a bout with unabridged anxiety, his prayer was answered. His pulse leveled off and his body calmed. For now the worst was over. He'd survived another attack and could finally face his objective. He breathed a sigh of relief, pulled a handkerchief from his pocket, dabbed beads of sweat from his brow, and turned to the vendor.

"You all right?" the toothless merchant asked. "You're pale as a ghost. You ain't sick or nothing, are you?"

"N-n-no," he said, searching his mind for a reasonable explanation for his odd behavior. "I'll be fine. It's that dreadful odor. It's enough to sicken anyone. Doesn't it bother you?"

"Nah," the merchant said. "I'm used to it." Without warning, he made a vulgar nasal sound, spit a clump of yellow phlegm to the ground, and wiped his mouth with his soiled shirtsleeve. "I can't afford to get sick or nothing. Selling is my business. I don't need no diseased person coming around here, spreading no germs."

"Yes, I can see that."

"Okay then, what can I get for you?"

He placed his order, leaned over the rickety counter, and watched with distaste as the impoverished man bagged his food. It appalled him to be in the company of another derelict, but realized he had no other choice. He knew, with God's guidance, things would eventually change. It would just take a little more time.

With the thought as a mild consolation, he faced the sky and uttered another private prayer.

"Anything else?" the merchant grumbled under his breath, placing the brown bag down with a thud. "I don't have all day, you know. If you want to stargaze, do it on your own time."

"No," he said with a stern glare. "That will be all."

"Okay then, you owes me twelve dollars."

Without disputing the price, he placed the money onto the counter, turned, and once again forced his way back through the hostile congestion. On reaching the safety of the familiar stone path, his chains of torment were instantly broken and a renewed sense of confidence replaced the uneasiness. It felt good to be in control. With a renewed sense of wellbeing, he strolled through the majestic pines until he reached a clearing. He stopped and faced the snow-capped, Canadian Rockies.

"Damn them," he said, shaking his fist in midair, reliving his previous fight for breathing space in the marketplace. "Damn them all to hell!"

Filled with negative emotion, his face turned red-hot. His temperature spiked; and his body trembled from head to toe. Rather than risk another war with nerves, he thought it best to rest. He lay beneath a skyscraping spruce, gazed up through the canopy of branches, and watched the marshmallow clouds float by until eventually sleep took a firm hold. Once locked deep within himself, he revisited the dream, which has plagued him since childhood.

A small boy cowers in a broom closet, crying while peeking through a slit in a chained door. His vision is blurred. The sickening scent of jasmine permeates the air. He hears the other's wail from an unseen room and immediately realizes he is not alone. God is also present. His heart beats wildly. He stares as God holds a crucifix up to heaven while chastising a woman who sits on a tattered, blue chaise.

"I expel you, Satan!" God screams. "For I am the vessel, the hand of justice. Release this woman and be gone!" God wields the cross like a dagger, striking her hard, releasing her evil. "Return to hell!"

The woman lets out a blood curdling scream and shields her face from the crucifix, which is covered in red.

"I punish you, woman, in the name of Daniel!" God shrieks above the distant thunder. "Do you repent for your sins of the flesh? For your copulation with the beast? For your evil offspring?"

Amidst the constant flashes of light, the woman moans, but does not respond.

"Do you repent?" God screams again.

As if the dark of night governed the setting, an unsettling umbra screens her face and her body falls limp. God drops the cross to the wood-planked floor and a tremendous clang echoes throughout. He then picks up a worn Bible, unchains the door, and drags the boy to the woman's feet.

"Feast your eyes on the whore, boy," God demands. "Witness what happens to the wicked and those who turn their backs on the church."

Through tear-filled eyes, the boy witnesses the woman's body slumped over the arm of the chair, bathed in red from head to chest.

"I won't be wicked, Father!" the boy cries aloud, his voice faltering amidst the constant cracks of thunder. "I promise."

"Good," God says, gently patting the boy's head. "You make me proud. But remember, son, you must always punish the sinners and only through a proper cleansing can the prophecy be fulfilled. For you are the chosen one!"

Without warning, God calls to Heaven and some rat-like minions appear. They claw the floor as they approach and emit a vile stench. After sounding a series of high-pitched screeches, they huddle close and wait for the order to pounce.

"Do not fear them," God tells the trembling boy. "For they only consume the wicked. Watch closely as they devour the earthly shell in search of her wretched soul."

Suddenly, out of the shadows, a beautiful angel appears. She's adorned in gold and white satin. Her skin is milky-white and her features are those of perfection. She weeps aloud and extends a shiny golden staff to the ceiling.

"Thou hast forsaken the one true Lord," she cries.

Instantly, she leans forward and expels a stream of fire from her fingertips, though nothing in the room burns. "Be penitent!"

"Be gone!" God bellows and faces her with a vengeful stare. "Be gone, soulless handmaiden!" He then raises His arms high above His head and screams, "For thou art the angel of the undead! Return from whence you came and allow the cleansing to continue!"

"Daniel," the angel declares high above God's cries. "Your final warning has come! Know that your demise is close at hand and your name shall be stricken from *The Book of Life*. In the end, the one true God shall triumph." On repeating her sermon for a second time, she floats up and vanishes into a thick blue mist, leaving the stench of sulfur in her wake.

God ignores her swift departure and returns his attention to the lifeless woman. In blood, He draws the sign of the cross on her forehead and steps back. "Carry on with the feast," He screams to his minions. "For the time is nigh."

The boy remains quiet until the woman's body is reduced to bone.

"Come, son," God says warmly, facing the boy with a satisfied expression. "Let us rejoice in the good words of the Bible."

Before the boy could respond, the dream ends.

Groggy, disoriented, and wet with perspiration, he flexed his arms until the tingles stopped. He could tell by the angle of the shadows that it was already mid-afternoon. The discovery alarmed him. He jumped to his feet, brushed the pine needles from his clothing, and picked up his groceries. Now, his only concern was to return to his hike. With the sun high overhead, he resumed his pace through the woods asking God for guidance and an end to his recurring nightmare.

Suddenly, an eerie breeze crept out of the dense woods, chilling his moist and sticky skin. A guttural whisper followed. Though the voice was barely audible, he recognized it. His spine tingled with excitement as he awaited the task, which he knew would be asked of him, but soon realized he was wrong. No orders came. Disappointed, he trekked on until the sounds returned. "Was it God again? Would His return enlighten me with great wisdom?" With growing anticipation, he fine-tuned his ears and looked from side to side, but saw nothing out of the ordinary.

"Who's there?" he called out, expecting an instant response. "I asked, who's there?"

He waited at least five minutes before calling again. This time, his voice faltered along with his determination. Disturbed by the strange, unseen presence, he cautiously continued down the unpaved, single-lane path. The sensation that someone or something was out there was great, but it wasn't God. Armed with only bare fists, he readied himself to battle the unknown. Just as he turned a sharp bend in the trail, a small brown pup darted out from beneath the thick underbrush, almost causing his heart to

7

stop.

"Well now," he said with a sigh as he picked up the meager animal. "Where did you come from?"

Before he could regain his composure, a child's voice called out. "Bijou! Here, Bijou. Where are you hiding? Come back here this instant, you naughty dog!"

As if on command, the pup wriggled furiously. It arched its back, growled, and bore its tiny, sharp teeth into his flesh. Crimson blood spewed to the ground.

"You little bastard!" he cried, his anger swelling red, like the blood that dripped from his arm. "You'll pay for this!"

Once again, the uncontrollable urge intensified. It festered in his mind and traveled swiftly through his veins until it reached his extremities. Prompted by the need to appease his escalated anxiety, he tightened his broad hands around the pup's scrawny neck and wrung it until it snapped. With building anticipation, he expeditiously discarded the broken creature into some nearby brush and awaited Bijou's young master.

CHAPTER 2

For generations, Saint Michael's Monastery sat at the foothills of the Canadian Rockies, just far enough away from Grande Cache, Alberta, to discourage much social influence. The hundred-acre, gated estate housed only two buildings, the chapel and residence. They were connected by a grand, hand-laid, cobblestone courtyard with a life-size, stone statue of Christ in its center.

Normally, life for the monastic community was simple. It involved prayer, meditation, and the administration of the sacraments to the nearby parish of Saint Bartholomew. However, due to a recent fire at Saint Bart's Church and the health hazard the metal scaffolding created, the brethren felt obligated to temporarily open their gates for Sunday services. Monsignor Valois, overseer of the brethren, believed the initial inconvenience was a small price to pay for the tidings that the church would reap in the end. But today was Saturday and most thoughts were on the delightful weather not income.

After surviving another interminable, harsh winter, it was no surprise that the brethren took pleasure in the splendor of the day. While some clergy enjoyed private meditation, others conversed in whispers, yet most of them strolled the grounds nodding to one another as they passed, resembling Japanese women in an Oriental garden. Overall, they were content with the serenity of their surroundings, which they perceived to be one of God's greatest gifts to them.

Although most of the priests were over fifty, gray, and balding, one of them, Father André Jeneau, didn't fit the general description. He was in his mid-thirties and had a full head of ebony hair. His chest was broad, his arms, thick and muscular. If not for his long, black cassock, he could have easily been mistaken for a weight lifter.

It was thought by most that he preferred exercise to prayer and today was no exception. Though he had begun his grueling cardiovascular workout later than usual, he felt especially pleased with the results. His abs tingled and his washboard stomach glistened, wet with perspiration. Brimming with pride over the temple he had created, he grabbed his towel from the lowest branch of an immense maple tree and threw it around his neck to absorb most of the moisture. At the same time, he noticed Father Xavier Fontaine ramble into the courtyard toting a large, brown, paper bag. He was weaving precariously from side to side in a zombie-like fashion.

"Do you need any help?" Father André asked, wiping the dampness from his forehead. "Is something wrong?"

Father Xavier meandered by, muttering incoherently under his breath. Droplets of sweat trickled down the sides of his face and a milky substance glazed his eyes. He appeared to be in one of his fixed states of agitation.

Father André took no offense at Father Xavier's lack of attention. It was becoming quite common. Though disturbing, he knew his gesture of good will was a waste of breath and would probably go unrecognized. During his short time at the monastery, he'd come to realize Xavier had mental problems and was most likely due for another dose of his daily medication.

Out of curiosity more than concern, he followed Father Xavier into the kitchen and was astounded to discover him lying on the floor, face down in a small puddle of blood. A leg of lamb lay by his side. Instantaneously, his head pounded and his lunch rose to his throat.

"What in heaven's name happened?" a voice called from behind.

Caught off guard, he spun around to see an older priest standing in the doorway. He had a large frame and his face was

11

pudgy. He was clutching a bible and rosary.

"Oh, Father Beaumont," Father André said, wiping bile from his chin. "It's Father Xavier. He's taken another fall."

"Oh, my heavens!" Father Beaumont said, shielding his eyes with his bible. "Is he all right? Is he dead? I can't bear to look."

"I don't think so," Father André said, slowly backing away from the scene. "But there's so much blood. Go, quick, find the monsignor. He'll know what to do."

"Yes! Right away."

Within minutes, Father Beaumont returned to the kitchen, Monsignor Valois on his heels. Everything appeared to be the same, but something felt different. He quickly scanned the room and realized Father André was nowhere to be found. He returned his attention to the matter at hand, Father Xavier.

"He's lying over there, Monsignor," he said, shielding his eyes once again. "What do you think? Will he be okay?"

"Good gracious!" Monsignor Valois said, kneeling by Father Xavier. "What do we have here?" He paused a moment to examine the wound. "He'll be fine. It doesn't appear to be very deep." He proceeded to wipe the blood from Father Xavier's face with a damp dishcloth and added, "It's only a surface wound." He then stood and searched the room. "He must have whacked his head on the edge of the counter while having another one of his attacks."

"You must be correct, Monsignor," Father Beaumont said nervously, placing the raw meat into the sink. "But Father André would know for sure."

"Where is Father André?" Monsignor Valois asked. "I thought you said he was here tending to Father Xavier's needs."

"H-h-he was," Father Beaumont replied. "I don't understand it. Maybe the excitement was too much for him. Remember how he reacted last week when I cut my hand with the carving knife? I thought he was going to drop dead at the sight of my blood. He's probably up in his chamber heaving as we speak."

"Father, must you be so graphic?"

"Sorry about that, Monsignor."

"In any case, take Father Xavier to his room and clean him up. I'll check in on him later. He's had these spells on more than one occasion since his arrival, and rest always seems to be the best remedy."

"Yes, Monsignor," Father Beaumont replied, relieved that he would not have to endure a lecture on appropriate monastic language. "However, I'll require the assistance of Father Pierre. Father Xavier looks awfully heavy and I don't believe I can manage him alone."

"You're probably right. I believe Father Pierre is in the courtyard. Hurry to get him."

"Yes, Monsignor," Father Beaumont said. "I'll be back in a flash." He gave a cordial nod and scurried from the room.

By the time the old grandfather clock had chimed the half hour, the task was carried out and both priests returned to the kitchen. Father Beaumont's face was red and it was obvious he was out of breath. Father Pierre, on the other hand, was fine.

"Did either of you see what happened to Father Xavier?" Monsignor Valois asked, adjusting his oval, wire-framed glasses.

"No," Father Beaumont replied hastily. "But I'm certain Father André has the answers."

"Yes, yes," Monsignor Valois said. "You did mention that Father André had witnessed the unfortunate incident. Amidst the confusion, I'd almost forgotten. I'll definitely have to speak with him later on." He turned his attention to the other priest and asked, "Father Pierre, did you notice anything strange about Father Xavier when he returned from town?"

"No," Father Pierre explained. "I was nowhere near the gate when he got back. So, I didn't see him."

"I see." Monsignor Valois said, disheartened by the response. "I see."

"Will there be anything else, Monsignor?" Father Beaumont asked with a note of excitement. "I'm ready, willing, and able to do anything I can."

"No, Father, I believe I can manage it from here. You may go back to whatever you were doing. Thank you for your help."

"Do you think Father Xavier will be all right?" Father Pierre asked, turning to leave. "He's had so many spells during his

14

short time at the monastery. It makes me a bit nervous."

"I'm certain he'll be fine," Monsignor Valois said, offering a sympathetic smile. "But if he's not feeling any better by morning, I'll phone Doctor Cartier. Go now, say a prayer for him."

CHAPTER 3

Norbert Piedmont had just settled down to read *The Evening Gazette* when his wife, Claudine, bolted into the living room. Tears rolled down her cheeks. Her face was red and swollen.

"What's happened, Claudine?" he asked, alarmed by her appearance. "For God's sake, what's wrong?"

"N-N-Nobby," Claudine stammered. "It's terrible news! I just got off the phone with Bob and Giselle Bourgeois. Something awful has happened. It's—"

"Spit it out, woman."

"—it's little Joline. She's missing."

"What?" he exclaimed. He threw his newspaper on the floor and jumped to his feet. "What the hell happened? Where is she?"

16

"I don't have all the details yet," she said, sobbing amid her words. "But she hasn't been seen since she took her new puppy for a walk."

"When was that?"

"Earlier today."

"How come I didn't hear about this at the station?"

"Giselle tried to file a police report but was told that Joline wouldn't be considered a missing person for at least forty-eight hours." She rushed over, grabbed the knot of his loosened tie, and yanked. "For Christ's sake, Norbert, you're the goddamned police inspector! Can't you do anything about the red tape? They're frantic!"

He pushed her away and squeezed his head with both hands. "No!" he cried, slumping back to his easy chair. "No, not again! This can't be happening! Not to Joline, too. What kind of animal would do this to children!"

"Nobby, pull yourself together. Don't jump to conclusions. There must be a logical explanation. There has to be. Come on, we've got to get over there to lend our support."

In slow motion, he faced her. He could feel an intense heat travel from his cheeks to his forehead, but ignored the sensation. Feeling light-headed, he nervously wiped the sweat from his brow and began to twist a lock of his bushy gray hair around his index finger.

"You know how kids are," she said, wiping her eyes.

"They get involved with games and lose track of time. That's probably all it is. Let's not think the worst."

"Claudine," he said softly, wanting with all his heart to accept her simple explanation. "Do you honestly believe that? Because I don't think I'd have the strength to go through it all over again if you're wrong."

"Don't worry," she said, smiling slightly. "You won't have to. History won't repeat itself."

"Yeah, and lightning never strikes the same place twice."

"Oh, Nobby, God wouldn't be that cruel."

"God has nothing to do with it!" he yelled, slamming his broad fist down on the Victorian end table. "He doesn't exist!" He moved his watery eyes to the top of the doorframe where he could still see the faded outline of the crucifix, which had hung there for as far back as he could remember. "He can't exist or Jacqueline would still be with us."

On finishing his sentence, visions of his little girl came flooding back. She was young, vibrant, and full of life. She was home and safe with her family. Even though she was a change of life child and not planned, she couldn't have been loved more.

"If only I'd done something different," he cried. "Maybe she'd be alive today." He searched his tortured brain for a logical explanation, but the memories were too painful. Overwhelmed by grief, he cradled his face in his hands and broke down.

"Nobby, settle down. You've come too far to regress to

18

that state. I love you and couldn't bear to lose you, too. My prayers were answered when you recovered the way you did."

"It wasn't prayer or your faith in God that snapped me out of it," he said slowly raising his head. "It took only a few days rest and a couple of pills. It was medical science, plain and simple. I've told you at least one hundred times, God doesn't exist!"

"Okay, have it your way. But I'm merely grateful that you're well again. Now, take a deep breath and try to relax."

"Don't worry, Claudine," he said reaching for a tissue. "I'll be fine. You're right. I shouldn't be so pessimistic." He smiled lovingly at her and added, "We don't even have all the facts yet. I've probably blown it all out of proportion."

"That's my Nobby," she said, smiling warmly. "That's my boy." She wrapped her chubby arms around his neck, kissed his cheek, licked her finger, and wiped away the lipstick smudge. "I promised Giselle we'd get over there as soon as possible. Are you up to it?"

"Yeah, yeah, I'll be fine. Just let me grab my briefcase. I'll meet you in the car."

She gave him another kiss, walked to the doorway, and thanked him.

"Thanks for what?" he asked, confused by the statement.

"For being the caring, wonderful man I married, that's all." Without saying anything more, she winked and hurried from the room.

19

CHAPTER 4

That evening, the suppertime atmosphere was unusually somber and the main topic of conversation was Father Xavier's weak condition. Though almost all of the brethren pitied him, a few voiced their doubts as to the severity of his illness. Overall, blessings for a swift recovery were the general consensus.

Monsignor Valois was no exception. He stood at the head of the table, offered a short prayer, excused himself, and slipped out of the room. Although his initial thoughts were on Father Xavier's well being, he ascended the stairs with a careful eye, fearful he would trip on the hem of his cassock. About midway up, he stopped, grabbed onto the highly polished banister, and recalled with painful clarity an incident on these same steps roughly two months prior. Sweat dripped from his brow as the memory flashed before his eyes.

It had been a Monday evening, approximately seven, during the height of an early spring snowstorm. He'd received an urgent telephone message about Mrs. Alice Varier. She was near death and in need of the Last Rites. She'd been a great contributor to the church, a devout Catholic, and a dear friend.

In his haste to reach her before she expired, he raced down the dimly lit stairs, simultaneously colliding with Father André, who seemingly appeared out of nowhere. Thankfully, God had been on duty that night and a small catastrophe had been diverted. Had it not been for Father Xavier's precise timing and strong arms, the collision could have been fatal.

He cleared his mind of the stressful memory, wiped his damp forehead, and returned his thoughts to the matter at hand, Father Xavier's poor health. It was plain to see that Xavier's medical condition had worsened since his arrival, but he believed in Doctor Cartier's keen capability as the house physician to improve the situation. On reaching the bedroom door, he tapped softly with his gold ring.

"Father Xavier?" he called in a whisper. "Are you awake?"

He paused, still gripping the knob, contemplating his choice of words before entering. He didn't wish to appear condescending and certainly had no desire to offend Father Xavier's oversensitive nature. Semi-confident that he could handle any unforeseen circumstance, he entered.

21

As he opened the door, he felt the rush of cool, night air filter into the dark room through the window. The drapes thrashed against the frame. Though chilled, for some odd reason, the breeze lifted his spirits and strengthened his belief that everything would turn out all right in the end. With a positive outlook, he walked over to the bed, lit the lamp, and examined Father Xavier closely. He saw that the wound had scabbed and his long, even breaths dictated he was in no apparent danger. Filled with certainty that a complete recovery was imminent, he recited a short prayer, made an invisible sign of the cross in mid air, and swiftly departed.

CHAPTER 5

The brethren were midway through the evening prayer service when the chosen one slipped into the candle-lit chapel. Certain he had arrived unnoticed; he took a seat off to the side and quietly studied the hand-carved Stations of the Cross, which hung along the stone walls. The candles, which rested in small wrought iron candelabras below each plaque, flickered. They cast eerie shadows over the ancient statuary, making them appear as though they were alive.

"Dear God, my Father," he whispered, comforted by the thought of being surrounded by religious ghosts. "Permit me to be the vessel of Your will, and give me the strength that I'll need to carry out Your commands. Your will be done."

Suddenly, the familiar voice called to him in a thunderous tone. "It is I," the voice said. "Your Lord, your Master."

23

He jumped in his seat, startled by the interruption, for God had never intentionally interfered with his benediction before. Elated by the impromptu visit, he settled back against the cold, wooden pew and waited. He knew it would only be a matter of time before God's message would be proclaimed. His anxiety escalated at the thought.

"You have abandoned your soul to Me," the voice said. "For thou art My beloved, My disciple, My chosen one. You must continue to carry out My will, and be grateful I have selected you from amongst the many candidates. Appreciate the honor, which I bestowed upon you. Open your eyes to My greatness, for I am the one true God, the Alpha and the Omega."

"For You, alone, are Holy," the chosen one said. "You, alone, are Lord. You, alone, are the Most High."

"It is right to give Me thanks and praise," the voice boasted.

"Amen," the chosen one replied, waiting for the ultimate reward, the culmination of the summit, the eternal glory that he had earned.

"You have sacrificed to Me the thirteenth and final innocence as promised in *The Book of Life*. One for each of the twelve disciples and one for My beloved, Judas. Thus far, you have done well. In addition, you have returned the other to the sacred ground, the place from whence the evil spawned. It is now time to make the escapee carry the burden of atonement for the sins of the past and present. For the time is nigh and you have suffered

long enough. But be warned. If My directives fall on deaf ears,
your punishment shall be great and I shall not be able to protect
you from the chastisements, which I am destined to inflict upon
this deserving world. Keep in mind that I am the only salvation,
the only hope for mankind. *Pro nostra et totius mundi salute com
odore suavitatis ascendat.*" The voice repeated the Latin words for
a time until they fused into the brethren's chants.

Sated by the hallowed homily, the chosen one surveyed the
chapel for a second time, pleased to see that everyone was still
engrossed in prayer. It was apparent that no one had eavesdropped
on his private conversation with God, for he knew they were not
worthy anyway. It was his right alone and his virtuous actions
placed him high above the rest.

CHAPTER 6

Through the dead of night, Father Xavier bolted up in bed, his vision blurred. Where am I? he thought, trying to focus. What happened to me? The more he wracked his brain, the more it throbbed. Nothing made sense. The last thing he could remember was his return from the marketplace and the fantastic pain.

He looked around, trying to re-associate himself with his surroundings and realized he was alone in his chamber, though something was amiss. The mood wasn't the peaceful solitude he had felt when he'd first arrived at the monastery only a few short months ago. It was different somehow. The tension was great.

On closer inspection, everything was as he'd left it, including the Bible on the nightstand, with its page still marked for the passage he'd been reading the previous night. Still uneasy with the finding, he slowly moved his eyes to the wooden crucifix that hung above his bed. Instead of soothing him as it had always done, for some mysterious reason, it frightened him, turning his skin to goose-flesh. Christ's eyes pierced straight through to his soul and a familiar scent of jasmine filled the room.

Before he could shake off the uneasiness, he heard barking dogs in the distance. He stumbled to the window through the darkness and was surprised to see flashes of golden illumination weave and bob amidst the trees throughout the woods. Before he had the chance to discover the reason for the uproar, a strong queasiness invaded his stomach. He ran to the toilet and vomited for nearly fifteen minutes, then leaned on the vanity and stared at his pale reflection in the mirror.

"Something's terribly wrong with me!" he cried, examining the deep crevasses that had formed on his face. "I feel it." In an effort to relieve the pain, he returned to his bed, pulled the covers up to his neck, and prayed, "Lord, Heavenly Father, grant me peace. Rid me of these blasted demons. Amen." Within the hour, he was asleep.

CHAPTER 7

Inspector Norbert Piedmont shined his flashlight down into the cavity of a large hollowed out tree and saw two, tiny fingers poking through some red-stained leaves. "Roget," he called above the deafening chirp of crickets. "Get over here quick. I've found something!"

"What is it?" Sergeant Major Jacques Roget asked.

"Take a look for yourself," Inspector Piedmont said, backing away, vomit inching up his throat. "I think we found her."

"Holy Jesus!" Sergeant Major Roget said, looking into the stump. "I'll get the photographer."

"You do that," Inspector Piedmont said, lowering his head. "I'll radio the coroner's office."

Within the hour, the medical examiner and his team of

professionals had arrived, carrying stretchers and life-saving equipment. But they were too late. After carefully probing through the wet debris, they pulled out the broken corpses of both Joline Bourgeois and her small dog. The smell of excrement saturated the atmosphere.

"Jesus Christ!" Piedmont said, instinctively covering his mouth with a handkerchief. "Not again! Not Joline, too! I don't know how much more of this I can stand. When will the madness stop?" He gagged as he witnessed the pitiful sight and grimaced when the men placed the bodies onto the dew-covered ground.

"Inspector," Roget said, gently squeezing his shoulder. "Snap out of it. I think you may be too personally involved to think straight. You might even be playing right into the killer's hands."

"What?" Piedmont exclaimed, wiping vomit from his mouth. "What the hell are you talking about?"

"In view of the fact that your daughter was the last victim, maybe someone else should handle this."

"Are you out of your mind, Roget?" Piedmont screamed. "Ever since Jacqueline's death, finding that son-of-a-bitch has been my only reason to get up in the morning. I can handle it. I'll be fine. Now lay off!"

"Okay," Roget said. "Simmer down. I only call it as I see it and I understand your pain."

Piedmont ignored his words, holding back tears while

29

watching the technician examine the girl's body. It was a bad dream, Jacqueline all over again, the same M.O. Entrails were stuffed in her oral cavity and a set of rosary beads dangled from her delicate neck. Her bones were broken, splintered, and piercing through her flesh.

"What kind of sick bastard could do this to innocent children?" Piedmont yelled, turning away from the scene, plowing his fist into a tree. Without expecting an answer, he composed himself, wiped the blood from his knuckles, and turned back to the medical examiner. "How long has she been dead?"

"Less than twelve hours, Inspector," the medical examiner said. "But I'll know more after the post mortem."

Piedmont leaned back against an evergreen until the medical team had finished placing the corpses into body bags. He stared blankly as they were carted away. "Son-of-a-bitch!" he mumbled under his breath. "I'll kill the bastard when I catch him!"

"What did you say?" Roget asked.

"Nothing."

"I know this must be rough on you. Are you going to be all right?"

"Sure," Piedmont answered. "Don't worry about me. It must be a touch of the flu."

"If you say so."

"I say so. What have we got so far?"

"It appears to be the same M.O.," Roget said. "The female

child, the organ, the rosary beads, and the cross in blood on the forehead. Everything's here. This makes number thirteen, all within the past eighteen months. The murders have spanned the whole country, from Montreal to Edmonton. It appears he's moving west. But that doesn't make sense. I thought the analysts had projected Vancouver to be his next target."

"Looks like those smart-ass, college grads were wrong," Piedmont said, popping a peppermint into his mouth. "I'm not surprised. It's not the first time. It appears our man is changing his pattern."

"Inspector?"

"Yeah, this is the first time there have been two victims found in the same area, Jacqueline and now Joline."

"You're right," Roget said. "He is changing. That means there's a good chance our serial killer is still in town. What's our next move?"

Piedmont shifted thoughts as he noticed the ambulance's flashing red lights disappear through the trees. "Christ, she was my daughter's best friend!" he said, clicking the mint hard against his teeth. "How the hell will I ever break the news to Bob and Giselle? For Christ's sake, it was almost six weeks to the day since they stood by us as we buried my little, Jacqueline. What the hell do I say to them?"

"I understand, Inspector. I'll do it if you like."

"No, I'll find a way. But thanks for the gesture."

31

Roget immediately turned to his subordinates. "I want these grounds carefully probed," he hollered. "Don't leave any stone unturned. We have a homicidal maniac to catch and the bastard must have left some shred of evidence behind. Find it!"

"Do you think we'll catch him before he strikes again?" an officer called out.

"You bet your ass I will," Piedmont interjected, his jaw set, eyes glittering furiously, punching his fist into his palm. "I'll get him if it's the last thing I do."

"Don't you mean we'll get him, Inspector?" Roget asked, raising an eyebrow.

"Yeah, yeah, that's what I meant," Piedmont said, spitting the half-chewed mint to the ground. "I hate peppermint. C'mon let's get the hell out of here."

CHAPTER 8

"Oh, good morning, Father André," Father Jean greeted, pouring his last bit of batter into a mammoth, enamel frying pan. "How are you today?"

"Tired, Father," Father André stated flatly, frowning as he approached the antique, cast iron stove. "Extremely tired."

"Oh, then you must have heard the racket outside," he said and rushed to the adjacent stove to flip the maple bacon. "Police ran amok on the grounds all night long. Do you have any idea as to what is going on?"

"No, I don't," Father André said indignantly. "Nor do I care." He took a few steps and stopped. "Though I do find it a sacrilege to have intruders here on a Sunday. Doesn't anyone respect the Lord's Day anymore?" Without awaiting an answer, he swiftly exited the kitchen, careful not to step on the grout in the tiled floor, and shoved the screen door into an unsuspecting police officer.

"Whoa!" the stocky policeman said, holding up his arms. "Where's the fire?"

"Pardon me, Officer," Father André said with a smile. I didn't see you hiding there. Are you all right?"

"Yeah, I'm fine," the officer said, steadying himself. "What's the rush?"

"Can't break mother's back, you know. In all my years on God's green Earth, I've never stepped on cracks. Now, if you'll excuse me, I'll be on my way. The chapel awaits."

"Wait a minute, Father," the officer said, holding him back. "I'd like a word with you. If I'm not mistaken, the next service doesn't begin for some time and this shouldn't take very long."

"Though this does violate my regular regime, go on. But make it fast. The Lord, God will not forgive me if I miss my personal meeting."

"Yeah, whatever you say, Father," the officer said, flipping through a worn, spiral notebook. "Maybe you can help me. I've been all over the monastery and can't seem to locate Monsignor Valois. Do you know where he is? It's imperative that I speak with him as soon as possible."

"Do I look like his secretary?" Father André said, pushing him aside and stepping out into the mid-morning sun. "It's

Sunday. Where else would he be but in the chapel celebrating The Eucharist. Obviously, you do not acknowledge the Sabbath. So, if you would be so kind as to have a seat in the sitting room, I'll inform him of your presence once Mass has ended. That should be within fifteen or twenty minutes, depending on how long-winded he is today. Nevertheless, when you do meet with him, you will only have a short time to speak. You see, he's saying mass again at eleven and will need time to prepare."

"You seem to know his itinerary pretty well. Maybe I should question you first."

"What questions could you possibly have for me?"

"Let me start by introducing myself. I'm Inspector Norbert Piedmont of the Grande Cache branch of the Royal Canadian Mounted Police."

"Mounted Police? This must be important."

"It is. And who are you?"

"I am Father André Jeneau."

"How long have you been stationed here?"

"I arrived at the beginning of April."

"April you say? Where did you come from?"

"Saint Clementine's in Montreal."

"Montreal, eh?" Piedmont said, drew in a deep breath, and started writing. "That's Father Andrew, from Saint Clementine's, right?"

"The name's André."

"Oh, sorry about that," Inspector Piedmont said, scratching his head with the end of the pencil. "It's been a long night. Have you ever been to Edmonton?"

"No," Father André said, folding his arms across his chest. "Is this going to take much longer?"

"Have you seen any strangers in the area recently?"

"No. I have not seen anyone unknown to me. I generally keep to myself and try to mind my own business. For the life of me, I don't understand why everyone else can't do the same. The world would be a lot less complicated. Wouldn't you agree?"

"Yeah, well life is full of complications," Inspector Piedmont said dryly. "There's been another murder in the area."

"Murder? Oh, my Lord! Where? When?"

"That's what I was hoping you'd be able to help me with."

"I don't understand. What would make you think I'd know anything?"

"Where were you yesterday between the hours of noon and six?"

"Why? Am I a suspect? Do I need an alibi?"

"No. It's just routine questioning. Awfully defensive though, eh Father?"

"Well, of course," Father André said, shifting his position, clutching tightly to his black prayer book. "Wouldn't you be? It's not every day that I'm accosted with questions pertaining to a murder."

"Please, Father, just answer the question."

"Certainly, Inspector, I'll try my best. Now let me see. Some of us went to the marketplace to do the weekly grocery shopping." He paused and added with a grin, "We do eat you know."

"What a revelation," Piedmont said, his eyes narrowing to slits. "I'd always thought that you priests lived on the host. Who went?"

"The monsignor selected Father Phillippe, Father Xavier, Father Thomas, and myself."

"Does it really take that many priests to do such a simple job?"

"Yeah, and it takes seventeen of us to change a battery in a transistor radio, too."

"You're a real comedian, aren't you, Father?"

"Sorry, I couldn't help myself."

"Well, cut the shit. This is a serious matter. Did you travel together?"

"No. We ventured out at different times."

"Different times? Why?"

"Due to our various duties and chores, it would have been almost impossible for us to make the trip together. Therefore, we split up the list and went out at our own pace."

"Isn't that an awful waste of gasoline? I mean, to make numerous trips to town. It doesn't make much sense."

"No, no!" Father André huffed. "You've got it all wrong. We didn't take the car."

"Why not?"

"If Father Thomas had had it repaired weeks ago when he was supposed to, instead of spending the money on the leaky roof, we would have. Due to his evident lack of reliability, we were forced to travel on foot."

"Oh, I see. During your walk, did you see or hear anything out of the ordinary? Such as a scream or a cry for help?"

"Hmmm," Father André said, shifting his weight from one foot to the other. "Come to think of it, I did see something. However, I can't be certain if it was on my way to or from the marketplace."

"What did you see?"

"Now I remember. It was on my return. I saw Father Xavier. He was ahead of me on the path. I called out and tried to hail him, but there must have been too much distance between us. He never acknowledged me."

"Xavier," Piedmont said, rubbing the end of his pencil on his chin. "I don't believe I know him."

"Probably not. He's new to the monastery as well."

"Okay, anything else?"

"Yes. About ten minutes later, I heard a girl's voice."

"A girl?" Piedmont asked. "Are you sure?"

"I think so, but it was far off."

"What did she say?"

"I think she was calling out for someone."

"Who was she calling for?"

"I haven't a clue. It was awfully breezy and between the rustling of the trees and the other woodland sounds, I couldn't make it out. And why would I want to try? It was certainly none of my business."

"Did the girl's voice sound distressed?"

"No, I wouldn't say that. It seemed innocent enough. I just assumed it was one of the local children playing hide-and-seek in the woods."

"Was this before or after you saw Xavier?"

"Didn't I just tell you that it was about ten minutes later?"

"Hmmm, yes, you did. Can you give me a description of this Xavier fellow?"

"With pleasure. He's about my height and weight, probably in his mid-twenties."

"How old are you?" Piedmont asked.

"Me?" Father André asked, eyeing him suspiciously. "Thirty-six. Why?"

"You're about six foot, one hundred and ninety pounds, correct?"

"Close enough, but I thought you were interested in him."

"I'm interested in everybody," Piedmont said. "You look quite strong. Do you work out much?"

"Sometimes. Why?"

"What color are his hair and eyes?"

"Who?"

"Xavier."

"Oh," Father André said, trying to maintain his wits. "His hair is definitely black, and I'd say his eyes are blue, though I've never actually studied them. He's neurotic and I wouldn't want to get that close."

"Would you say this Xavier fellow looks similar to you?"

"No! We are nothing alike. And I find it highly insulting that you would attempt to compare me to that inferior imbecile."

"Is there anything else you can tell me about yesterday?" Piedmont asked.

"Well, let me see. I was almost at the gates when Father Xavier whizzed past me, heading back toward town. I grabbed his arm and asked him what was wrong. He said he'd forgotten the roast, and due to the fact it was to be our dinner last night, he had to return for it."

"What time was that?" Piedmont asked.

"I can't recall."

"Were you the first to arrive back here?"

"No. When I arrived, Father Thomas was already in the kitchen. I helped him put away the groceries and proceeded to the courtyard for some exercise. Do you need a description of Father Thomas and Father Phillippe as well?"

"No," Piedmont said. "We're acquainted. Did Xavier or Thomas mention anything about encountering a child on the road?"

"No. Of course not," Father André said. "Wait a minute! You don't think Father Xavier had anything to do with the murder, do you? Although it makes sense. He did go back to town."

"I'm not accusing anyone at this point. I'm just trying to get all the facts. At about what time of day did you hear the child scream?"

"I never said I heard a scream. What are you trying to do? Isn't this what they call entrapment?"

"My mistake. Let me rephrase the question. At about what time of day did you hear a child's voice?"

"That's more like it," Father André said in a calmer tone. "It was about three or three-thirty."

"What time did you get back to the monastery?"

"Me? Uh, it must have been around four-thirty, though don't quote me."

"What did you purchase at the market?"

"Some produce. Why?"

"I don't really know that it's important, but it may be."

"Is there anything else, Inspector? I'd like to get going."

"Are you definitely convinced you heard a girl's voice?"

"I've already answered that question. That's the problem with today's society. Everyone talks and no one listens. Yes, it was a girl's voice."

"No need for sarcasm, Father. It's not necessary. It's just that I have to make sure all the facts are straight. You can understand that, can't you?"

"I suppose," Father André said. "I apologize for the remark. It's almost time for the next Mass and I didn't sleep well last night."

"Why is that?"

"My chamber window faces the woods where the ruckus came from. Between the dogs' constant wails and the annoying flashes from the searchlights, I'm a bit edgy today."

"I apologize for the disruption, but under the circumstances, it was necessary. Did anyone see you at the marketplace?"

"Of course, about half the countryside. It seems that all of Alberta had shopping in mind."

"Then I guess Thomas and Xavier will be next on my list. You didn't mention Father Phillippe. Why?"

"There's a simple explanation for that. I have no idea what time he left for town. I hadn't seen him since the meeting with the monsignor on the previous night."

"Well, I guess we're finished for now. Thank you for your time. If I have any more questions, I'll be in touch."

"Good day, Inspector. If I can be of any further service to you, don't hesitate to ask."

With a sigh, Father André smiled and scurried across the cobblestones toward the chapel. He could feel the Inspector's eyes on his back, but he wasn't concerned.

"Oh, Father," Piedmont yelled from behind. "Don't step on the cracks."

Without offering a response, he grabbed the slightly tarnished, brass handle, pulled open the door, and dashed into the chapel.

CHAPTER 9

It was ten thirty-five a.m. when Father Xavier entered the chapel and searched for an obscure corner to await the departure of the crowd. Mass would end soon and rather than be trampled, he tiptoed over to the choir loft door, stood in the recess, and began to say his prayers. During his second *Hail Mary*, the sound of a woman's soft voice broke his concentration.

"Pardon me, Father," she said. "Would you mind if I joined you? I thought maybe I could wait here, out of the way, if it's no bother."

He whipped around and gave a half smile, pleasantly surprised by the beauty which stood before him. She was an attractive young novice with the face of an angel. Wisps of golden-brown hair innocently escaped her wimple and her blue-green eyes sparkled like vast oceans.

"Uh, no. It's no bother at all. I was simply passing the time with a few prayers until mass is over. I'm Father Xavier. And you are?"

"Sister Domenique Rondeau," the small-framed woman said and extended her hand in a graceful fashion. "I'm pleased to make your acquaintance."

"My, what a beautiful name," he said, giving her hand a gentle squeeze before releasing it. "The name, Domenique was derived from Saint Dominic of France back in the early thirteenth century. He is the patron saint of the propagation of the faith, whose feast day is August fourth. However, Saint Domenique was canonized in her own right on July sixth." He smirked and leaned back against the wall, confident she'd be astonished by his knowledge.

"My, you certainly are a Theologian," she said.

"I suppose you cold say that."

"I'm impressed."

"I hope you'll excuse me for asking this, but how old are you? You don't appear old enough to be in God's service." He shook his head and continued, "What I meant to say is you are so young."

"Pardon me, Xavier," André interrupted in a bold fashion. "May we have a word with you? I promise it won't take long."

"Excuse me, Domenique," Xavier said and turned to the

men. He chatted privately with the brethren for a few moments, and promptly returned to her side. "Sorry for the interruption, but it was important. I've just been informed that the police wish to speak with me later this afternoon."

"Goodness!" she said. "What could they have to ask you about? Do you know why they're here?"

"I don't really know," Xavier said. "But I'm certain I'll find out in due time. No need for concern." He drew in a deep breath and watched closely as Father André and Father Thomas walked out of view. "Now, where were we?" he said, turning his full attention back to her.

"You'd asked me my age," she said. "And thank you for the compliment, but I'm not as young as I look. I'm twenty-five. How old are you?"

"Twenty-seven. How long have you lived at Saint Bartholomew's?"

"I've been there ever since I can remember."

"That's odd. I've said a few masses there and I've never noticed you before. I thought Reverend Mother had introduced me to all of the nuns. Obviously, I'm mistaken."

"That may be because I've only recently come out of seclusion. Before last month's fire, I'd always attended the seven o'clock mass. So, this is the first time I've ever been to the monastery."

"That's probably it," he said, smiling. "I only celebrated

the ten o'clock mass. It's as if we were two boats afloat on different currents, amidst the fog of urban renewal."

"That's a poetic way of putting it," she said, smiling coyly.

"How much longer will the church's renovations take?" he asked.

"It should be completed by year's end. In any case, that's the contractor's latest prediction."

"Wonderful. Some of my colleagues will be so happy to hear the news. Some consider holding mass for the public here to be a great intrusion. However, I believe that your misfortune has become our blessing."

"Excuse me?" she said with a note of alarm.

"Oh, I didn't mean to sound so callous. I meant to say that even if it's only once a week, I'm grateful that your church's congregation has brought this place out of the dark ages. To see so many smiling faces is definitely a joy."

"But didn't you choose this location for the solitude?"

"No," he said emphatically. "I had no say in the matter. I'm here on a mandatory sabbatical. Unexpectedly, my bishop wrote to me saying he felt as though I needed a rest."

"Oh," she said. "I'm certain he had your best interest in mind when he made his decision."

"Yes, you're probably right," he said with a smile. "And why are you here? What do your parents think about your calling?"

"They're dead," she said softly, lowering her head. "The sisters took me in when they died. I've been in their care ever since I was a small child."

"It saddens me to hear that," he said, gently caressing her shoulder. "Do you have many memories of your family?"

"Actually, no. I was only an infant when they passed on."

"That's too bad," he said, facing the marble floor. "Please disregard my constant prodding. But it's in my nature. Sometimes I can be extremely tactless. Forgive me."

"No offense taken," she said, smiling again. "In fact, it's been a pleasure to converse with someone other than the sisters. Strangely enough, I welcome the opportunity."

"I, too, am happy to have made a new friend."

"Have you been here long?" she asked.

"I arrived at the end of March."

"What church did you come from?"

"Saint Alban's in Winnipeg."

"I've never been to Winnipeg, yet I've heard the city is beautiful."

"Bah! It's a veritable rat race. It's much more beautiful here. The Rocky Mountains are so picturesque in my estimation. I suppose Bishop LaVallee was correct in sending me here."

Once mass had ended and the stampede of parishioners had vanished through the exits, they proceeded to the wooden pews, seated themselves next to Father André and Father Thomas, and continued their conversation in a whisper.

"Would you do me the honor of staying after the service?" he asked. "I'd like it if we could talk some more. You're a definite breath of fresh air, Domenique."

"Thank you," she replied, picking up a missalette. "I'd love to."

They spoke for a while longer until the participants of the next mass scurried in. Once everyone had taken their seats and Monsignor Valois had entered with his entourage, they faced the altar. Mass was about to begin.

During the mass, Xavier closely observed her features and mannerisms. He sensed something was vaguely familiar about her, yet he couldn't place it. He saw it in her eyes, something haunting and inescapable. He listened to her sweet voice as she recited the rituals and watched as she moistened her lips between sentences. He was so preoccupied with her that it was difficult to concentrate on the sermon, let alone follow the mass. Before he knew it, the service had ended. Without any remorse for his impropriety, he escorted her to the courtyard.

"What a glorious day!" he said, facing upward, allowing the warm rays to touch his skin. "For some strange reason, I feel lucky to be alive!"

"What a peculiar sentiment," she said.

"No, not really. It's because I haven't felt this good in such a long time. And I believe it's due to you."

Jamian Snow

"What do you mean?"

"I have a mild case of epilepsy and it sometimes affects my moods."

"Epilepsy? I'm truly sorry to hear that."

"Don't be. Thank God, it's only a mild case of petit mal. I've been under a doctor's care for the past fourteen years and my seizures aren't as frequent as they used to be."

"It must be awful for you. How do you endure it?"

"Oh, it's not that bad. The worst part is that it's extremely difficult for me to get close to anyone or to talk about it. When I do speak of my illness, most people think I'm going to explode at any moment."

"I find that difficult to believe. I'd hate to think that most people could be so ignorant."

"Well, you're special. You're not like most people. There is something warm about you, something unique. I haven't found that in many people."

"That's extremely generous of you to say," she said. "I believe that if you allowed yourself, you'd find that there are many others who care about people as much as I do."

"Maybe so," he said. "But enough about others. I'm simply delighted to have met you." He led her around the Italian, marble statue of Christ to a stone bench. "We'll be more comfortable here. Sit and tell me more about yourself."

"There's not much more to add," she said. "I've already

50

told you what little I know of my past and I'm afraid that the rest of my life isn't quite that colorful or exciting."

"I'll be the judge of that," he said, pulling a new leaf from a large oak tree. "When did you take your vows?"

"I haven't yet."

"Why the long face?"

"Well, I sometimes doubt my calling."

"What do you mean?"

"I've often thought of falling in love and of marriage. I feel as though something's missing, but I can't be sure."

"What's wrong with that? It's a normal sentiment. I used to have the same thoughts."

"Really?"

"Yes."

"How did you come to your decision?" she asked.

"That was simple. I put it on the Lord's shoulders and eventually everything fell into place."

"You make it sound awfully simplistic."

"It is. All you have to do is allow the Lord to guide you. I believe our lives and the paths we take are predestined, even though our religion suggests otherwise."

"You know, I have an extraordinary feeling that you may be right."

"I sure am. And as your namesake did, I'm certain you will bring the masses closer to the Lord in one way or another."

"Okay Xavier, I've told you enough about me, now it's your turn."

"Me? I really don't care to talk about my past."

"Why not?"

"Because you're so happy and I don't wish to cloud this beautiful day with my tales of woe."

"Oh, it can't be that bad," she said. "How can you expect us to become better friends if you're uncomfortable sharing your feelings? I've been told that I make a great sounding board."

"Okay," he said. "For you, I'll make an exception. But remember, I've warned you." He stood and began pacing with his hands behind his back. "My story's a bit different, though similar to yours in some ways. I, the same as you, never knew my natural parents either. I was adopted by some horrible people who were extremely abusive. But that was before I entered the church."

"That must have been terrible for you."

"I can't find the words to describe my pain."

"I'm sorry. I'd always dreamt that adoption would have been wonderful, though now I'm not so sure. After hearing of your experience, maybe I was better off in the convent."

"You were," Xavier said, staring off into space. "My adoptive parents hated me, though I never understood why. They beat me savagely and called me a bastard child on a daily basis. They would lock me away in my room for days without any food or drink, without any sunshine or friends to play with. I felt

52

abandoned and alone."

"Good Lord," she said, her eyes filled with tears. "How did you finally escape the horror?"

"Here's where my story exceeds the limits of strange. I can recall it with total clarity. I had just turned thirteen. It was a Friday afternoon and I had lollygagged on my way home from school, praying that they were already dead drunk, asleep so sound that I would be safe for a while. The anxiety I'd felt when I climbed the steps of the porch was overwhelming. I remember turning the cold doorknob, holding my breath, expecting the profanities to accompany the thrashings, but when I entered, my life changed dramatically. All of my pain and suffering was carted away on stretchers, covered with white sheets."

"I don't understand."

"They were dead. They'd been murdered."

"What a tragic blessing," she said, gripping her rosary beads. "Where did you go from there?"

"I was placed in a catholic orphanage in Montreal. It was the best thing that could have ever happened to me. From out of the rubble of my turmoil, I found God. I was placed in his hands and have been safe ever since."

Xavier's jet-black hair moved with the breeze as he sat and reflected his past. It was painful to rehash the old memories, but he did. He could not understand how he could have allowed this woman to dig so deep, to unlock the door to that private domain of his childhood torment. He feared the consequences of releasing the ghosts he had buried for all those years, yet felt confident he'd done the right thing.

"Well, enough of this morbidity," he said. "It's all behind me, and that's where I want it to stay."

"I understand," she said. "I had no idea. I regret making you relive such an ordeal."

"No problem. Let's change the subject and I'll be fine. Would you like me to give you some background information on Saint Michael's Monastery? I did some research before I arrived."

"Please do. I'd love to hear it."

"The Gothic architecture of the buildings resembles the style developed in Western Europe during the Middle Ages. If you'll notice, the columns extend into the roofs, curving out like the ribs of an open umbrella."

"It's beautiful."

"The flying buttresses of stone support the arched walls, which are lined with those picturesque stained-glass windows."

"Yes, I see. The craftsmanship is exquisite."

"Did you know Medieval Christians believed, in a symbolic sense, that those carvings of saints and Christian heroes encrusted over the doorways were to strengthen the holy buildings?"

"Really? I'd never heard that."

"Yes. Amazingly enough, Catholicism is based on numerous archaic beliefs. But, I suppose we had to start somewhere."

"You're absolutely right, I never thought about it that way," she said and giggled.

"But the most interesting fact I stumbled upon was that behind the monastery is a door, which leads down to an amazing tunnel system, much like the catacombs of ancient Rome."

"Wow! Have you explored them?"

"Yes, a few times. I've begun to draw a map, but it's a poor facsimile. There are numerous passages and it will take months to complete with the accuracy needed for a comprehensive probe of the area."

"Can I see it?" she asked, jumping up with the excitement of a child. "Do you have it with you?"

"No, I keep it hidden in my room."

"Why so cryptic?"

"Well, when I informed Monsignor Valois as to my finding, he became infuriated and forbade me to explore areas below the monastery's gates. He said they were of no concern to me and I shouldn't involve myself in this church's ancient past."

"How strange," she said. "Do you think they were built to bury the dead or to conceal some deep, dark secret?"

"No. I don't think so," he said and chuckled. "I haven't come across any graves or skeletons as of yet."

"Then, what do you suppose they were used for?"

"Probably for seclusion and meditation. I found several

chambers with make-shift beds, basins, and antique candle holders still covered with wax."

As they continued to discuss the ancient design, a shadow moved from around the corner of the residence. Xavier caught a glimpse of it from out of the corner of his eye and watched as it crawled along the bricks toward the bushes. Suddenly, the breeze picked up and an uneasy feeling swept over him from head to toe.

"Who's there?" he called out, his voice quivering. "Come out of there this instant!"

"What is it, Xavier?" Domenique asked. "Who are you talking to?"

Before Xavier had the opportunity to explain, Father André tapped him on the shoulder. "What seems to be the problem, Xavier?" he asked. "Seeing things again?"

"Oh, it's you, Father André," he said. "I should have known you'd be lurking somewhere close by."

"It must be your magnetic personality," André said. He acknowledged Sister Domenique with a nod and walked around the bench to face them. "But don't flatter yourself. I tend to believe that it's just my unfortunate luck and bad timing."

"What do you want?" Xavier asked, perturbed by the intrusion. "Don't you have anyone else to spy on?"

"My, my. Touchy, aren't we?"

"No, I just don't like the fact that you're always snooping around me."

"Oh, please!" André said, rolling his eyes. "You really are unhinged. It just happens that I was standing by the chapel with the monsignor when I heard you yell. Naturally, I assumed you were taking another one of your fits."

Instantly, the sun emerged from behind a cloud, distorting Xavier's vision. It cast an unnatural umbra on André's face, making his eyes appear black instead of their usual brilliant blue. He was unnerved by the strange occurrence and feared another bout with his infliction would ensue. He didn't know how he would handle the embarrassment if it were to transpire in front of Sister Domenique, so he held his breath and hoped for the best.

"Are you all right, Xavier?" Domenique asked. "You're trembling."

"She asked you a question," André blurted, not giving him the chance to respond. "How can you just sit there and ignore this angelic creature's compassion for you?"

"Oh, I apologize, Domenique," Xavier said, rubbing his eyes. "It's just that I'm convinced I saw something or someone standing over there by the rose bushes."

A moment later, Father Thomas materialized from out of the shadows, brushing bits of leaves and dried earth from his clothing. His hair was tousled and adorned with twigs. He appeared to be in a state of confusion.

"See, it's not my imagination," Xavier said, glaring at André, attempting to keep his voice calm. "I'm not crazy, even though you constantly insinuate it."

"Who said anything about being crazy?" André said, smirking. "But if the sandal fits, wear it."

"What in God's name were you doing back there, Father Thomas?" Xavier asked. "Why were you hiding in the shadows? Were you eavesdropping? Were you taking notes of our personal conversation?"

"For heaven's sake," Father Thomas said. "Don't be so cynical. I was only looking for my missalette. I'd dropped it earlier on my way to mass and returned to look for it."

André dashed to the spot where Father Thomas had been. He knelt down, fished through the dry leaves, and stood, waving a black book in the air. "He was telling the truth, Xavier. It's right here," he said, surrendering the book to Father Thomas.

"Thank you, Father André," Father Thomas said, eyeing Xavier queerly. "Let's go. Our brunch should be ready."

"Yes. Go on. I'll be there shortly."

"Okay," Father Thomas said, heading for the building. "I'll meet you inside."

Once Father Thomas was out of earshot, André again addressed Xavier. "You really ought to work on your paranoid disposition. Your defensiveness marks you as a casualty of the classic textbook case. Only those who have something to hide or do evil deeds react in that manner. If I were you, I'd make another appointment with your psychiatrist." Without adding anything more, he strolled away.

Xavier was infuriated by the incident. He hated the fact that Sister Domenique was there to witness it and realized his special moment with her was ruined. It was André's fault. He was jealous of his new-found friend and had to interfere. It was his way. He had been disagreeable ever since he had arrived.

"Pay no attention to Father André," Xavier said, smiling at Domenique. "He has a knack for undermining everything I say or do. He always makes me feel inadequate. I apologize for the turmoil and I wouldn't blame you if you never spoke to me again."

"Don't be ridiculous," she said. "It was simply a foolish misunderstanding and a lack of communication. It could have happened to anyone."

"Thank you for your understanding, Domenique. I can't imagine what came over me, or why I overreact to everything these days. Honestly, it doesn't make any sense. This never happened to me when I resided at Saint Alban's."

"There's probably a simple explanation. Maybe it's due to the change in altitude. I know that it affects the way a cake bakes."

"Surely, you jest," he said laughing, relieved that the tension had been broken. "Are you saying that I should throw myself into the oven to find out?" He laughed aloud and added, "Seriously, can't we put this unfortunate incident behind us? I promise it will never be repeated."

"Of course," she said. "There was no harm done. You are

only human and it was an honest mistake. I'm positive God won't hold it against you. But, you have to lose the bitterness. Let it go. Perhaps if you did, you'd achieve some reasonable balance in your life and find it easier to make friends."

"You're right and thank you for giving me the opportunity to redeem myself. You won't regret it. I'm sure we'll become great friends in time."

"That would be nice," she said and glanced at her watch. "My goodness, where has the day gone? I must return to the abbey."

"Okay, but can we get together on Wednesday? I'd appreciate it if our friendship could get off to a new start. Besides, there's something I'd love to show you. I think you'd find it exciting."

"What is it?" she asked.

"Some of the walls and ceilings in the underground chambers are painted with Christian murals. Though some of the paint has worn away, you can still make out the beautiful artistry. Will you come? It could be quite an adventure. Maybe, if we're lucky, we'll uncover some ancient artifacts."

"Sounds like fun. I've never been on an archeological dig before. But what about Monsignor Valois? Didn't he forbid you from going there?"

"Well, what he doesn't know won't hurt him," he said and laughed aloud. "And if he finds out, I'll blame it on my innocent curiosity. What do you say?"

"Okay, what time?"

"Around two."

"I'd like that, but I can't. One of the new girls, Mary, is having a problem adjusting to her new surroundings. I need to counsel her. Could we make it a little later?"

"How about four?"

"Okay, see you Wednesday at four," she said and darted off the grounds through the iron gates.

CHAPTER 10

Domenique replayed the unorthodox scene of Xavier battling André many times in her mind as she made her way down the earthen path back toward the abbey. She reflected on how high-strung and rough around the edges Xavier was and on André's bitter remarks. Though she did not agree with the rivalry, she could totally understand Xavier's cynicism. Having to deal with André's horrible attitude on a daily basis and all that Xavier had gone through during his miserable childhood was enough to confuse anyone.

"That poor man," she said to herself. "He's totally alone in the world. I honestly believe he needs a sincere friend. Someone who would listen and care. Someone like me."

Having made up her mind to pursue the friendship with

Xavier, she dismissed the negative aspects of the day and focused only on the positive. It was uplifting to know that she would be a good influence on his life. She promised herself that she would be there for him if he needed her and believed he would do the same.

CHAPTER II

Bothered by his earlier confrontation with Father André, Xavier decided to eat dinner in his chamber rather than risk the chance of another argument at the supper table. To look foolish in front of the brethren would be too much embarrassment for one day, especially when André made a habit of antagonizing at every possible moment. It was only a hunch, but he believed André was out to get him. Assuming the worst, he quickly mounded his plate with food and scurried from the room, hopeful not to be seen. The fewer questions, the better, he thought as he dashed up the wooden staircase toward his room.

In his room, he found the air unusually thick. The lack of ventilation was suffocating. "What the heck?" he said, 7positive he'd left the window open. "It's hotter than Hades in here!" He set down his tray, pushed the window up as far as it would go, and allowed the cool evening air to saturate the room. Within seconds, his feeling of asphyxiation was alleviated. He sat on the edge of the bed, gave thanks for the food, and ravenously devoured his meal. Feeling somewhat sated, he pushed the tray aside, knelt on one knee, and thanked the Lord once again.

Instantly, he was overwhelmed by an uncomfortable sensation, a heaviness. It originated in his chest and swiftly traveled throughout his body. With mounting anxiety, he tore off his clothes, extinguished the light, and buried his face deep in his pillow, desperate to alleviate the discomfort. He shifted his thoughts to Domenique and their happy union. It helped to ease his mind and his pain. After a time, he drifted off to sleep.

CHAPTER 12

Saint Bartholomew's compound was located only two kilometers to the south of Saint Michael's. It sat protected from the outside world by a high, stone wall, lined with lush foliage, wildflowers, and multi-colored rose bushes. Within the barrier, a limestone fountain graced the center of a petite, bricked courtyard. It was stained a green gangrene and hadn't flowed in years, though it definitely added an old world charm.

The main building, the convent, was more than just a home for would-be sisters. Though exclusively female, the residents were not all nuns. In recent years, it had become a safe haven for many abused and homeless girls from every province in Canada.

"I understand what you're saying," Domenique said, sitting Indian style on the edge of her bed, twisting the fringe of her satin pillow, wondering where it would all lead.

Reverend Mother stood by the bureau in her usual influential manner, features sharp and well defined. "Do you realize how truly special you are to us?" she asked, wrinkles forming on her brow. "If it weren't for you and your unique ability to touch the heart, we wouldn't have the rapport that we have with the girls. You've brought them all nearer to the Lord, especially when they were at their lowest points, abandoned and alone in the world. You gave them a reason to go on."

"What a wonderful thing to say," Domenique said, watching her distorted reflection move in Mother's clear, plastic-framed glasses. "Although, I honestly don't believe I'm worthy of such praise."

"And what of the fund-raisers you're chairing? If the donations had not been as generous as they were, what would have become of the church's restoration project? You even convinced an old skinflint like Mr. Poirier to dip into his pocket for one of the new stained glass windows. For the life of me, I don't know how you did it."

"It comes naturally," Domenique said, covering her face with the pillow.

"That's what I'm trying to say. You would make a wonderful nun, and we love you. I believe it's your calling, but I can't make the decision for you."

"I love you, too, Reverend Mother. This has been the only

family I've ever had, and the girls are a joy to me. I can't imagine living any place else."

"Then you've made up your mind to stay with us?"

"Almost," she said, pausing to give thought to the rest of her reply. "As a new friend recently told me, if it's meant to be, I'll receive some sort of sign from heaven. Then and only then will I make my decision."

"Well, let's pray your sign comes before the end of the week."

"Why? What's so important about this week?"

"Don't you remember? The archbishop will be visiting, and I was hoping to have good news for him. The church definitely needs devoted people such as you, Domenique."

"I know what you're saying, but—"

"Well, it's fruit for thought," Reverend Mother said, rushing to the door. "Sleep on it. We'll discuss it in the morning. Goodnight, my dear." Abruptly ending the conversation, she hurried from the room.

Finally alone to sort through the emotions Reverend Mother had ignited, she sauntered to the window, gazed up at the hazy moon, and sighed. Her heart burned with indecision and confusion. She felt as though, if she were to leave, she would be abandoning the post she had been destined to man.

"Dear Lord," she prayed into the gentle breeze. "Guide me. Help me to choose the correct path so that my potential will be

used to the fullest. In your name, I plead for a sign. Amen."
While drawing the drapes she remembered something and added,
"God, I almost forgot. Thank you for introducing me to Father
Xavier. I certainly believe he needs my help and friend—"

Before she had the chance to end her prayer, her bedroom
door swung open and crashed against the wall. She whipped
around and gasped, paralyzed by the sight. In the doorway stood a
strange young girl with long, blonde hair tied back with rose satin
ribbons. Her eyes were jet-black, lifeless, and hollow.

"Beware," the girl said in a low, guttural tone. "Evil is
afoot. Allow not the void of eternal hell to consume your soul.
Pay heed to the elders, for they know what is best." The child
floated up and pulsated within a greenish glow. "This shall be
your one and only warning."

Domenique stood frozen in place as the ethereal child
dissipated into a dense gray fog and exited swiftly through the open
window on a sudden gale force wind. She blinked repeatedly, not
believing her eyes. Without thinking, she slammed the window
down and yanked the drapes together. She stumbled to the
doorway in a confused state, hesitated, and nervously peered out
into the hall. No one was there. She immediately stepped back
into the room, bolted the door, and shot back to the window,
trembling.

"What in God's name was that?" she said, cautiously
peeking through a slit in the drapes. "Was it a warning or was it

only the sign I'd asked for? I've had visions before, but nothing like this. It must've been brought on by my extreme fatigue and confusion."

She knelt, said another prayer, and settled back into bed. Still trembling, she reached to turn off the light, but decided against it. She knew it would be hours before she could fall asleep, if she could fall asleep at all, and things were more positive with the light on.

CHAPTER 13

Through the night, the chosen one's vivid dreams followed no set patterns. He tossed and turned while visions of past victims, including Joline Bourgeois, flashed across his mind. His blood-laden hands appeared exaggerated, then swelled to enormous proportions.

Without warning, the scene changed. He was now in a brook. He tried frantically to scrub his soiled hands, but couldn't remove the scarlet stains that plagued them. The red was blinding and he knew the rats would soon come.

His mind then shifted to apparitions of Sister Domenique. She laughed in an insane, high-pitched cackle and called to him with her eyes. She enticed him with lust as she moved her delicate, slender hands slowly up from her knees toward her forbidden zone. "Feast your eyes," she said as she raised her black skirt high to

71

reveal her nakedness. She continued on, exposing her supple breasts beneath her disheveled habit. She teased and taunted. Suddenly, her laughter amplified. Louder. Harder. More threatening. "You're not a man!" she screamed. "You're a diseased animal! You drove me into Satan's arms!"

A dead silence followed as the image faded.

He was alone and cold.

From out of the blackness, another image flickered in his head. The toothless marketplace vendor loomed before him, clad in rags. He held a mangled pup within his outstretched arms. "You want me to wrap it up for you?" he asked with a mocking smile. "Will there be anything else, Sir?" The wrinkled, aged man moved nearer and hurled the bloody animal at him, cackling wildly.

Once again, Sister Domenique materialized before him. She now held Joline's tortured body close to her flawless bosom. Her angelic wings fluttered in slow motion, and crystalline tears streamed down her cream-complexioned cheeks. "Why?" she wailed with a forlorn expression. "Why? Why?"

The multitude of words echoed through his head, crisscrossing in his brain, making them incomprehensible. Crazed, he fled into the darkness of his subconscious with a vengeance and speed. Though he raced from the vague images, he gained no distance. His legs ached like a constant migraine. His mind twisted. He tried desperately to retreat from the madness that engulfed his psyche.

Suddenly, the chosen one sprang up in his bed, hyperventilating, gasping for breath. "My God!" he cried into the darkness of his chamber. "Rid me of these blasted demons!"

He punched full force into his pillow, cold sweat streaming from every pore. With lips dry and mouth desiccated, relieving his anxiety was paramount. He knew how important it was to lower his pulse and calm his nerves before the attack spiraled out of control. Frantic for closure, he reached for the plastic pitcher on the night table and poured some lukewarm water into a goblet. It took four hard swallows before he could quench his thirst and eventually, he felt relaxed enough to drift back into semi-consciousness. Not long thereafter, he heard the familiar voice call to him as it had always done.

"My chosen one," the voice called. "It is I, your Lord and Master. I have come to cast away your demons. You must not blame yourself. You have only done what I have asked of you, but you must remain focused on My divine plan. Do not allow false guilt to cloud your vision or judgment, for you are My vessel. Think only of her. Remember the past and bring Me the handmaiden. For she is the angel of purification and rebirth. My will shall be done!"

Between breaths, his mind transported him back to the chapel and Sister Domenique. What perfection, he thought. She's the one. The angel. He kept his stare trained on her mouth as she moved her moist, pink lips to the psalms, yet he heard nothing. He continued to scan her every feature until his eyes froze at the rosary, which draped from her hip. Suddenly, harsh reality slapped him in the face. He cleared his mind of her disturbing beauty and replayed her earlier conversation, adding the responses he knew she would give, for he was the chosen one and knew all.

It was a bittersweet story, the line about being an orphan and the nuns taking her in. It almost brought tears to his eyes, but he supposed she could have done worse. He shut his eyes tight to alleviate the growing anxiety, which churned in the pit of his stomach, and when he opened them, he found the chapel empty.

"Where are you? Where did you go?"

He turned in slow motion and there she was, dipping her fingers into the font, her majestic wings outstretched. He stood and watched as she delicately made the sign of the cross on her forehead and waited until the holy water turned blood-red before he approached her.

"There you are. I've been searching everywhere for you."

She tilted her head and smiled, forehead still moist.

"You've been here all the time, haven't you? Did you know that I am a chosen disciple of the Lord? No, you couldn't possibly have such knowledge."

She moved her sapphire eyes to the floor.

"You're not certain as to your calling, are you? Well, that's understandable. You haven't worked hard enough or long enough to be a nun. You're probably thinking of raising a family and of sex, aren't you?"

A river of tears flowed down her creamy cheeks.

"You poor, confused child. You've been praying for our Lord's guidance, haven't you? He doesn't seem to hear you though, does He? Well, that's why I'm here. I am the divine intervention you requested."

She raised her head, cheeks glistening in the fragmented light.

"Allow me to wipe away your tears of sorrow. Allow me to purify your soul. For you are young. You have your whole life ahead of you to serve my Lord, my Master. Repent and recant all of your doubts and nefarious thoughts before it is too late."

She timidly looked away.

"You're a sinner! Repent! For our Father proclaimed that I am the only means of your salvation."

She stared blankly at him, squeezing the beads of her rosary.

"I can tell what you're thinking. You think I'm awful, don't you? You're asking yourself, 'how can he know me as well as he does?'"

She turned away and faded into the blackness.

"Come back! I want to know you inside and out. I need to cleanse you. Don't think badly of me. I'm sure you'll agree with me once I've had the chance to explain. Can't you understand?

I'm here to save your soul. There's still time, unlike mother. Mother. Mother. . . ."

Her clouded image exploded into a burst of brilliant blue then completely disappeared.

CHAP†ER 14

Wednesday morning, Father Xavier woke to find himself standing at the far end of the courtyard fully clothed, in his bare feet. Good God, he thought. How did I get here? How could this be happening to me again? His body was numb, paralyzed with fear. He teetered from side to side, sucked in the cool, damp dawn air, and watched the haze hover inches above the dew-laden grass. It chilled his already moist feet. It sent twinges up his legs to the base of his spine. What will I say if anyone sees me? They'll think I'm crazy. How could I explain?

He closed his eyes to rid himself of the constant uneasiness and prayed that when he opened them, he would be back in the safety of his room. His stomach churned violently. He felt as though he would heave at any moment. Once the inexplicable

77

sensation subsided, embarrassment set in. He charged through the kitchen door, bolted it, and stumbled up to his room.

"I'll be fine," he kept saying to himself. "No one saw me. Everything will be okay."

About to throw himself down on his bed, he heard voices coming from the courtyard. He dashed to the window, pulled back the drapes, and stared out in disbelief. It looked as though half of the Canadian countryside was present and policemen were scattered about the grounds.

His mind reeled with instant confusion. This cannot be possible, he thought. I would have seen them. I was down there only moments ago. My feet are still wet. His eyes dropped to his feet to see that he was wearing shoes, though the laces were untied. He glanced at his clock and was astounded by the time. It was already nine-thirty.

"What's happening to me?" he exclaimed, applying pressure to his head with both hands. "Am I going mad?"

Unable to rationalize the bizarre happenings, he sat in the window seat and watched the crowd mill around a long, black hearse as it pulled up to the main entrance of the chapel.

"Sweet, Jesus! Today is Joline's funeral! How could I have forgotten?"

He bolted down to the chapel, dipped his fingers into the font, made the sign of the cross, and stormed through the assembly of mourners toward Joline's small walnut coffin. He could not understand what propelled him or why, but knew he was needed. Whether it was instinct or premonition, he was certain he was the only one capable of releasing her soul from the evil that had snatched her from this world.

He stopped short at the foot of the open casket and shrieked. Monsignor Valois was standing over it, holding a bejeweled dagger. He pushed the pallbearers aside and dove at him, ripping the weapon from his hand.

"What's the meaning of this?" Monsignor screamed, falling back against a pew. "Father Xavier, have you lost your mind?"

Xavier knew the timing was crucial. Her soul had but seconds left. He closed his eyes and chanted in Latin over the body. Once finished with the prayer, he opened them and screamed. His eyes bulged. His body quaked. Instantly, his heart surged with excruciating pain. He felt faint. Without time to grasp its meaning, he was grabbed from behind by Inspector Piedmont and Monsignor Valois and was swiftly escorted to the sacristy.

"Good God, Father Xavier," Monsignor said, panting, as he seated him in a wooden chair. "What's happened to you? Don't you realize the damage you've caused the Bourgeois family? Not to mention the monastery. What were you thinking?"

"You're asking me?" Xavier said, lips quivering. "You, the one who was about to commit a grave sacrilege. How dare you! And how do you explain the fact that Sister Domenique Rondeau is in that coffin? What the hell have you done to her?"

79

"Excuse me?" Piedmont asked, looking puzzled. He turned to the monsignor, whispered something, and then turned back to Xavier. "What the hell are you babbling about? The body of Joline Bourgeois is in the coffin. Why would you think otherwise?"

"Because the coffin was open," Xavier answered. "I saw it with my own eyes." He grabbed Inspector Piedmont's sleeve. "He killed her. Or—he was going to kill her. Oh, I know this sounds bizarre, but you were there. You must have seen it." Remembering the dagger, he held his hand up and waved it. "I have the proof right here."

"What in God's name are you talking about?" Monsignor asked. He gently slid the crucifix out of Xavier's hand and gave him a soothing pat on the back. "It'll be all right, Father."

"It was a dagger," Xavier exclaimed, his face contorting. "I know it was. I took it from you."

"You've obviously experienced another one of your hallucinations," Monsignor said. "It'll be all right. We'll contact the doctor."

Xavier's reality was shattered. His logic was gone. He could only remember fragments of the desperate actions he'd taken only minutes before.

"Is there anything I can do, Monsignor?" Father André said from the doorway.

"Yes," Monsignor said, turning around. "Please escort

Father Xavier back to his room and stay with him. He's had another attack."

"Okay," Father André replied. "Do you want me to call the doctor?"

"No, I'll phone for Doctor Cartier once we're through with the funeral. I wish to speak with him personally. I'm certain he'll be able to explain this insane outburst and prescribe something to calm him down."

"Something strong," Father André said, winking at Xavier. "Something very strong."

"Yes," Monsignor Valois said.

"I know just what to do." Father André said. "The last time Doctor Cartier visited, he left me Xavier's medication and instructions on how to administer it in the event something like this ever happened."

"I wasn't aware of that," Monsignor said. "But I'm glad to hear the doctor had the foresight to prepare you for such a situation." He turned back to Xavier and continued, "Go, get some rest, Father. I'm sure you'll be fine once you've had your medication. I'll be up to see you later. Until then, Father André will watch over you."

"No!" Xavier hollered as Father André escorted him from the sacristy. "Don't touch me!"

"What was that all about, Monsignor?" Piedmont asked once Xavier was gone. "Does he act like this often?"

"Oh my, yes!" Monsignor said, with a note of excitement. "But it's never been this extreme."

"I don't follow you," Inspector Piedmont said.

"You see, prior to his arrival at the end of March, I received a letter from his bishop informing me that he was susceptible to these attacks of epilepsy, but he hadn't mentioned they'd be this frequent or this violent. He just wrote that it was a mild case and would be of no bother to us."

"The end of March, eh? Isn't that around the same time Father André arrived?"

"Yes, I'd have to say you're nearly correct. If I'm not mistaken, they arrived within two weeks of each other. Why do you ask?"

"No special reason. I just found it odd André was so sympathetic to Xavier's medical needs. I was under the assumption they didn't care much for each other."

"What gave you that idea, Inspector?"

"It was during my interviews with them, but obviously I'm mistaken. Do you know if they knew each other before they arrived at the monastery?"

"I don't believe so," Monsignor said. "I can't see how. They came from separate parishes in different provinces."

"You said Xavier's spells were frequent. How frequent?"

"Well, the last one took place on the day of poor Joline Bourgeois' murder."

"Really?" Inspector Piedmont said, raising his voice an octave. "Do tell."

"Oh, Inspector! I don't want you to get the wrong idea. I forget sometimes that your mind is always calculating and ticking away on your work. The only reason I remembered his last attack was because it had occurred on such a solemn day."

"Yeah, right. Saturday was a solemn day. Your God must have been looking the other way. He has a tendency to do such things."

"God doesn't sleep, He only rests His eyes," Monsignor said with a smile. "He's aware of every aspect of everyone. He misses nothing."

"Yeah, whatever," Inspector Piedmont said, his eyes shifting toward the door. "Don't you think it would be proper to get on with the funeral? This has been tough enough as it is on Bob and Giselle and I certainly know what they're going through."

"I know you do," Monsignor said, resting his hand on the inspector's shoulder. "I know you do. Let's get on with it. Shall we?"

CHAPTER 15

It was well after four when Domenique finally sauntered through the monastery's iron gates. She realized she was off schedule, but figured Xavier wouldn't mind. She saw him standing a few yards away, leaning against a tree, with his back to her. Excited about getting the excursion underway, she ran up to him.

"I apologize for being late," she said, tugging at the back of his brown robe, ready to explain.

Xavier mumbled something under his breath and dashed around the corner of the mammoth building into the darkness.

"Xavier, wait!" she hollered, tracing his steps. "I truly am sorry. Don't let it spoil our day."

She stopped short at the edge of the thicket, uncertain as to whether or not she should continue. It was a battlefield of entangled vines and overgrown branches. For reasons she could not rationalize, she half-expected the greenery to come alive, seize her, and devour all of her connections to the here and now. The sense of abandonment was overwhelming. With unmistakable hesitation, she pulled away some of the tree's leafy arms, hoping to discover him hiding beneath the thicket, playing an innocent game of hide-and-seek, but he wasn't there. Her mind whirled with confusion and her stomach contracted. She called out again, but he didn't answer. Just as she was about to head back, something came from behind and anchored securely over her mouth. Instantly, her eyes widened and her heart slammed hard against her ribcage.

"Peek-a-boo!" a man whispered. "I'm so glad you finally arrived. I've been here waiting for what seems a lifetime. I thought you'd had a change of heart."

Mind running wild, she elbowed his gut, grinding her small heel down hard into his foot.

"It's no use, Domenique," he said gutturally, reinforcing his grasp. "Don't fight fate."

Before she had a chance to inflict any damage, she was shoved into some prickly shrubs along the backside of the building. A gauzy material was fastened over her eyes and mouth. Her hands were bound in front with rope.

"Don't move," he muttered, thrusting her face-first into the rough foliage, which climbed the dry mortar toward the spires. "Or you'll regret the day you were born!"

Crippled with fear, her brain malfunctioned. She didn't know what to think or how to react. Though a voice inside kept repeating that it was all a bad dream, reality dominated the situation with tension and fear. Paralyzed, unable to focus her motor skills, she stood trembling, petrified of what lay ahead. She listened intently to his respiration as it turned labored, his constant pants mingling with the rustling of dried leaves. She thought he may be experiencing a seizure, but soon realized he was working at something.

She heard the creaking of rusty hinges and felt a rush of cool, stale air blast toward her. She surmised by the drastic drop in temperature and the musty odors that she had entered an ossuary, hidden away from the outside world for generations. How could I have been so blind, she thought as scenes of Sunday's conversation with Xavier flashed before her eyes. How could I have been so stupid?

"Domenique," he whispered close, holding a bright light up to her face. "Don't be such a child. You look like a scared rabbit." He kissed her cheek, expelling hot breath. "There's no reason to be frightened. I don't want to harm you. I'm just following my father's orders. Now, relax and be careful as I guide you down this narrow stairwell. The rock steps are steep and I wouldn't want you to trip and kill yourself."

She hesitated, each step more uncertain than the last, concerned that her feet wouldn't land squarely on the stone slabs. Her trepidation resulted in a cold sweat, dampening the gauze, and stinging her eyes. She could feel the fear rise from the pit of her stomach and course through her veins, eating red and white blood cells as it traveled.

"You're almost home, my angel," he said, embracing her as they reached the bottom.

With her feet on solid ground, the terror she'd been experiencing erupted into anger so intense that her small frame shook from the force. Perspiration streamed from every pore and she trembled from head to toe. Like hell I'm home, she thought, spontaneously kneeing him in the groin.

"You bitch!" he shrieked, releasing his hold. "You little bitch!"

In her haste to escape, she stumbled on the edge of the lowest step, and landed on the base of her spine. Instant pain flashed through her body. Before she had the chance to regain her footing, his hand tightened around her waist and her hope for freedom disintegrated into his powerful grip.

"Where the hell did you think you were going?" he whispered, pulling her close. He slammed her against a cold, wet wall and continued, "There's no way out, Domenique. In time, you shall come to realize that I am your only salvation. Have trust in me, for I am the chosen one. We must all pay our debts to the

Lord, and your time has come. Your only means of redemption is through me. I knew this the first time I laid eyes on you. You are the one. The handmaiden. The angel."

Her mind reeled and her backside throbbed. Why, she thought frantically. Why me? Why are you doing this, Xavier? Why do you hate me so?

"Enough, damn you!" he yelled. "Stop your babbling!"

Can he read my mind? Does he hear what I'm thinking? What kind of monster is he?

"Words, words, words," he yelled, his voice reverberating back like a boomerang. "You're trying to confuse me with your words, but you won't succeed! No, no, you won't succeed. For in the end, you shall do as I say! Now be quiet!"

Overwhelmed with doom, she realized that it wasn't her thoughts he was responding to, but voices in his own mind. He's a madman, she thought. He's going to kill me. I just know it. If only I could speak, I could reason with him. Oh, God, please help me to escape.

"Silence!" he screamed, squeezing her neck. "You're the one who'll pay, not I!" His voice once again returned to a whisper as he moved his hands to her waist. "Domenique, my dear, I don't know what overcame me. You have to look at the whole picture and try to understand. You see, I have an important job to do and you are going to help me. Do you understand? Don't take it personal. I really do admire you, but nothing can alter the fact that

I have my orders." He swung the lantern at her head, knocking her to the floor. "Oh, Domenique, this is too easy. You didn't even put up a fight." He kicked her repeatedly in the ribcage.

Excruciating pain surged through her midsection. Her head throbbed. The bittersweet taste of blood moistened her lips and her mind was about to shut down.

"Get up! I'm not finished with you yet." He yelled, yanking her to her feet and removing her gag. "Why must you torture me this way? You know I don't want to hurt you and yet you torment me so."

"Xavier," she croaked. "Please, I beg you."

"Shut up, Domenique! Have you no respect? Can't you hear Him? My Lord, my Father, how good of you to come, even to a place like this. Tell me. Tell me, Father, what am I to do? Answer me."

Trapped within the terror, which enveloped her, she waited, expecting to hear the answer, but only heard more of his mad ranting. "Xavier, stop this madness!"

"You wretch!" he yelled, pulling her close once again. "You've sent Him away! You've destroyed the moment." He slapped her in the face and continued, "You bitch! Haven't you caused enough turmoil for one day? Let's go. There's much to be done and very little time left."

He propelled her forward through a Gordian maze; a tunnel system so vast and complex that she thought it would never end.

89

Her mind capitulated toward collapse with each agonizing step. Her constant pain made it almost impossible to maintain a firm thought pattern.

"Where are you taking me?" she asked in a faint whisper, laboring to sustain his swift pace.

"Quiet, or I'll leave you here to rot. We are in so deep, you would never find your way out. Do I make myself clear?"

She concentrated through the soiled fibers of the blindfold, but could only make out his vague silhouette. His height reaffirmed that her captor was indeed Xavier. Though she couldn't see his face, she could only imagine how distorted it must look.

"Xavier," she said, choking back her tears. "Please talk to me. Tell me why you're doing this?"

"It's the will of God."

"What have I done to deserve this? I implore you, please, let me go."

"What? Have you taken leave of your senses? You can't go. You're my ticket to heaven."

"No!" she cried, charging at him, ceaselessly hammering her tied fists against his chest. "No!"

She bit through his garment's fabric, tearing through his flesh. His blood tasted foul. The more he screamed, the more she ripped into him. If only she could reach his heart. Then, and only then would she stop.

"You vile swine!" he screamed.

90

With the bitter taste of his blood on her lips, she wrestled him to the ground, causing him to lose control of the lantern. It rocked back and forth across the stony floor, creating the illusion of a flickering fire. Repeatedly, she jabbed her elbow into his side until she tore away from his constant clutch. She scrambled to her feet, ready to take flight, but he snatched her foot, once again regaining control. In an instant, she was smashed down to the rocky ground, the cracking sound of her facial bones echoing throughout. Defeated, she could feel her warm blood gush from her mangled features.

"You foolish woman!" he yelled shrilly. "You can't fight me. You could never kill me. You're weak and pathetic. Your iniquitous actions only demonstrate that the rogue rules your soul. You definitely need purification." Without permitting her to respond, he muscled her onward to a reinforced metal door. "Ah, here we are. I hope you'll find your new accommodations adequate." He unlocked it, wiped the bloody hair from her face, removed her blindfold, and bulldozed her into the room.

She stumbled forward and attempted to focus, but could only see her distorted shadow on the bulky, rock wall. She stood and shivered, afraid to turn and face him again. Slowly, her eyes adjusted to the dim lighting. In the corner, she saw a small wood-framed bed, shrouded in multi-layers of dust, the covering to the ancient straw mattress worn and tattered. Dried straw from within escaped to the floor, leaving the bland bedding unleveled. She moved her eyes a fraction and noticed an unlit oil lamp and Bible sitting on a tiny, splintered table. These, curiously enough, were the only items in the room free of dirt. On the earthen floor lay an opened medical bag.

"You like it?" he whispered, kissing the nape of her neck.

Her body became rigid at his touch. Her legs shook. It took everything she had to continue to stand on her own two feet. In an attempt to escape his vile lips, she moved a step forward.

"Don't be that way, Domenique. Mother always liked it. And you remind me so much of mother." A high shrill cackle escaped from his throat. "Don't act naive. You know why you're here. You're the handmaiden, the angel of rebirth. Your enigmatic ways shall bring the masses together for His joyous return."

Her mind instantly shifted to the chapel and his haunting description of her namesake, Saint Domenique. He's deranged, she thought. I have to get out of here. Her body stiffened as she found the courage to face-off with him once again. With mounting trepidation, she slowly twisted her head in his direction and encountered a sharp slug to the jaw. The excruciating pain instantly traveled through her head. Her eyes rolled back and she dropped to the floor.

"Now, now, Sister, you shouldn't have done that," he said as he lifted her limp body and hurled it onto the decrepit bed. "You're just not ready to gaze upon me yet."

He refastened the blindfold and watched as a peculiar

calmness swept over her disfigured face. It was as if there had been no passage of time. She hasn't changed a bit, he thought, admiring her seraphic beauty. He felt exhilarated by the knowledge he would never have to share her with another human being as long as she lived. Motivated by her impotent position, he reached into the medical bag, grabbed some bandages, and gingerly dressed her wounds. He then proceeded to bind her hands and feet firmly to the raw bedposts.

"Oh, I almost forgot the *pièce de résistance*!" he said, pulling a purple stole from his pocket and anchoring it over her mouth. "There, that should hold you."

Inordinately self-gratified by his benevolent act of doctoring, he immediately deserted the chamber, re-secured the latch, and made his way back up to his room.

CHAPTER 16

"Good heavens!" Xavier cried, jumping up in his bed. "It's after five. I'm late."

He sprinted to the door and noticed a slip of white paper on his dresser. It was another note from Father André. Though the words were curt, the reminder was the same. It was time to take his medication. Anxious to get down to the front gate, he hurriedly poured himself a tall glass of cool water and downed the pill. He crumpled the note, shoved it into his top drawer, flew down the flight of stairs to the kitchen, and rushed through the door, whizzing by Father Thomas as he exited the building to the courtyard.

"Whoa!" Thomas called after him, picking up the church bulletins, which had flown from his hands. "What's your hurry?

Get back here and help me!"

Xavier ignored his pleas for help and continued his sprint across the long stretch of lawn, never breaking his stride until he finally reached the gate. Panting arduously, he grabbed the iron bars and stuck his face between them with hopes of catching a glimpse of her strolling down the gravel path, yet there was no sign of her.

"Domenique," he cried aloud. "Don't abandon me!"

He dropped to his knees and wailed loud and hard, disenchanted by the fact he had missed his chance at friendship. He was late and she'd already come and gone. He wracked his brain, trying to figure out where he'd gone wrong and why she didn't wait.

Suddenly, the intense ache he had grown accustomed to only since his arrival at the monastery took hold. His stomach churned and his vision blurred. He strained to bring the vague images into focus, but only saw wavy outlines of the trees and gate. He clamped his eyes shut and vigorously massaged his temples, yet the distortion lingered. As his illness progressed, he saw a vision of Domenique. She was bound, gagged, and in pain. He could not make out her features, but was positive she was in danger and needed him.

CHAPTER 17

Reverend Mother peered through the convent's tiny attic window at the network of metal, which surrounded the church, reminiscing the tragic day, the day of the inferno. She shuddered as she recalled with haunting clarity, the firemen as they lifted the charred remains of Sister Abadelia from the blaze. In an attempt to dismiss the unpleasant memory, she left the window and returned her attention to her boxes of treasures, which were strewn all over the wood-planked floor.

While sifting through the numerous wooden crates for old photographs for her scrapbook, she stumbled across a green felt scapular which was adorned with a picture of the Blessed Mother. Its inscription read, 'My Mother, My Confidence'. Her recollection of a time not so long ago came flooding back with special fondness. It was the day Domenique had given her this precious possession, the day of her First Communion.

"Lord in heaven," she said, her eyes starting to fill. "Thank you for bringing such an angelic child to my doorstep on that rainy, August night. I have cherished every challenge while raising her. Please aid her in making the right decision to stay with us. I don't think I could bear the thought of losing her. Amen."

She wiped her eyes, placed the scapular around her neck, and descended the stairs to the second floor. Feeling a tad vacant, the cheerful murals, which lined the length of the hall, brought a smile to her face as she remembered the previous summer. Domenique had supervised the whole ordeal. Though more paint landed on her clothes than the artwork, only a few splatters of blue and red remained in the difficult to reach corners as a reminder of the mess that had accompanied the job. But in the end, the finished product was superb and the artistry impeccable. Before entering Domenique's bedroom, she stopped to admire the late afternoon sun dancing across the expansive canvas. It was a soothing kaleidoscope of vibrant colors.

"Sister Domenique," she called out on entering the bedroom. "It's imperative I speak with you."

To her surprise, she wasn't there. Anxious to locate her, she hustled down the grand staircase to the pristine dining room. She scanned the massive room expecting to find her helping one of the nuns prepare for dinner, yet she was nowhere to be seen.

"Sister Helen," she said, walking up to the buffet. "Have you seen Sister Domenique this afternoon? It's imperative I find her."

"No, Reverend Mother," Sister Helen said, shaking her aged head from side to side. "I haven't seen her since early this morning."

"Oh, well, if you run into her, please mention that I'd like to speak with her."

"Okay, Mother," Sister Helen said. "But knowing Sister Domenique and her avid enthusiasm, I wouldn't be at all surprised if we ran into each other, literally."

"I know exactly what you mean," Reverend Mother said with laughter in her voice. "That child is extremely impetuous. She's quite a fireball."

Having no luck in the dining room, she continued her tedious quest throughout the scores of rooms in the abbey, asking everyone she met if they had seen her and no one had. It's not like her to disappear this way, she thought to herself, after exhausting all other possibilities. Feeling flustered and disheartened, she cast her pursuit aside and returned to the dining room to offer assistance with the last of the suppertime preparations. The conversation would just have to wait until after dinner.

An hour later, an entourage of nuns and bubbly young girls filtered into the room and quickly settled themselves on the wooden benches alongside the medieval-looking tables. Reverend

Mother stood and watched for Domenique to enter; for today was a most important day, hopefully, a momentous occasion in the abbey. Domenique would either commit her life to the church or go out into the world as a layperson. She had always known that this special child had been destined for greatness, but realized that in the end the decision was ultimately Domenique's.

She tapped a fork to her glass and cleared her throat. "May I have your attention please?" she shouted above the ruckus. "Would you please simmer down?" She waited, but it appeared that no one had heard her. "Quiet!" she yelled again, slamming her fist firmly on the table. "Quiet down!"

The clamor came to an abrupt halt. Everyone turned their attention her way and the silence was so deafening that one could almost hear the butter melting on the green beans. With confused expressions, they waited.

"Thank you," Reverend Mother began. "Now that I have your attention, is there anyone who could tell me if they've seen or heard from Sister Domenique today?"

She eyed the group with hopeful anticipation, waiting for a favorable response. By now, her hands were clammy and her patience wore thin. After a brief pause, a grumble of noes hovered throughout and she felt as though something was definitely wrong.

"Someone must have seen her," she said with a sinking feeling. "She certainly must have told someone where she was going. For heaven's sake, take a moment and think!"

"Let me see," Sister Agnes Fredette said. She stood and leaned against the edge of the table. "Hmmm, I remember now. It was earlier. Sister Domenique told me she was going to meet a friend at Saint Michael's at noontime."

"Noontime?" Reverend Mother asked. "Are you certain?"

"Well, of course I'm certain. I may be old, but I still have all my faculties."

"Thank you, Sister," Reverend Mother said. "I've been out of my mind with worry. You may be seated."

"Wait a minute," Sister Agnes said, removing her wimple and scratching her nearly bald scalp. "Maybe I'm mistaken. My memory isn't what it used to be. I believe she was to meet someone at four. Yes, four o'clock."

"Are you absolutely sure this time?"

"As sure as I'm standing here," Sister Agnes said, wobbling from side to side. She replaced her wimple and went on, "Oh, dear, I'm a bit dizzy. I think it's these darn prescription glasses. May I sit now?"

"Yes, certainly," Reverend Mother said. "Did she happen to mention what time she'd be back?"

"Who?" Sister Agnes asked, wrinkling her nose.

"Sister Domenique," Reverend Mother belted out with an exasperated huff.

"Oh, Sister Domenique," Sister Agnes said with a smile. "She's a lovely girl. What was that question again?"

"Did she tell you what time she would be back?"

"No, Reverend Mother. She didn't say."

"Okay, if she hasn't returned by the time we're through with dinner, we'll take a drive to the monastery to retrieve her. Something about this bothers me. It's all highly peculiar."

"I don't think there's any cause for alarm," Sister Agnes said. "You know how Sister Domenique is. She probably just lost track of time. Youngsters of today are oblivious to details."

"I hope you're right, Sister. Thank you. Now I'll begin the dinner blessing."

After dinner, there was still no sign of Sister Domenique and worry began to eat away at Reverend Mother's stomach. With high hopes of finding her, she instructed Sisters Agnes, Angelina, and Marie Louise to accompany her. It was only a short drive to the monastery, but she was glad to have the company.

"We must hurry, Sisters," Reverend Mother said, looking at the tarnished sun falling slowly behind the peaks of the mountains. "We haven't much daylight left and I don't like to drive after dark."

When they arrived, Monsignor Valois was tending his garden by the broad iron gates. His plump body was adorned with a large straw hat and his face looked flushed. After an acknowledging smile, he took off his gloves and walked over to them.

"Good evening, Sisters," he said. "Good evening. To what

do I owe this honor?"

"Hello, Monsignor," Reverend Mother said. "Your garden is growing beautifully. It's lovely."

"Well," Monsignor said. "It will be beautiful after I replant some of these chrysanthemums. It appears someone has trampled them."

"Yes," Reverend Mother said, pointing to the ground. "I see the footprints. I'm sorry for your misfortune."

"Okay, Mother," he said, looking above the rim of his glasses. "Although it's always wonderful to see you, I'm sure you're not here this late in the day to compliment an old man's garden." He chuckled and slapped his gloves together, releasing the dry earth from them. "So, what can I do for you?"

"Pardon our intrusion," Reverend Mother said. "We're here on a personal matter."

"Really?" he said, raising his eyebrows. "Now you've peaked my curiosity. Come, let's go inside and I'll put on a kettle. We can talk in a more comfortable setting." On their approval, he ushered them into the sitting room and proceeded to the kitchen to prepare some tea.

"This room is wonderful," Sister Agnes said, resting back in a comfortable overstuffed chair by the mammoth hearth. "Isn't the fire pretty?"

"Definitely," Sister Angelina said. "The subtle snapping of the fresh kindling adds to the setting of this most beautiful room.

It is quite cozy."

"Yes, I agree," Sister Agnes said. "I love the fragrance of charred wood. It always creates such a euphoric atmosphere. It reminds me of when my house burned down as a child and of the church."

"Oh, Sister Agnes!" Reverend Mother said with a note of distaste in her voice. "How utterly morbid!"

"No, no, no. You misunderstand me. The fires were terrible experiences, but they sure smelled good."

Reverend Mother shook her head and rested her arm on the thick, solid oak mantle, which was ornately adorned with intricately carved angels. From this familiar vantage point, she admired the fine collection of aged oil paintings, which surrounded them with timeless beauty. This room had always been her favorite and she loved the way it was decorated in an enchanted era of long ago.

"Ah, here we are," Monsignor Valois announced, breaking her concentration. He set a sterling silver tea service down on the coffee table and smiled warmly. "Now, what can I do for you, Sisters?"

"We apologize for such a late visit," Reverend Mother began, smoothing the wrinkles from her habit. "It seems as though we've misplaced a novice."

"A novice?" he said, pouring the piping hot brew. "My, this could be a problem."

"It's Sister Domenique," Reverend Mother said. "Sister Agnes told me she was to meet someone here earlier today."

"Yes, yes," Sister Agnes interrupted. "Those were her exact words. She was to meet someone at the monastery."

"Is she still here?" Reverend Mother asked, eyeing the older nun. "She's been gone for quite some time and missed her dinner. She's never done anything like this before and I'm a tad worried."

"Hmmm," he said, adjusting his glasses. "Let me see." He took a long sip of tea and wiped his mouth with a green, linen napkin. "I don't know her, but let me check with the other brethren. I'm sure we can get this cleared up expeditiously. If she's here, we'll find her." He promptly placed his cup on the tray and barreled out of the room.

Forty-five minutes later, he returned to the sitting room. He was out of breath and had a peculiar expression on his face. He sauntered to the center of the room and faced the nuns.

"Sorry for the delay," he said, nervously. "It was unavoidable."

"Any sign of Sister Domenique?" Reverend Mother asked, holding tightly to her black rosary beads. "Any information as to where she is?"

"No, Mother," he replied. "I'm sorry. Hercule Poirot, I'm not. And it seems no one has seen her today. I certainly wish I could have been of more help to you. But don't fret. I'm sure she'll turn up eventually."

"How utterly unfortunate," Sister Angelina said. "Where could she be? I hope nothing has happened to her."

"Mother," Sister Marie Louise said in a sad tone. "What should we do now? With Joline Bourgeois' recent murder, I'm a little worried for her."

"Calm down now, Sisters," Reverend Mother said. "Let's keep our wits about us, shall we? I'm positive we'll find her. There must be some logical explanation as to where she is."

"If you'll pardon me, Sisters," Monsignor said. "I do have a clue. It isn't much, but at least it's something."

"What is it, Monsignor?" Reverend Mother asked, her upper lip twitching. "Please, tell us anything you know."

"While questioning the residents, I ran into Father André. He reminded me that Father Xavier was the last person seen with her. Now that I think of it, he may be right. I remember noticing Father Xavier talking with a nun in the courtyard on Sunday morning. It could have been Sister Domenique."

"Do you think so?" Sister Agnes asked. "How could you be certain? It's so easy to get everything mixed up. I do it all the time."

"Hush, Sister," Reverend Mother stated flatly. "Go on, Monsignor."

"It's all coming back to me. Yes. They were sitting on a stone bench with their backs to me. If my memory serves me correctly, Father Thomas was speaking with them as well."

"Have you spoken with Father Thomas or Father Xavier about this?" Reverend Mother asked. "Maybe they can tell us where she is."

"Yes," he said. "I did. Father Thomas hasn't seen her at all today. And Father Xavier claims he was to have met with her this afternoon, but he overslept and the meeting never took place."

"I knew I had it right!" Sister Agnes said. "But wasn't he the one who went crazy at the funeral?"

"I'm afraid you're right," Monsignor said, lowering his head. "He's been quite ill."

"Ill?" Sister Agnes said. "He acted more like a raving lunatic! I shudder to think that Sister Domenique was going to meet such a man. I think he belongs in a straightjacket. He totally disrupted the requiem. And poor Mr. and Mrs. Bourgeois, I thought they were going to faint."

"Watch your tongue, Sister," Reverend Mother said, offering a stern glare. "You must remember Father Xavier is still a man of the cloth. Instead of criticizing, say a little prayer for him."

"Reverend Mother is absolutely correct," Monsignor said. "He does need our prayers. He has definite medical conditions that plague him, but I do believe he has a sincere and loving heart."

"Where should we go from here?" Reverend Mother asked. "It's awful to think, and I hate to say it, but I have a strong sense of foul play."

"Come now, Mother," Monsignor said. "Let's not have any negative thoughts. We should start by probing the grounds."

"I agree," Reverend Mother said, following him out into the courtyard. "Come, Sisters, we'll find her."

After two hours of scanning the area in the dark, Sister Agnes cried, "Why did I ever let her go? I should have insisted she take someone along with her. I knew there had been a murder in the area recently and it could be dangerous. Why didn't I stop her? I'm the one to blame."

"Now, now, Sister Agnes," Reverend Mother said. "We can't have any of this. It is certainly not your fault. She'll return to us, don't you worry."

"It's getting late, Mother," Sister Angelina said above a rumble of thunder.

"You're right," Reverend Mother said. "I didn't expect to stay here this long. And I suppose we've done everything we can for tonight. Come, we should head back to the abbey before it rains."

"I just had a thought," Monsignor said, walking them to the iron gates. "Maybe Sister Domenique has already returned to the abbey. There's a good possibility she's already at home, snug in her bed as we speak."

"I pray you're right," Reverend Mother said, offering a half smile. "But if she's not there and I haven't heard from her by morning, I'm certainly going to inform the authorities. It's too late to head into town this evening. Besides, it appears there is a storm brewing on the horizon. Thank you for all of your time and help, Monsignor. I'll keep you posted."

"I'd appreciate that," he replied, waving to them as they got into their black station wagon.

Thick black clouds slowly blocked out the moonlight as Reverend Mother cranked the engine. Lightning discharged across the distant sky, outlining the mountaintops. The breeze picked up with an increasing velocity, carrying moans from deep within the woods. Each gust, which blew through the open window, reached to them like invisible hands, sending chills randomly up their spines.

"Drive careful," Monsignor yelled through the howling wind. "It appears that this one will be a bona fide beast."

"We will," Mother called back, glancing once again at the ominous sky. "Take care."

Before pulling away, she adjusted the rearview mirror and flinched as a flash of lightning silhouetted the monsignor's large frame. It had a haunting effect, re-igniting visions, which had long been forgotten. There was something oddly familiar about the scene, something strange and frightening. It was Vivian standing back there in the pouring rain, waving goodbye all over again. Yet how could it be possible? She'd been dead for years and time had buried the memories. With a sense of abandonment, she revved the engine, wiped her tears, and turned on the windshield wipers.

"What's wrong?" Sister Agnes asked with a queer expression on her face.

"Oh, it's nothing, Sister," Mother answered, glancing once again at the sky. "It's the storm and my sweet Domenique may be lost in it."

Without looking back, she sped down the dark, narrow road toward the woods.

CHAPTER 18

"I look horrendous," the chosen one said, gritting his teeth, staring at his worn reflection in the mirror. "She'll pay for this. I swear it!" He pounded his fist down hard on the vanity, causing the toiletries to topple and jingle on the counter. "She has the manners of a wild beast, but I'll soon change that. As my Father cast out the demons from the whores, so shall I."

With the swiftness of a cheetah, he changed clothes, rolled the bloody robe into a ball, and with cautious steps, left the bathroom and descended the back stairwell to the sitting room. He tiptoed over to the fireplace, tossed the ripped garment in, and watched the brown fibers burn until they were reduced to ashes. He then proceeded to the kitchen, shifted some things around in the icebox, and to his good fortune, discovered some leftover liver and onions. Elated by the find, he piled the food onto a plate, grabbed a candle, shifted his eyes back and forth, and cautiously left the room.

Once down in the wine cellar, he walked to the far wall, pressed his weight against an ancient wine rack, and moved a stone slab to reveal a hidden path. That was easier than I expected, he thought, grinning from ear to ear. He continued through the opening and descended the rock steps with careful ease, retracing his steps through the underground labyrinth.

At the locked room, he unlatched the door and entered. He ignited the lamp with the candle, placed the food on the table, and directed his attention to Domenique. "What perfection," he whispered. To his surprise, he saw she still lay unconscious. With untold excitement, he sat on the bed, placed a gentle kiss on her forehead, and readjusted her blindfold. He proceeded to remove her gag while listening to the peaceful rhythmicity of her respiration.

"What a shame," he whispered, pulling hard at his groin. "Too bad it has to be this way. I would have preferred your cooperation."

Droplets of perspiration formed on his brow while heated twinges raged through his moist, sweaty body. His blood boiled. He hurriedly shed his costume, discarding it to the floor. Feeling a sudden chill, he reached for the black medical bag, pulled out a pair of scissors, and with slow snips, peeled away the cloth to expose her smooth flesh. With hands trembling, he released the scissors, let out a deep sigh, and moved his hands ever so slowly over her breasts, caressing her nipples.

"Domenique," he whispered softly in her ear. "My sweet angel."

A terrified expression shot across her face. Her body writhed. "Xavier," she said, her voice rasp. "Stop!"

"Hush," he whispered, placing two fingers on her lips. "It'll be all right. I'm not here to harm you. I'm here to cleanse. You mustn't utter another word."

She choked on her next breath, drew in another, and whispered, "Xavier, they'll find me. They'll put you away. If you let me go, I promise I won't tell anybody. I'll see you get help."

"You fool!" he screamed, pulling back. "No one will find you! You'll never leave. Not until the cleansing is complete."

With harsh movements, he retied the gag and continued his ravenous descent, pillaging, penetrating her innocence. He moaned with each forceful thrust, thighs held rigid. Consumed with ecstasy, he repeatedly slammed his muscular body against hers until his urge was sated.

"Father," he exclaimed, sagging to the floor, drained of all energy. "Your will be done." He stood, leisurely redressed, and turned his attention back to her. "See what you've made me do. You're no better than mother. Like Eve who tempted Adam with the apple, you, too, used your femininity as a tool of evil against man and God. You, as all women, were born corrupt and need purification. Redemption is your only means of salvation, for the Father's will must be done."

Having chastised her with quotes from the Bible, he grabbed a dilapidated wool blanket from under the bed and covered her. He then yanked off her gag for a second time. To his delight, her pain was obvious and warranted.

"Are you hungry?" he whispered. "Take this nourishment. Eat it, for you shall be fed but once a day for your penance. The purification of your soul has begun." He grinned while shoveling the food into her open mouth. "Ah, that's a good girl. Eat up."

"W-w-why are you doing this to me?" she asked between sobs. "What have I done to deserve this? Xavier, can't you remove my blindfold? My eyes are stinging."

"No!" his voice echoed. "It's God's will. I, the chosen one, shall abide by His word."

"Listen to yourself, Xavier. God's not talking to you. It's in your mind. God wouldn't tell you to do such horrible things to me! Why do you hate me so?"

"Repeatedly, you ask the same things," he said. "Why are you doing this to me? What have I done to deserve this? You want answers? Okay, I'll give them to you. Not that it matters. You're not going anywhere." He stood, and with outstretched arms, looked toward the stone ceiling. "I am the tool by which my Father is working. I am the chosen one. It is my job to cleanse your sinful soul."

"Xavier, those aren't your words. You're regressing back to your tormented childhood. You're using God as an excuse. You feel guilt for the abuse and the deaths of your adoptive parents. It's not your fault, but theirs. They did this to you."

"You are half correct," he said in a whisper. "Yes, it all began when I was but a child. I was witness to His glory. At that time, He asked me to be His servant for my entire mortal life. And of course, I accepted the responsibility without reservation. Motivated by His unconditional love for me, I have already purified the souls of many sinful girls across this corrupt country. All of this has been done in His name. But I had to move quickly, for the purification process had to be completed before they reached womanhood, before they could spread their disease of the flesh. In the end, my Father will grant me immortality. I look forward to His second coming. It is near. It is destined."

"Xavier, listen to what you're saying. You've killed innocent children. You're a priest for God's sake!"

"Silence!" he screamed. "Or you'll get no answers." He paused to wipe her mouth, and went on, "When we met, you said you were looking for guidance. Well, my angel, I, the chosen one, shall be your guide. I have known of your existence and destiny since childhood. When you dishonored Father, your fate was sealed. Though you witnessed His love, you continued to denounce Him. You are the soulless handmaiden." He took a deep breath, backed away and continued, "You had thoughts of leaving the sisterhood, didn't you? In essence, you wanted to leave God's family. For this, I believe you deserve damnation, but it appears our Father has other plans for you. You also aroused forbidden desires in me. You tempted me. You're a contemptuous whore and must pay for your transgressions of the past and present!"

"Please, Xavier, come to your senses."

Ignoring her constant pleas, he refastened the muzzle and prayed aloud, "Heavenly Father, have I not done all that You have asked of me? Have I not met all of Your expectations? I've detained her in Your name. I beseech You, please give me the strength to cleanse her soul and ready her for the important role she is about to play. Help me to return her to Your beloved family before it is too late."

Confident that his prayer had been heard, he wiped his tears, doused the light, and left with the resonance of his footsteps trailing behind.

CHAPTER 19

Domenique lay in the uncomfortable bed for hours, reliving the torture and replaying Xavier's crazed words repeatedly in her mind. At first, she thought it was all a bad dream until her stinging muscles brought her to the painful reality that the attack really happened. Desperate for freedom, she wriggled and thrashed her body until the binding straps loosened a bit, though not enough leeway was made to slip through. The torment of her exertion was fierce, causing sharp pains to travel briskly up and down her arms. Her abdomen ached and she didn't know how much more of the agony she could withstand. It appalled her to realize she had been stripped of her virginity as well as her pride. Though the cuts and bruises would heal in time, she knew the desecration would haunt her for the rest of her life. Inching closer to her breaking point with every painful thought and movement, she burrowed into the far reaches of her mind in search of answers and peace.

Chapter 20

The steady tick of the old grandfather clock was the only sound that pierced the silence as the chosen one climbed the stairs to his room. He was weary from the day's tribulations and was anxious to shed his garments, slip into bed, and dive headfirst into dreams of his upcoming reward. He'd earned it, the power and glory, and relished the fact that an immeasurable honor would be bestowed upon him in the near future. He'd come so far and was so close to achieving his goal, his divine right. While meditating, distant rumbles of thunder broke his concentration, scattering his idyllic visions to the four corners of the globe. "To hell with this!" he shouted, sprinting to the open window. Before he had the chance to shut out the racket, something changed. The anger that had peaked only moments before disbursed amidst the howling wind. The scene was awe inspiring, wild, yet somehow mesmerizing. With eyes fixed on the horizon, he witnessed a solid line of threatening storm clouds closing in at phenomenal speed. It was as if the normally serene setting had run amok. The starry canvas had been replaced with shades of black and dark grey and bolts of electricity ripped across the night sky. Suddenly, the heavens opened up and unleashed a torrential downpour, soaking him to the skin.

"My Lord," he cried aloud, charged with exhilaration. "Thy fury is upon us. Send down Your wrath in all its glory! Cleanse this world of sin!"

As if his prayer was heard in the heavens, the wind gusted with tornadic ferocity and a thunderous voice boomed within the raging storm. "My chosen one," the voice said. "It is I, your beloved Father. Hark, for My time is nigh!"

Euphoric, he leaned out over the sill and allowed the biting rain to pelt mercilessly against him. His face stung and his eyes blurred. Though his vision was distorted, he observed a glowing, fire-like mass bobbing in the distance. It danced from side to side in an unthreatening fashion before rushing up to the window. For fear of being burned, he jumped back and hid behind the soaked drapes.

"It's the fires of hell," he cried, peeking through the fabric. "Please, Lord, not me!"

The spirited orb ignored his pleas and pulsated nearby,

emitting a warm glow. It was soothing and invited him to bask in its light. Though the flames burned high, the temperature remained cool. And for a moment, the storm ceased.

"Have no fear," the familiar voice said. "Rejoice! For your time has come to see Me in all My glory!"

"Are You my Lord?" he asked, excited by the strange visit. "Or are you the demon from hell, the unforsaken one?"

As his words were spoken, the storm re-intensified with hail and tremendous winds. The drapes whipped about him and huge bolts of lightning crashed with thunderous claps. Immediately, the warmth was gone and replaced with a bitter cold.

"Come to Me, My son," the voice beckoned. "Take flight with Me."

He neared the apparition. Body trembling, he hesitantly climbed out onto the sill uncertain as to whether or not it was blatant curiosity or desperation to put closure to the bizarre scene which motivated him. For some odd reason, he just felt as though he must play it out to the end. He must stand up with eyes open wide, ready to face the unknown with total faith. Faith was all he had. And he knew that in the end faith would be his salvation.

"Trust in Me," the voice said calmly. "For I am your God and you are my servant. Walk with Me this celebrated night, for you shall finally meet My Holy Family."

Sedated by the gentle tone, he stepped off the ledge and soared downward into the raging storm. His adrenalin raced, yet an odd calmness enveloped him. Although he hurled toward Earth with remarkable speed, he had no fear. His conscious mind was consumed with a new confidence and his beliefs were stronger than ever. Just as he was about to hit the ground with deadly accuracy, an icy hand reached out of the electrically charged fireball obstructing the impact. This divine intervention was the final sign that his Lord was his Master and ruled all situations. Now filled with unchained anxiety, he grabbed tight to his savior and ascended toward the heavens.

"Come," the voice said. "Time is of the essence. You shall finally know your Lord."

Leaving all hesitation behind, he was spirited off to a caliginous location where faint moans of tortured souls agonized from out of the darkness. Although the confines of this realm included roads paved with good intentions, unmistakable sounds of sorrow could be heard. The disturbed cries reflected numerous visions of suffering and torment, obviously a payback for sins committed. This kingdom with its mix of sadistic satires and darkened images was strange, yet somewhat stimulating, though reason escaped him. It was full of contradictions, but obvious that his Lord in all His glory dominated the situation.

"My chosen one," the voice said. "Cast your eyes downward. Gaze upon your Fathers and sisters. Watch as they revel in the splendor of anathema, for they are all My children. They are reaping their just rewards for their devout service to Me."

121

This was a forgotten island, where thousands of generations amassed as one. It was a lonely place set far off the beaten path, a place where sins were forgiven. The souls trapped in this holy void were numerous, too many to count, and all striving for the same outcome, salvation.

"You are truly My chosen apostle," the voice said. You have led many new souls to Me. And for this, I am pleased. Now, raise the sword of decision and glorify My name!"

"My Father," the chosen one said with glee spewing from his very essence. "I am truly honored to be Your chosen one. I realize my duties now. I am Your faithful servant for now and for all eternity. I have served you since that day long ago and I surrender my soul without reservation. I am consumed by Your word and I devote my life to Your cause. Your will be done."

The chosen one sealed the covenant with blood from his right forefinger, which he smeared onto an ancient, black book. The pact was definite and provided him with the catharsis he so longed for. On signing his fate, the resonance of dying laughter filled the air and the mood became somber. Human sacrifices were offered from marble alters and black hooded beings marched along the perimeter of the domain carrying torches. It was a delectable sight with the sweet aroma of burning flesh feeding his appetite for a renewed subscription to euphoria. Once the ceremony had ended and God's minions had crept back into the blackness, he was replaced in his bed and cast into a much-deserved cataleptic sleep.

CHAPTER 21

The mammoth storm raged through the night, dispensing windswept rains and torrential downpours throughout the foothills of the Canadian Rockies. The temperature had dropped drastically and it looked as if winter had returned with a vengeance. Flash floods had washed out several of the major roadways, and on last report, the tempest was to continue until at least midday.

At dawn, the intermittent hail pelted unmercifully against the old convent, provoking its splintered shutters to flap violently with each intense gust. Great flashes of brilliant white discharged from the ever-billowing sky accentuating the building's inconsistencies. And if the menacing storm continued, it wouldn't be long before new damage would add to its already tarnished glamour.

"Oh, my Lord!" Reverend Mother exclaimed, unnerved by the constant racket. "When will this blasted storm end?"

With extreme caution, she peered through her ecru, eyelet curtains, afraid of each thunderous crash of lightning. Wide-eyed and amazed, she stood frozen in place as the powerful gale screamed from the other side of the moist pane of glass. Out of fear of being struck by the high voltage, she backed away and gasped.

"Come now, Sister," she said. Get hold of yourself."

Determined more than ever to overcome the uneasiness, she changed her attention to Domenique. It had been almost a day since she'd seen her; and she was certain she'd fine her in the dining room helping with the breakfast preparations. She quickly pulled off her cotton nightgown, donned her habit, and raced down to the first floor.

"Where's Sister Domenique?" she blurted to Sister Anne who was placing the silverware on the table.

"Good morning, Mother," Sister Anne said, her face solemn. "I'm sorry, but I'm afraid there's been no sign of her today. The chatter around here is that she's left the nest."

"Hush, Sister," Mother bellowed. "She wouldn't just leave. I mean more to her than that. If she'd chosen a different life, I'd have known about it."

"Sorry, Mother. They're only rumors. Personally, I believe something's amiss."

Rather than discuss the morbid possibilities, she dismissed the older nun and began to design a proper course of action. It was dispiriting, but all was not lost. Without allowing her imagination to run away, she strolled up to the buffet and nudged Sister Agnes.

"Good morning, Mother," Sister Agnes said. "Would you care for a cup of coffee?"

"Yes, thank you," Mother said, with a renewed sense of hope. "Have you had any word on Sister Domenique?"

"No Mother, nothing," she said, wincing as another crack of thunder shook the building. "Though I certainly pray that she found shelter from this storm. It's hell out there."

"I agree," Mother said as dozens of hungry girls burst into the room. "I haven't seen a storm this fierce in years."

"Oh, well," Sister Agnes said with a frown. "I suppose it's time for you to give some sort of explanation to the household. But be gentle with your words. You know how fragile some of the girls are and we wouldn't want to scare them."

"Sister," Mother said, shooting a glare. "It's not necessary for you to dictate how I am to speak or what I am to say. Have I made myself clear?"

"Perfectly."

"Ladies," Mother began, not wishing to get into an argument. "Please remain quiet for a moment. I have something terribly important to discuss with you. It appears Sister Domenique is missing. She never returned to the abbey last night and I'm very concerned. Has anyone seen or heard anything pertaining to her disappearance? I'm in a quandary and I desperately need your help."

A sudden hush fell over the room.

"I see," Mother said after a long pause. "I suppose the next step will be for Sister Agnes and I to set out for the RCMP when the storm subsides. Now, let's begin with the blessing."

Several hours later, the storm abated. It was barely long enough for Reverend Mother and her travel companion to risk the drive into town. Anxious for closure, they slipped into their overcoats, grabbed large black umbrellas, and carefully walked across the soggy terrain toward the car, encountering many deep puddles along the way.

"Be careful, Sister," Mother said, gripping the handle of her umbrella. "This ground is treacherous!"

"For goodness sake," Sister Agnes called from behind. "I'd appreciate a hand. I can only travel as fast as these old bones will carry me."

"I'm sorry, Sister Agnes," Mother yelled dashing to her side. "I don't know where my mind is today. Here, take hold of my arm."

Dodging the raindrops, she expeditiously escorted her to the old station wagon and deposited her into the passenger seat. After fastening her in, she dashed around the car, slid behind the wheel, and pumped the gas pedal. It took a while, but eventually the tired engine whirred, spit, and kicked into gear. On hearing it crank, a sense of relief swam over her. Ready to brave the storm, she gripped the wheel with both hands and began her toilsome trek over the puddled ruts along the winding, unsurfaced road into town.

Within the hour, she was parked in front of the police station. She'd made the trip without incident and could now focus on her dilemma. Eager for aid, she helped Sister Agnes navigate the steep flight of brick steps to the main lobby. She plopped the nun down on a bench and flew up to the counter where a handsome, young officer was standing.

"Excuse me, Sir," Mother said, nearly out of breath. "We're here on urgent business. We must speak to Inspector Piedmont at once."

"Would you mind taking a seat over there," he replied, pointing to the long, wooden bench where Sister Agnes sat. "I'll inform him that you're here."

"Thank you," Mother said. "You're very kind."

Unable to do anything else, she proceeded to the seat and acquainted herself with the surroundings. The station buzzed with conversations of the wicked storm. Telephones rang from unseen rooms. The thick, wood doors squeaked and squealed as employees went in and out about their business. It appeared that the building was in dire need of renovation, though it seemed to operate capably.

"Inspector Piedmont can see you now," the officer said, ushering them into a large office. "Please, have a seat."

The nuns took their seats and looked around. The office was in great disarray and poisoned with the thick stench of cigar smoke. A hodgepodge of papers and soiled manila folders towered high in every corner. A number of dented filing cabinets lined the paint-chipped walls, making the room seem smaller than it actually was. The only window was dressed in partially opened, gray, Venetian blinds, which emphasized the utter dullness of the day.

Minutes later, a plump, middle-aged man with a neatly trimmed, pen-lined mustache entered the room carrying a large cardboard box. He smelled of smoke. A ring of bushy, gray hair crowned his balding head, and his uniform seemed well maintained. He smiled as he placed the carton on his disorganized desk.

"Good day, Sisters," he said. "I see you've received my message. Thank you for coming in."

"Message?" Mother asked. "I'm a bit confused, Inspector. There must be some misunderstanding."

"Didn't Corporal LaPorte stop by the convent earlier today? I told him to call you to ask if you wouldn't mind stopping by my office. I wanted to speak with you regarding the Bourgeois child's death."

"No, Inspector," Mother said. "We haven't seen him. However, we did see a police car race past us on our way into town."

"That must have been him," he said, toying with the end of his moustache. "In any case, I'm glad you've made it here."

"I suppose," Mother said, miffed by the misunderstanding. "But I'm afraid we're here on a different matter. One of our sisters is missing!"

"Tell me about it, Mother," he said, sitting behind his desk.

"It's Sister Domenique Rondeau," Mother said. "We haven't seen her since yesterday morning."

"Domenique? Hmmm, I've heard that name before. Can't seem to place it, though. In any case, go on. I'm sure it'll come to me in time."

"She had told Sister Agnes she was to meet someone yesterday afternoon at Saint Michael's Monastery and hasn't been seen or heard from since. You see, she has never done anything like this before and I'm worried. I feel something is terribly wrong! I beg you, Inspector, please help us find her!"

"Okay, Reverend Mother, settle down," he said, jotting something in a spiral notepad. "We'll figure this out. Let's take it one step at a time." He turned to Agnes and smiled. "Sister Agnes, what time did you last see Sister Domenique?"

"Let me see," she said, adjusting her whimple. "I think it was nine o'clock when she told me of the meeting. Wait a minute. No, I'm mistaken. It was around noontime. Yes, it was yesterday at noontime. I remember it emphatically."

"Are you sure about the time?" he asked.

"Yes," she replied. "Yes, I'm sure of it. Didn't I just say that?"

"Did she say with whom she was to meet?"

"No, Sir," Agnes replied. "She didn't say."

"Did she mention the time of the alleged meeting?"

"Yes. I remember her saying something about four o'clock yesterday afternoon. I'm certain those were her words. I truly hope this information will help you to locate her."

"Thank you, Sister. I'm sure it will," he said, turning to Reverend Mother. "Has anyone else seen or spoken with her since that time?"

"No, Inspector," Mother answered. "I've questioned everyone at the convent and no one claims to have seen her since yesterday morning. And when she didn't show up for dinner last night, we went directly to the monastery in search of her. There, we spoke with Monsignor Valois about the situation."

"Did he have any clues as to her whereabouts?"

"No," Mother said. "He questioned the brethren, but no one had seen her since mass on Sunday morning."

"What did you do next?" he asked, tapping his pencil on the notepad.

"On Monsignor's suggestion, we scoured the grounds, but found no trace of her. She has merely vanished! I have a dreadful feeling something awful has happened to her."

"Aren't you being a bit premature with your assumption, Reverend Mother?" he asked.

"No, not at all," Mother said flatly. "With the Bourgeois child's murder and last night's horrendous storm, I feel more than justified for my bleak outlook. You don't have to be a physicist to figure out that she could be in some sort of danger."

"I understand your reasoning," he said. "Did you happen to bring a photograph of her? It would make things a whole lot easier if we knew who we were looking for."

"Yes, I did," Mother said and handed it to him. "It's an old one, but it's all I have."

"Hmmm," he said, placing it on his desk and massaging his chin. "Not to change the subject, but the Bourgeois girl is the reason I needed to speak with you. If you'd indulge me for just a moment, we'll get right back to Sister Domenique."

"How can we possibly help?" Mother asked, perturbed by his lack of concern for Sister Domenique's whereabouts. "We only know that which we've read in the *Gazette*. I've already given you this information prior to the funeral. But at the risk of being redundant, the last time I had seen any of the Bourgeois' was before the reconstruction of our church had begun."

"Are you certain no one from the convent has seen any strange characters in the vicinity? Even a small clue could aid us. Thus far, we have no leads as to the identity of her murderer."

"Yes, Inspector," Mother answered. "I'm positive. We

have seen no strangers lurking in the woods. I wish there was something more I could add."

"Okay then," he said, flipping through his notes. "Let's get back to Domenique. You're certain no one had seen her at the monastery yesterday?"

"Correct," Mother said. "That's what the monsignor told us. I've known him for many years and have no reason to doubt his word. He's a stickler for details. Therefore, I'm certain he has questioned his household thoroughly."

"All right," he said. "Maybe there's a possibility someone has seen her on the road, either arriving or departing from the monastery. I'll have to check it out."

"I pray you're right," Mother said.

"Does she have any family?" he asked. "There's always the chance she went home for a visit. Have you made any inquiries as to that theory?"

"No," Mother said, scanning his face for any sign of compassion. "She's an orphan."

"Really?"

"Yes, Inspector," she said, not wishing to delve into any complicated explanation. "I believe we've told you just about everything we know. Do you think it will help you to locate her?"

"I hope so, Mother."

"Remember," Mother said. "Every minute that passes is crucial. And at this very moment, she could be in a life-threatening situation."

"I'm not so sure it's that dire, but we'll be by the convent later to go through her belongings. If we're lucky, we'll find a lead. At the least, it's a good place to start. I'll also post her picture with a missing person's ad in the *Gazette*. I'm certain someone will have seen her."

"What a splendid idea," Mother said and gracefully rose to her feet. "We appreciate anything you can do for us."

"That's what we're here for," he said, escorting them to the door. "Good day, Sisters."

As the nuns were about to leave the building, Reverend Mother stopped short and turned back. "Inspector," she said. "I almost forgot. While at the monastery last night, Monsignor Valois mentioned that some of the priests had seen Sister Domenique talking privately with Father Xavier on Sunday morning. I don't know if it means anything, but maybe it will help."

"Really?" he said, jotting down this new information. "Is there anything more?"

"Yes. It seems that she had a conversation with Father André and Father Thomas as well."

"Hmmm," he said raising an eyebrow. "How interesting. I've spoken with them before. I found Father André to be extremely odd. And that Father Xavier seems to have a few misplaced screws."

"I think he's crazy," Sister Agnes said, leaning against the doorframe.

"Hush, Sister," Mother said sternly. "You know that Monsignor told us he's been ill since his arrival."

"Well," Inspector Piedmont said. "I'll definitely have to go a second round with them. I'll also have my men check the area between the convent and the monastery. We may find some clue as to her whereabouts. Thank you for the new information."

The nuns bid their adieus and exited swiftly. En route to the abbey, Reverend Mother could only think of Domenique. "Where could she be?" she said with sadness, wiping tears from her eyes. At that moment, all she had left was her strong faith and hope the police would find her.

CHAPTER 22

In four days time, investigations ground to a halt. Though several anonymous leads had streamed into the department, most of them turned out to be dead ends. The stacks of reports and unanswered questions multiplied and the police were no closer to solving either of the two cases. With nothing new to go on, it appeared the Bourgeois girl would just be another statistic added to the violent killing spree, which plagued the nation for the past year and a half. And it seemed all efforts were in vain as to the location of Sister Domenique.

Piedmont had concluded his preliminary interrogation of Saint Michael's brethren, but sensed something wasn't quite right. Though all of their alibis had checked out for the most part, some inconsistencies were prevalent and warranted closer examination.

After compiling the data, he came to the decision that he'd begin his re-interrogation with Father Xavier.

On Monday afternoon, Inspector Piedmont and Sergeant Major Roget once again set off for the monastery. Despite Piedmont's solemn promise made on the day of his daughter's funeral to never step foot on the monastery's grounds again, he found himself back for another spin on what he called, 'the Catholic carousel of fate', for he strongly believed that the entire morbid scenario was predestined. A sick joke orchestrated by God as a means of persecution for those, like himself, who have lost their faith. Plagued by his analytical frame of mind, he pushed his personal anguish aside and pressed down hard on the pedal. At that exact moment, the blinding sun burned his hot cheeks as an icy breeze slapped his exposed skin. He supposed that being attacked by the drastic variations in temperature was a reflection of his opinions on the cases, which filled his docket and shifted his thoughts to the matter at hand, the questions he'd ask. To his astonishment, as he turned onto the last stretch of pavement, he encountered a multitude of television vans parked haphazardly along the normally lazy lane. His skin crawled to see such lack of law and order, but he couldn't muster the nerve to add ticketing to his hectic schedule. It appeared that every city in each province was represented by a news crew searching for new leads as to the disappearance of Sister Domenique Rondeau.

"Christ!" Piedmont said, quickly raising his window in a

136

feeble attempt to block out the constant shouts for answers. "I'd ticket the lot of them if I thought it'd do any good."

"Nah, it wouldn't hold them off," Roget said, offering a half smile. "They're like leeches, ready to blood suck anything newsworthy."

"But, how the hell did they got wind of this so quickly? The ink isn't even dry yet."

"It's radar," Roget joked. "Their antennas spread across the country, coast to coast."

"You know it. Like a cancer. But how did they figure out that we'd end up back here?"

"Beats me," Roget said. "Can't decipher that one. But it's obvious their expecting something."

"Yeah, it looks as though the world is watching our investigation. We'd best watch our asses."

"You'd better bend over and put on your best smile."

"Right," Piedmont said, shaking his head. "I'll do that. Come on, let's get this over with."

As they approached, they were instantly mobbed by reporters, all adorned with press passes and badges from their respective employers. Careful not to injure anyone, Piedmont inched his way through the sea of flashing cameras and up to the iron gates, eyes kept trained on the entrance. Ignoring the barrage of questions, he landed his hand down on the horn.

"Where the hell are they?" he asked above the din.

"Don't know," Roget answered. "Didn't you call first? Aren't they expecting us?"

Before he had the chance to respond, an older priest strolled down the stone path, unlocked the gate, and ushered the vehicle onto the grounds, barring the reporters from entering.

"About time," Piedmont barked, and sped up the drive, never offering the priest a lift. "They were really getting on my nerves." He parked the vehicle and followed Roget to the massive, dark mahogany doors.

"Good afternoon, gentlemen," Monsignor Valois greeted. "I see you've brought along quite an entourage."

"Entourage?" Piedmont said, looking over his shoulder, and back toward the gate. "Oh, them. They've been hounding us like flies on shit ever since the missing nun article hit the papers. I guess they assumed this would be our next stop."

"Well, it appears their assumptions were correct," Monsignor said, ushering them into his private office. "Flies are never far behind, when words resemble trash. You really should clean up your vocabulary, Inspector. As you know, the good Lord respects those who respect others."

"Don't try to preach that crap to me. Whether or not I respect you or the church has nothing to do with why we're here. And it's certainly not going to help find the nun, so let's stick to business." He took a seat next to Roget and continued, "Like I told you on the phone, I'm here to find some answers."

"Certainly," Monsignor said, shuffling some papers on his desk. "But as I told you earlier, I don't know how much more I can say on the subject."

"Okay then, I guess we'll have to go over everything again to make sure we have all the facts straight. And the sooner we can get through this, the sooner we'll be out of here."

"I understand, Inspector."

"Let's begin with the rosary beads," Piedmont said, "Are there any missing?"

"No," Monsignor said, "All rosary beads are accounted for. I even went as far as to insist upon seeing everyone's set for personal verification."

"Were any identical to the set I showed you on my last visit?"

"Almost all of them. I'd have to say that most clergy from around the globe have the same kind or very similar. It's a common make."

"So much for that angle," Piedmont said sourly, returning to his notes. "As you know, a few days ago, Reverend Mother informed me of Sister Domenique's disappearance and of an alleged meeting with someone here at the monastery. We now believe it was to be with Father Xavier. Do you have any new information for me? Any small detail would be helpful."

"No, Inspector. I wish I had. I've questioned and requestioned everyone and no one has seen her since Sunday."

139

"What about this Father Xavier?" Piedmont asked. "When I spoke with him, he claimed she never showed up. Is he still sticking to his bullshit story? He was jumpy and I can't forget how he acted at the funeral. He's definitely hiding something."

"Though I understand your skepticism, Inspector, you can't possibly hold him accountable for all the world's little imperfections due to his delicate medical condition. And referring to his 'bullshit story' as you so delicately put it, I have no reason to question his word."

"Listen here, you pompous jerk!" Piedmont yelled, leaning forward, banging his fist on the desk, and knocking a potted mum to the floor. "There's a goddamned killer on the loose! He's already butchered thirteen little girls, including mine. And Domenique may well have been his latest victim. So don't give me that shit about this priest and his fragility. He may be the goddamned one we're after."

"Please, Inspector," Monsignor said. "Retreat to your corner. If there were any question as to the behavior of one of our clergymen, I and the church would recognize it and act accordingly."

"Bullshit!" Piedmont shouted, holding back his urge to shove his fist down the monsignor's throat. "I know how the hell the Catholic Church works. It wasn't so long ago that a bishop in the states was accused of molesting young boys. If I'm not mistaken, it was somewhere in New England. Remember? It was

140

all over the wires. And that was only the first. Since then, accusations have popped up all over. But in the end, the charges are always miraculously dropped. Instead of being officially condemned and excommunicated as a heretic, they're martyred. I guess that's where your religious mysteries fit into the scheme of things. Is it just coincidence or an act of God?"

"Inspector! You can't possibly believe there's a connection. That's a preposterous insinuation. Are you implying that the whole Catholic Church is involved in this foul play?"

"I'm not implying anything of the sort," Piedmont said, trying to resituate his animosities. "I'm just trying to make the point that I know the lengths the church will go to protect one of their own. Indeed, it's quite a fellowship."

"Inspector," Roget blurted. "Don't you think it's time to interrogate Xavier? I'm sure Monsignor Valois has helped us as much as he can."

"Don't ever interrupt me again!" Piedmont said, glaring at Roget. He then turned and faced the Monsignor. "Sergeant Major Roget is right. Where is he? We have some unfinished business to discuss."

"Once again," Monsignor said. "I'm sorry to have to be the barer of bad news, but it won't be possible to speak with him at this time."

"Why not?" Piedmont said.

"Well, you see, Father Xavier's been in and out of

141

consciousness ever since he learned Sister Domenique was missing. Obviously, the news devastated him. He's been under doctor's care since."

"What the hell kind of shit are you giving me now? When I spoke with him on Friday, he was healthy enough. Flakey, but healthy all the same."

"This is true, Inspector. But there's a good possibility your visit only aggravated his medical condition. You have a tendency to aggravate no matter what the circumstance."

"Really?" Piedmont exclaimed, eyes bulging, veins swelling in his temples. "You want aggravation? Well, I'll cause you some goddamned aggravation. It would be my pleasure to drag the bunch of you frustrated bastards down to the station. I'm sure those reporters outside would have a field day with that! Who would they crucify then?"

"Now, now, Inspector," Monsignor said. "Settle down. There's no need for threats. If Doctor Cartier gives his approval, I'll allow you to speak with him."

"Did you get all that, Roget?" Piedmont asked. "We wouldn't want to misquote his holiness, now would we?"

"Uh, word for word, Inspector," Roget said, scribbling in a notepad. "It's been quite an interview."

"Is the doctor with him now?" Piedmont asked.

"No," Monsignor said. "He's come and gone and is not due back until tomorrow morning. You'll have to wait until then.

Do we have an agreement?"

"For the moment," Piedmont said. "But my gut instinct tells me that this Xavier character is faking it. You know there are some people who can control their own heart rate. It's just possible he's one of them. Maybe he kidnapped the nun and came up with this cock and bull story about never meeting her. Maybe they have a thing going. It has been known to happen. I'm sure there are some of you who still like women."

"Inspector," Monsignor bellowed. "I believe you've gone too far. You're grasping at straws. If you had anything concrete to go on, you'd have arrested him already."

"These things take time," Piedmont said with a grin.

"Inspector, I can understand your lack of faith in God due to the loss of your daughter. It must weigh heavy on your mind. As much as I dislike your new attitude, I truly understand the defensiveness. But we're not the monsters or the enemies. Though some clergy are not cut out for a life in the church, you can't assume we're all evil."

"Well, we won't know anything for sure until we speak with the doctor," Piedmont said, walking to the door. "What time will he be in?"

"Around seven o'clock."

"Okay, we'll see you then."

Piedmont followed Roget to the vehicle, uncertain if he had made the correct decision. His instinct told him to dash back into the building, find Xavier, and force him to talk, but he suppressed the gnawing urge and opted to honor the accursed agreement. He felt as though he had just made a pact with the devil and believed he would live to regret it. Agitated at how the day had progressed, he revved the engine and sped off the property, giving the reporters the finger as he passed.

"Good thing the gate was open," Roget said. "Or we'd be waiting for an ambulance."

"Can you believe that asshole?" Piedmont said, gripping tight to the wheel. "His attitude sucks. I don't trust that bastard, never have."

"Don't you think you may be overreacting a bit, Norbert?"

"No!" Piedmont said, focusing on the road. "He just burns my ass. Don't you think it's strange that the last two murders occurred only after Xavier entered the picture? And he was seen with the missing nun."

"Is it possible the two cases are connected?"

"Maybe."

"It's somewhat far fetched, but I suppose anything's possible at this point," Roget said.

"I guess we won't know until tomorrow."

CHAPTER 23

Diffused rays of predawn sun crept over the horizon leaning sluggishly against the rugged slopes of the Rockies. Its normal brilliance, obscured by the leaden sky, made the transition from the blackness of night to the pewter of morning seem almost inconspicuous. The forecast was for another Pacific storm to rage in nearby British Columbia, but it was too early to discern if its effects would be felt locally.

"Dammit!" the chosen one yelled, springing from his bed to the window, "What's happening to me?"

Short of breath, he threw open the sash and detected the barely visible, canopy of thin clouds. The humidity was thick and choked off his oxygen supply. Struggling to breathe, he inhaled hard, massaging his temples, but the pressure in his head remained. His mind was awhirl with confusion, his memory fragmented.

145

Trying desperately to ascertain whether his rendezvous with God was a reality or dream, he focused beyond his angst and re-enacted the role he played on that celebrated night. Instantly, it all came flooding back. His mind drew a perspicuous picture.

"My Father!" he cried aloud, not caring if he woke the world. "I remember it all! It was true! You did call on me. It was the night of the great tempest. You summoned me in the same manner as the ghosts of Ebenezer Scrooge. I, too, was fortunate enough to see my true destiny and am blessed. My thoughts are finally clear and I have no doubts. So, if it is Your will, I shall aid You. I shall pave the way for Your return. I only pray for the strength to persevere over the trials and tribulations which lie ahead. Amen."

Ignited with a reborn energy, he closed the window, picked up his rosary from the nightstand, and covertly proceeded through the dark hall down to the pantry. It pleased him to find the kitchen vacant. Careful not to make any noise, he assembled a tray of food, poured the last few drops of milk into a golden chalice, and lit a candle. Once again, it was time to visit Domenique.

On his arrival to her bedside, he immediately placed the food down and held the candle close to her. Even in the inadequate light, he could see her features were worn and her skin was a pale gray. A deep crimson stained her blindfold, and purple marks encircled her wrists and ankles. Her condition had deteriorated and she appeared to be acting like an injured animal.

146

"You're a pitiful heap of flesh and bones," he muttered irritably, while setting the candle down on the antique table. "You're pathetic!" He removed her gag with a quick pull and laughed aloud. "Oh, stop your whining."

"Xavier," she whispered, words barely audible. "Why are you doing this to me? You're supposed to be a man of the cloth. For God's sake, have mercy on me."

"Do not lament, my dear. For mercy only comes to those who repent their sins. Doesn't the remorse burn deep within your soul? Well? Haven't you anything to say?"

"Y-y-yes, I'll repent. I'll do anything."

"Excellent! Then, do you offer your wretched life up to God, our Father?"

"Yes," she cried, tears rolling off her face. "Now, let me go! I beg you! Please, I won't leave your side. I promise to help you in any way I can."

"How can you help me?"

"We can help each other. We're both sinners. Untie me and we'll cleanse the world together."

"Hmmm," he said, sitting down on the bed, placing the tray on his lap. "Maybe this is what our Father meant by referring to you as the handmaiden."

"That's right," she said, squirming from side to side. "That's exactly what he meant. You're the chosen one. You said as much, yourself. You and I are destined to bring about his return.

147

God told me, too."

"Did he?"

"Yes, yes. He came to me in my sleep. It was a vision."

"What message did He relay, pray tell?"

"He told me that I am the handmaiden. He ordered you to release me. Quick, untie me. We can go to the abbey together and continue with the purification process."

"You deceitful bitch!" he screamed, a brittle laugh rising from his throat. "Did you think I would fall prey to your lies, your trickery? Hah! You know nothing of His plan."

"No," she cried, thrashing about the bed. "You have it all wrong. I'm not lying to you. Let me go and I'll prove it."

"Hush," he said softly, pressing two fingers on her lips. "Enough talk. It's time to eat."

He shoveled the food into her mouth stifling her annoying utterances, while studying her struggle to devour the meal. It amused him. Normally, the sound of her chewing would be bothersome, but tonight his thoughts were on her upcoming deliverance. Once finished, he took the Bible from the night table, turned to *Revelations* 17:7,8; and read aloud:

> *"And the angel said unto me,*
> *Wherefore didst thou marvel? I will*
> *tell the mystery of the woman, and of*
> *the beast that carrieth   her, which*
> *hath the seven heads and ten horns.*
> *   The beast that thou sawest*
> *was, and is not; and shall ascend out*

of the bottomless pit, and go into
perdition: and they that dwell on the
earth shall wonder, whose names
were not written in the book of life
from the foundation of the world,
when they behold the beast that was,
and is not, and yet is."

"You are that woman, Domenique!" he said, slamming the Bible onto the table. "You are our Lord's handmaiden!" He picked up his rosary, and continued, "You shall be His vessel! And I, the chosen one, must bring you to salvation!" He proceeded to heat the rosary's crucifix in the candle's flame then firmly pressed it into her forehead, leaving the bloody impression of Christ.

"Aargh!" she shrieked, kicking up in her bed, blindfold moist with tears.

"Silence!" he yelled, slapping her repeatedly. "Offer yourself as a sacrifice to our Lord and stop your sniveling. Offer your pain and suffering to Him so that this world may be saved! For you must pave the way to salvation with cobblestones made from your own blood."

"Never!" she screeched.

Before another word was uttered, he cast the rosary aside, straddled her, and pillaged her innocence once again. Visions of glory flashed across his mind. The scenes of his mysterious encounter with the Lord only heightened his excitement. His

149

senses were rampant. With each plunge, he screamed, "Let my blessed, life-giving fluid fill you! Cleanse you! Redeem you!"

After a time, she let out a muffled shriek and then laid still. Her muscles relaxed and her body went limp. The constant trembling stopped and silence replaced her whimpers.

Angered by her noncompliance, he dismounted and scoffed. He would have to postpone the cleansing procedure for another time. Without looking at her again, he hastily redressed, assembled his belongings, locked the door, and raced back through the tunnels toward his room. On the stairway, he overheard voices coming from the kitchen and stopped to listen.

"As soon as I'm finished with my tea, I'll go up and check on him," he heard the monsignor say. "I certainly hope he's better. He's been in and out of consciousness for such an awfully long time and I'm a tad worried."

"I pray you're right," Father Beaumont said. "Lately, he's had mounting problems. I believe the poor soul is mentally unstable, but that's for the doctor to decide. What time is he expected in?"

"In a little while," Monsignor said.

"Are the officers here yet?"

"No, but they should be here momentarily."

"What sort of questions do you think they'll ask him?" Father Beaumont asked.

"As distasteful as they may be, I'm certain they will pertain to Sister Domenique and her whereabouts."

"You can't seriously believe that he had anything to do with it. Can you?"

"No, of course not. It's utter nonsense."

"It's a frightening thought, though," Father Beaumont said.

"What is?"

"The fact that this whole unfortunate mess could injure the Catholic Church's reputation. It's all so distasteful."

"Don't fret, Father. Nothing will stand in the way of our good name. Saint Michael's has been around for generations and I will not allow any adverse publicity to come between our devoted, charitable contributors and us. Go now, you have a mass to serve."

Without waiting, the chosen one swiftly ascended the stairs to his room. He had heard enough. It felt marvelous to have witnessed the monsignor's true colors. It was all out in the open. He was to be commended for his brazen candidness, and his love of the almighty dollar. It was a comfort to know that on the Monsignor's day of atonement, the Father would give him what he rightfully deserved. A punishment to fit the crime. Exuberant with his hypothesis, he slipped into bed, pulled the covers up around his neck, and prayed, "Almighty Father, Your will be done!"

CHAPTER 24

"Gentlemen," Father Pierre said to Inspector Piedmont and Sergeant Major Roget. "Make yourselves at home. I'll inform the monsignor of your arrival. I know he's been expecting you." Before they could respond, he offered a broad smile and closed the sitting room door.

"He was in a bit of a hurry," Roget said. "Don't you think? But he did seem happy."

"Yeah, it must be something in the food," Piedmont said with sarcasm. "LSD maybe?"

"You really do despise these fellows, don't you?"

"I guess."

"Why is that, Sir?"

"Because they're all tight-lipped, tight-asses. They stand

by their own private code without any regard for the rest of us. And I wouldn't trust my dog's life to them.

"Always on your guard, eh?" Roget said, taking his seat on a small, Victorian divan. "Can't even give them a bit of slack."

Piedmont ignored him and scanned the room. He noted the Persian rug and suspected it probably cost more than all of the furniture in the office combined. He surmised that the costly frivolities were no doubt generous donations from loyal parishioners trying to pave their way to heaven and it appalled him. How the church could be so callous with so much hunger and suffering in the world was detestable, he thought. Brimming with animosity, he scoffed and picked up a religious magazine from the antique coffee table. He'd hoped it would change his mood.

"Hey, Jacques," he said, a little later, while flipping through the pages. "Maybe you should subscribe to this one. Real interesting, but a girlie magazine it ain't. I'd bet my annual salary that they keep the hardcore stuff in their rooms."

"Yeah, and maybe if we hang around here long enough, they can even convert your taste in reading material. I'm certain Claudine would appreciate that, eh?"

"When icebergs form in hell."

Twenty minutes later, Monsignor Valois entered with a tray of coffee and biscuits. "Ah!" he said, nodding to them. "Welcome back, gentlemen."

"Good morning, Monsignor," the officers chimed.

"In view of the fact that you're a bit early," Monsignor Valois began. "And Doctor Cartier hasn't arrived yet, I thought you might enjoy a little breakfast."

"Thanks," Piedmont said, grinning. "Don't mind if I do. It's about time you gave something back to the community, even if it is only a free breakfast."

"Uh, yeah, thank you," Roget choked, eyeing his commander in chief as he reached for a biscuit. "We really appreciate this. It smells great." He picked up one of the buns and downed it without taking time to breathe, then licked his fingers and dove for another.

"Where are your manners, man?" Piedmont bellowed. "Did you forget them in the car?"

"Now, Inspector," Monsignor said, "That's perfectly all right. I admire a man with honest enthusiasm."

"Yeah," Piedmont said. "I'm sure you do. Isn't honesty next to Godliness? And isn't Godliness what you priests strive for?"

"Oh, Inspector," Monsignor said. "It seems nothing has changed. It appears you still have that bug lodged in your nose. You should think about having it surgically removed. It may even brighten your charming disposition."

"Okay, gentlemen," Roget said, holding up his hands. "Enough is enough! Lay down the swords. We're here on business, not for a sparring match."

"The Sergeant's absolutely right," Monsignor said taking a biscuit. "A change of subject is definitely in order and I have some news that I think may release some tension. It appears that Father Xavier is awake at last.

"That's terrific," Roget exclaimed.

"Yes, but something bothers me," Monsignor said. "It seems he doesn't recall what happened to him or what prompted his latest collapse. I'll feel much better when Doctor Cartier re-examines him."

"Really?" Piedmont said. "No recollection, eh?"

"None," Monsignor answered flatly. "So, once the doctor arrives and finishes with Father Xavier, we'll be able to spend a little time with him."

"Not so fast, Valois," Piedmont said, wiping the corner of his mouth with a green linen napkin. "If you don't mind, I want to speak with the doctor before I speak to Xavier. And you're not invited to the pow-wow. So, when the time is right, make yourself scarce."

"Of course," Monsignor said. "I wouldn't think otherwise. The doctor should be here shortly."

Piedmont was delighted to hear the news. He believed that maybe now he would get the answers to his ever-growing list of questions. Satisfied that today would be a day of resolution, he sat in wait.

A short while later, an older gentleman, fashionably dressed in a white, linen suit, approached the doorway. He sported a pair of expensive-looking beige alligator boots, probably Italian, and carried a shiny, black medical bag. His wrinkled face looked worn and he gave the impression that his feathers were a bit ruffled.

"Excuse me, gentlemen," the man said. "Father Pierre told me that a pair of policemen wish to speak with me. Unfortunately, I won't have time for them. I'm already running late and my schedule is extremely tight. Now, if you'll excuse me, I must see to Father Xavier."

"Hold on one minute!" Piedmont said, standing and walking toward the man. "You must be Doctor Cartier."

"That's correct," the man retorted.

"I'm Inspector Norbert Piedmont of the Royal Canadian Mounted Police, and this is my partner, Sergeant Major Jacques Roget," he said, flashing his badge. "We apologize for the inconvenience, but we have some important questions to ask. Now, if you'll come in and take a seat, we'll get on with it."

"Hmph!" Doctor Cartier grunted. "It seems I have no choice. Make it quick."

"We'll make this as brief as possible, Doctor," Roget said. "Now, please be seated."

"Very well," Doctor Cartier said, sitting by the fireplace. "What are these important questions?"

"Thank you for your cooperation, Doctor," Piedmont said,

thumbing through his notepad. "We're conducting a formal investigation into the disappearance of a nun. Her name is Sister Domenique Rondeau."

"I'm sorry, Inspector, but I have no information regarding this individual. To my recollection, she has never been a patient of mine, nor have we met socially."

"I see," Piedmont said, never releasing his stare. "But you are the attending physician to Father Xavier, correct?"

"Yes, but I don't see the connection."

"How did you come to be his physician?"

"Is this really necessary, Inspector?"

"It is," Piedmont said. "Would you kindly keep your answers to the questions asked."

"I've been the house doctor for years. The monsignor summoned me here a few nights back. He told me that Father Xavier had had another bad experience and was unconscious. Therefore, I came as quickly as possible. Didn't the monsignor inform you of this already?"

"In your estimation, Doctor, what do you believe happened to him? Do you have a prognosis?"

"When I arrived he was unconscious, with no detectable signs of trauma to the cranium. He had no bumps or bruises, but that didn't rule out a possible concussion or it may have been the result of a lack of oxygen from one of his seizures." He stopped, lit a pipe, and continued, "Yes, my diagnosis is that he passed out due to his frail condition."

"What exactly is this frail condition everyone talks about?" Piedmont asked.

"Now, let me see," Doctor Cartier said. He faced the ceiling and puffed out smoke rings, which encircled his head. "We're speaking about Father Xavier."

"What do you mean by that?" Piedmont asked.

"The fact is, at my age, it's easy to get my patients' conditions mixed up without reviewing their files. This is highly unorthodox and dangerously close to a form of malpractice. Now, if you'll allow me to continue, other brethren have medical conditions as well and it would be an injustice if I were to disclose inaccurate information."

"I understand," Piedmont said, fearful he was on the verge of losing his most valuable informant to a technicality. "I won't hold you liable. Please, do your best."

"Okay, I'll try to piece together what I can recall of Father Xavier's medical history."

"I'd appreciate that," Piedmont said.

"You see, Father Xavier is a victim of epilepsy. The two major types are grand mal and petit mal. He suffers from the latter. Petit mal is a disease of childhood that does not usually persist past late adolescence, but there is always an exception to the rule. The basic symptom is a brief, abnormal phase of behavior commonly known as a seizure, fit, or convulsion. A person with this form of epilepsy sometimes stops in the middle of whatever activity he's involved in and stares blankly into space. This can sometimes last up to a few minutes. During this blank interval, he is unaware of his surroundings. He may make slight jerking motions of the head or arm, but petit mal seizures do not generally involve falling to the ground. Usually, the victim of such a condition hasn't even realized that the blank spell ever occurred."

"This doesn't make any sense," Piedmont said. "Xavier's so-called seizures have lasted for days. How can you account for this?"

"There's a simple explanation," Doctor Cartier said calmly. "Of course, I can't be sure, due to the fact that I've only been treating him for a short time, but I believe his condition has worsened. It's not the norm, but I think he's progressed to grand mal."

"Is that possible?" Roget asked.

"It certainly is. The most characteristic symptom of grand mal epilepsy is a much more dramatic seizure. The person falls to the ground unconscious. His entire body stiffens. In most cases, he twitches uncontrollably. This can last for up to several minutes and is usually followed by a long period of deep sleep and a state of mental confusion."

"Is there any warning?" Piedmont asked, eager to learn more.

"Yes, most certainly. The impending seizure begins with

159

strange sensations, headaches if you will, before losing consciousness. It could start with a slight tension or some other ill-defined feeling. But other epileptics have quite specific auras such as an impression of smelling unpleasant odors or hearing peculiar sounds."

"Voices maybe?"

"Could be. Not everyone's the same."

"So, anything's possible with this fellow?" Roget asked.

"I don't know what you mean, but it could account for his strange behavior."

"When will you know for sure if this is what he suffers from?" Piedmont asked.

"Well, here's where my problem lies. I've spoken with him regarding this topic on numerous occasions. I've advised him that the sensible thing to do would be for him to allow me to admit him to the hospital in order for me to run the appropriate tests. You know, EEG's, CAT scans, and such. I wanted to refer him to a good neurosurgeon, but he wouldn't hear of it. Therefore, my only other option was to treat him here the best I could."

"I understand," Piedmont said. "But I need to speak with him today. I can't wait any longer. There are many variables and too many unanswered questions. Questions only he can account for."

"Well," Doctor Cartier said, "I won't know anything for certain until I reexamine him. In any case, may I see my patient now?"

"In a moment, Doctor," Piedmont said. "I still have a few more questions. Do you know of Sister Domenique Rondeau?"

"No, Inspector. I've already told you that I do not. Of course, I've read numerous articles about the unfortunate incident, and so has half of North America. Her face has been plastered in all the papers for days."

"Have any amnesiacs fitting her description been admitted to the hospital recently? I know I'm grasping, but I must ask."

"No, Inspector. It's hospital policy for the staff to alert the police department of any suspicious or unknown persons who have been admitted. Especially those with no identity."

"Okay, one last question. Can a person with this type of epilepsy perform violent acts or crimes while under the influence of a seizure?"

"In all earnestness, I don't believe so," Doctor Cartier said and rose to his feet. "But I'm certainly not an authority on the subject. I'm only a general practitioner."

"I thank you for your time, Doctor. If we have any further questions, we'll be in touch."

"Very well, Inspector," Doctor Cartier said, moving toward the door. "By the way, Monsignor, have you come across my old medical bag?"

"No, Doctor," Monsignor said. "I've searched to high heaven and it hasn't turned up. Are you certain you left it here?"

"I'm almost positive, but I suppose I could be mistaken," Doctor Cartier said. He huffed and swiftly exited the room.

"It won't be much longer now, Jacques," Piedmont said, rubbing his hands together. "Maybe now we can finally get some answers."

"Let's hope Father Xavier's the one who has them," Roget said.

"He is," Piedmont said. "I feel it."

"I pray you're wrong, Inspector," Monsignor said. "In any case, I'll allow you to visit him once the doctor finishes his examination, but you must make it brief. Is that understood?"

"Perfectly," Piedmont said, smiling wryly, mulling over all of the information the doctor had relayed. He sat back and began to play with the end of his mustache. "Perfectly."

CHAPTER 25

"How's my patient today?" Doctor Cartier asked as he closed the chamber door and pulled a straight chair up to Xavier's bed. "I'm glad to see you're finally coherent. You've had quite a long nap."

"Am I glad to see you," Xavier said, jumping up in his bed, his face ashen. "What happened to me? How did I get here?"

"Come now, Father Xavier, lay back and relax. Can't you remember anything?"

Xavier's mind whirled with confusion. Though he concentrated hard on the question, nothing surfaced. His head throbbed and even though he held tight to it, the pain persisted. Suddenly, the room spun and his eyes rolled back.

"Father, are you experiencing another migraine?" the

doctor asked, reaching for his stethoscope.

"I can't take it any more!" Xavier screamed, wishing with all his might that he could escape his body and be released from the dreaded torment. "Doctor, for God's sake, help me!"

He grabbed the doctor's coat sleeve as a sudden, frigid blast of air burst through the partially opened window, tearing at the drapes. The door creaked from the force and its rusty hinges moaned. Instantly, the temperature plummeted and it was as if an unseen visitor had entered on a gust of supernatural breath.

"My, Lord, it's freezing in here," Doctor Cartier said rushing over to the window and slamming it shut. "You'll catch your death." He pivoted back toward the bed and gasped. "Oh, sweet Jesus!"

"What's wrong, Doctor?" Xavier asked, his heart racing.

"N-n-nothing. It must have been my eyes. They must be playing tricks on me."

"What did you think you saw?"

"It was a shadow."

"A what?"

"A shadow. Standing by the door." He inched over to the door and closed it. "I closed this already when I first arrived. I'm positive." He reseated himself by the bed and continued, "I have this uncanny feeling we're not alone. It's as if an eerie presence is watching our every move."

"What?" Xavier asked. "You sense it too?"

"Come now, Father, disregard the ramblings of an old man. It must be my overactive imagination due to my growling stomach. I didn't eat much this morning and my blood sugar is probably low. Now, let's forget about it and see what we can do about these blasted seizures of yours." He placed the stethoscope on Xavier's chest and continued, "Hmmm, it's a bit rapid, but I suppose, under the circumstances, it's to be expected. Now take deep breaths. It will surely help to slow your heart rate."

Xavier wanted to continue on with the conversation, but did as he was told. Though he tried to relax, he couldn't take his mind off of the doctor's peculiar statement. He'd heard it correctly. He'd felt it too. Filled with inordinate fear, he gradually shifted his pulsing eyes to the door, half expecting someone to be standing there, but the space was empty. Incarcerated by the mounting paranoia, he drew in another deep breath, but the attempt failed. The overwhelming dread remained.

"Have you been taking your medication as I prescribed, Father Xavier?" Doctor Cartier asked.

"Yes, of course," Xavier replied, closing his eyes and burrowing back into the cool pillow, concerned that his condition was worsening. "Why am I always so damned anxious? Why can't I remember anything? Why is my memory full of bits and pieces? It's insane, but the more I try, the more fragmented the picture becomes. Doctor, what the hell is happening to me?"

"Just take it slow. Don't push it. Your memories will

come back to you in time. You've had a trauma." He replaced his equipment in the medical bag and sighed. "What is the last thing you remember?"

"Well," Xavier began, knocking his brain for answers. "The very last thing I recall is . . ."

"Why do you hesitate? What is it? Think. Try to remember."

" . . . Sister Domenique."

On mentioning her name, his brain banged full force against his skull, butchering his only memory. His body quivered and his pale complexion disintegrated. Within seconds, he once again reverted to a comatose state.

"Father Xavier!" Doctor Cartier yelled, jumping from his seat. "Stay with me."

He pulled out his stethoscope again and banged it onto Xavier's chest, listening for a heartbeat. To his surprise, the rhythm was strong and steady, but his breathing was curiously shallow. Transfixed on the body, he took a step back in disbelief. His finding wasn't at all as he'd expected. It defied his medical logic. Helpless, he watched his patient's health disintegrate before his eyes and assumed that his tortured subconscious was wrestling with unseen demons. It was hard to believe that even with all the advances in modern medicine, he was powerless to remove the curse, which held Xavier captive.

"You need to be in a hospital," Doctor Cartier said.

"There's no way that I can treat your condition any longer. You need a specialist. Hang in there, Father. I'll phone for the ambulance at once." He repacked his medical bag, turned for the door, and stopped short. "I could have sworn I'd closed the door twice before." He shook his head and rubbed his eyes. "Something is definitely amiss today. I should have remained in bed."

Before he could exit, a strange sensation invaded his being. His body quaked and strange tingles traveled the route of his spine. Nausea erupted and his legs went numb. Though he wasn't prone to the jitters, the uneasiness seemed to progress with each tick of time.

Several minutes later, adequate circulation returned to his legs and he was able to make it to the door. With trepidation, he stepped out into the hallway and felt as though a million eyes were spying on him. Assuming the worst, he slowly turned his head, but encountered nothing. He raced to the stairs, anxious to find a phone, but as he descended the first few steps, something crashed down hard on his skull. The pain was intense and all went dark. He tumbled to the base of the stairs, and lay still in a growing pool of crimson.

CHAPTER 26

"He was murdered!" Piedmont screamed at the medical examiner. "I'm positive! This whole goddamned incident stinks of foul play."

"Won't know for sure until I perform the autopsy, Inspector. But you may be right. Never can tell with these things. I'll contact you as soon as I have the results."

"Thanks, Pete," Piedmont said. "I believe it's cut and dry, but I'll wait for your report." He spoke privately with him for a few moments longer and then returned to the monsignor's side. "So, you still think your man is innocent?"

"I can't believe Doctor Cartier is gone," Monsignor said somberly. "We were with him less than three hours ago."

"Yeah," Piedmont said. "It's a damn shame."

"I simply can't understand how this unfortunate accident could have happened."

"Accident? Where the hell did you come up with that? This was no accident!"

"What are you saying, Inspector? You cannot possibly believe this was anything other than an accident. Your implication is utterly absurd."

"I'm not implying anything," Piedmont said. He skirted the bloodstain and stared at the chalked outline. "Something's not right. In my estimation, this is just a little too convenient. I find it odd that one minute he's upstairs, examining Father Xavier, and the next, he's dead at the bottom of the stairs."

"Oh, Inspector," Monsignor said. "I think you've read too many detective novels. Wouldn't we have heard him call out if someone had attacked him? For goodness sake, we were only in the other room."

"Who said anything about an attack?" Piedmont said, his eyes narrowing into thin slits. "You came to that conclusion too, eh, your Holiness?"

"Stop it, Inspector! You're playing with my words. You were the one who gave the impression of skullduggery, not I."

"I always listen to what my nose tells me," Piedmont said, tapping two fingers against the side of his nose. "And it's telling me that Doctor Cartier's so-called accident was no accident at all. Of course, I'll know more after the examiner is finished with him.

169

But know this, if he did meet with foul play, I'll tear this place upside down until I get answers. By the way, don't touch anything. Forensics will be here for quite some time yet. Have I made myself clear?"

"Yes, Inspector," Monsignor said. "I receive your message loud and clear. Now for my warning. If nothing comes of this and your nose is broken, I will see that the church presses charges against you for harassment and whatever else we deem appropriate. Did you get that, Inspector?"

"Are you threatening me?" Piedmont asked, twisting his lips scornfully, eyes gleaming angrily.

"No, Inspector, it's a promise!"

Roget shot down the stairs before Piedmont could respond. "Inspector," he called. "Father Xavier's no good to us now. He's out cold again. But he keeps mumbling something about eyes crawling all over him and being watched by the devil's spawn. He's making no sense."

"Great!" Piedmont said, scratching his head. "How convenient. He'll probably plead insanity."

"Do you honestly believe Father Xavier had a hand in this unfortunate affair?" Monsignor asked. "How utterly preposterous!"

"I'd bet my life on it," Piedmont said and followed Roget to the front door. He stopped, turned back, and smiled. "But I promise you, Monsignor, we'll get to the bottom of this unholy event."

"Then I'll certainly look forward to our next meeting," Monsignor said. "Maybe by that time, the medical examiner will have disproved your insane theory and Father Xavier will be cleared of all insinuation. Then, the church's lawsuit against you can be set into motion."

"Oh, by the way, Monsignor," Piedmont said. "I almost forgot. I've assigned an officer to stand watch over Xavier. He'll inform me when he regains consciousness. Maybe you can have one of your boys whip him up a batch of those terrific biscuits. I'm sure he'd appreciate it. I've also given the order that no one is to leave the area. Have a great day." Without awaiting a rebuttal, he left.

CHAPTER 27

The chosen one lay in a fetal position, thinking only of his broken angel, revisiting the day he had tracked her to the abbey. It's almost cruel, he thought. She had no idea that I was always there, watching, ready to spring her back to the harsh reality of her past whenever I chose. It appears that her mind has blocked out the memories, but soon they shall resurface. No longer will she be able to hide behind her false innocence.

He cocked his head and looked up at the cracked ceiling. "I'll break her," he said. "I'll bring her to her knees. I shall make her repent for the sins of the past and make everything right. Like that meddling physician, I'll dispose of anyone who gets in the way of my Lord's plan." Confident he hadn't forgotten any details, he picked up his Bible and began to read.

CHAPTER 28

"Damn!" Piedmont said, shoving a stack of reports off of his desk. "Nothing fits. Nothing's falling into place."

"You've got to take it easy, Norbert," Roget said. "You'll have a heart attack."

"Look at this goddamned coroner's report. It has to be wrong. Someone must have tampered with it."

"How can you say that? You know how thorough Pete is. He's been working his butt off for the past three days."

"I know, I know. But it's all too coincidental."

"Maybe you're right. But you'll have to accept the fact that there was no evidence to the contrary. I'm positive forensics went over everything with a fine-toothed comb."

173

"Where the hell is it?" Piedmont asked, thumbing through the file again. "How did he explain Cartier's smashed skull?"

"It's right here in black and white," Roget said, pointing to some bold print on the document. "It says that the forensic team found a large chunk of the banister had broken off, obviously during the doctor's fall. Splinters of wood, oak I might add, the same wood which the banister is made of, were lodged in his head. They concluded that he stumbled on the threshold, lost his balance, and fell from the landing. He apparently hit his head many times. His blood was found on the wall and banister. Taking into account his weight and the speed at which his body descended, it appears to be cut and dry. The blows to his cranium were the cause of death."

"I can read, but something still smells fishy," Piedmont said, slamming the file down on the desk. "It's those goddamned priests. They did this. They're hiding something. I know it. Cartier probably stumbled onto one of their secrets and never lived to tell about it."

"What the hell are you saying, Inspector?" Roget asked as he moved back to his seat. "Does everything have to be a damned conspiracy? Can't you take anything for face value? Do you really believe that the Catholic Church is behind all of the recent killings and accidents?"

"I do, Jacques."

"Do you know how absurd you sound? Listen to yourself, man. You're becoming paranoid. You have to resign yourself to the fact that the doctor's accident was just that, an accident. And you have to realize that the murders are the result of a madman, not the church. There's no connection." He ran his fingers through his dark curly hair and continued, "For Christ's sake, Norbert, you're a damn good inspector. You can't throw away your twenty-eight years on the force because your daughter was murdered. Remember, I loved her, too. I want to catch the son-of-a-bitch as badly as you do, but it's not the church's fault."

"You're probably right, Jacques," Piedmont said, lowering his head. "I don't know what's happening to me, but I'll be okay. I'll just be relieved once justice is served."

"Now, there's the inspector I know," Roget said, smiling. "From here on out, we'll take it nice and slow. We'll find the answers, don't you worry." He flipped through a notepad and continued, "Did you find out who's taken over Cartier's case load?"

"Yeah, a man named Petrie. He informed me yesterday that Xavier should be up to an interrogation later this afternoon and will call when he's coherent. This is one meeting I've been dying to conduct and this time nothing will stand in my way."

"Man, you still consider this a private battle."

"Come on, Jacques, you know what I mean. I'm certain we'll find the evidence we're looking for."

"I won't hold my breath," Roget answered dryly. "I still doubt he's involved."

175

"Okay, have it your way, but if he is, I'll make you eat those words."

"What?"

"Don't look so injured, Jacques. It's just a figure of speech. You can't take it literally."

CHAPTER 29

Piedmont's day had been relatively uneventful until Doctor Petrie's phone call. After receiving a short synopsis of Xavier's current condition, he learned that he was awake and finally able to manage a brief conversation. It wasn't what he'd hoped to hear, but figured a brief conversation was better than none at all. With renewed enthusiasm, he hung up the phone, grabbed the file, tossed it into his briefcase, and told his secretary to inform Sergeant Major Roget to meet him at the car.

Within the hour, they were back at the monastery, seated in straight chairs by Xavier's bed, ready to begin their questioning when a tall, lanky gentleman entered the room. He wore a white smock speckled with brownish-red stains and spoke in a familiar monotone. Straight away, Piedmont discerned that it was Doctor

Petrie.

"What now?" Piedmont said, his face flushed. "Make it fast, and it had better be good. With all of these damned interruptions, I'll never be able to successfully question this suspect.

"I'm terribly sorry for the intrusion, Inspector," the man said, extending his hand. "I'm Doctor Petrie and you must be Inspector Piedmont." After giving a quick shake of his hand, he proceeded to the open window, drew in a deep breath, and sat on the sill. "Under the circumstances, I thought it wise to be present during the interrogation. I'm sure you won't mind if I sit in."

"You've got to be kidding!" Piedmont said, veins protruding in his neck. "How'd you get past the guard? You just can't waltz in on police business. Now get the hell out of here!"

"Come now, Inspector, I'm not trying to interfere with your investigation. I just have Father Xavier's health in mind. As his physician it may be necessary to administer an injection on the remote chance my patient has a relapse. Wouldn't you agree that this makes the most sense?"

"Yeah, I guess," Piedmont said, not wishing to agree. "But understand that you don't administer anything without my consent. I want him coherent with no interference from you. It's highly irregular, but I'll allow it."

"Understood," Doctor Petrie said, folding his arms across his chest. "You won't even know I'm here."

"Okay, Jacques, is the recorder ready?" Piedmont asked, eyeing Father Xavier.

"Sure is," Roget said.

"Fine. Just make sure you get every word."

"I won't miss a syllable, Inspector," Roget said, placing the tape recorder onto the bedside table, close to Xavier's head. "Not one syllable."

"Good gracious," Doctor Petrie said, leaning forward. "This must be extremely important. I mean, to tape the conversation and all. But isn't it appropriate for you to inform him of his rights first? I realize I'm no police officer, but I do watch television and I am versed in the law."

"You worry about your job, Doctor, and let me do mine," Piedmont said through clenched teeth. He turned his attention to Xavier and continued, "Father Xavier, with your permission, we'll record your statements. Do you have a problem with that?"

"No, Inspector, that'll be fine," Xavier said, dragging his words. "I understand you have a job to do and the pressure must be immense."

"Please understand this is only a preliminary interrogation," Piedmont said in a matter-of-fact tone. "We're here looking for any answers or leads as to the whereabouts of a friend of yours, Sister Domenique Rondeau. You do remember her, don't you?"

"Yes," Xavier responded, "but I don't know where she is."

"Well, that remains to be seen," Piedmont said. "What did

you do with her?"

"What? Nothing."

"Where is she?"

"I-I-I already told you that I don't know."

"You were the last person to see her, right?"

"No. I told you before, I overslept and never met with her."

"How do we know that to be fact? Do you have any proof? Is there anyone who can corroborate your story?"

"Wait one minute!" Doctor Petrie said. "You're badgering my patient. I believe you're walking a thin line between infringement of his rights and outright entrapment. If you ask me, I believe he should have an attorney present."

"Nobody asked you, Doctor!" Piedmont yelled. He turned back to Xavier and continued, "Answer the questions."

"I'm trying, Inspector," Xavier said, holding his head. "But I have no information. I want to find Sister Domenique as badly as you. She's a friend."

"Bullshit!" Piedmont blurted. "You're not being straight with me. Now, we can do this down at the station with lawyers and all that crap, or we can handle it here quietly. It's your call."

"If it's all the same, Inspector," Xavier said, sitting erect, "I'd rather give my statement right here. I trust you, but you're trailing the wrong man." He faced the recorder and continued, "I, Father Xavier Fontaine, do solemnly swear that the statement I am about to give will be true to the best of my knowledge. I am of sound mind at this moment."

"Did you hear what he said, Doctor?" Piedmont asked. "He's given his permission to proceed. Now, shut up and sit your ass down!"

"Whatever!" Doctor Petrie said. He huffed, picked up his medical bag, marched to the door, opened it, and turned back to Xavier. "It's your funeral. I was only trying to help. In my opinion you're being railroaded."

"Well, Doctor," Piedmont said. "You know what they say. Opinions are like assholes. We all have them."

Doctor Petrie grunted and slammed the door on his way out.

"Now, Xavier, do you want to try this again?" Piedmont asked.

"Yes, Inspector." Xavier answered. "I'm ready."

"Okay. Let's go back to the day of Joline Bourgeois' funeral. Do you remember that day?"

"Yes, Inspector."

"Can you recall what happened?"

"Yes, unfortunately I can."

"Excellent. Now, please explain to me in detail all of the events which led to your being restrained?"

"Okay, I'll do my best, but everything's extremely vague. It was the day I was to meet with Sister Domenique."

"Correct," Piedmont said. "You told me that the last time

we spoke, but you're getting ahead of yourself. I'm only interested in the episode, which took place in the chapel. We'll get back to Domenique in a little bit."

"Okay, Inspector. You must forgive me. Lately, I've had some difficulty maintaining dates and times. Please have patience with me."

"I understand. Take your time."

Before Xavier had the chance to go any further, Father André barged into the room carrying a silver tray. "How are we today, Father Xavier?" he asked. "I'm here to administer your medication."

"Wait a goddamned minute," Piedmont exclaimed, holding up his arms. "What the hell's going on here? What medication?"

"My, Inspector," André said, holding a pill and a glass of water toward Xavier. "We are testy today. Did we get up on the wrong side of the bed this morning, or are we always this touchy?"

"Hold on!" Piedmont shouted, wedging his body between Xavier and the glass. "You're not the doctor. He just left here. What kind of medication?"

"It's an anticonvulsant," André said, rolling his eyes.

"A what?" Piedmont asked. "Speak English."

"It's a drug to prevent an epileptic seizure," André stated flatly. "It was given to me by Doctor Cartier some time ago. He told me, in the event of his absence, I was to administer it as prescribed." He looked down at his watch and continued, "And it's three-ten. I'm already ten minutes late. I sincerely hope this will not affect his treatment."

"Let me see those pills," Piedmont said, reaching for the bottle.

"Fine," André said. As he was about to hand over the bottle, it slipped out of his hand and fell to the floor. "See what you've made me do, Inspector. Now they're probably contaminated. I'll hold you personally responsible if Father Xavier has another relapse."

"Shouldn't Doctor Petrie be the one to administer these drugs?" Piedmont asked, helping André to replace the pills into the container. "He is his attending physician."

"That isn't necessary, Inspector," André said. "As I was the one who was chosen by Doctor Cartier for this task, I believe it is my responsibility."

"But this is Doctor Petrie's job."

"You're absolutely right, but as you can see, he's not here. He flew out of here so fast that I never had the chance to consult with him. Was it you who chased him away with your irritating charm? Or was it something you said."

"Okay, smart ass, enough of the backtalk," Piedmont said, exasperated by this latest intrusion. "Do what you must and make it quick."

"You're the boss," André said. He immediately administered the medicine and scurried from the room.

"What a jerk!" Piedmont said, watching the door close. "Xavier, do you remember the last question I asked?"

"Yes, of course I do," Xavier said and placed the empty glass on the nightstand. "That was a strange day. I was late for the funeral. I should have already been in the sacristy by the time I'd arrived. Nothing was right."

"Why were you late?"

"I'd overslept."

"You do a lot of that, don't you? Go on."

"I can't say why, but I had an overwhelming impulse to pray over the poor child's body. It was as if the Almighty Father had chosen me to guide her into heaven."

"What do you mean by that?" Piedmont asked, looking over at Roget.

"Honestly, I can't explain it. The sensation was too strong to ignore. As a priest, I believed it to be my duty."

"If you say so."

"When I arrived at the chapel, something happened to me. My vision distorted. I truly believed that I had seen Monsignor Valois standing over the coffin holding a jeweled dagger. As he was about to strike the Bourgeois child, I grabbed it from him. Then I looked into the coffin. The Bourgeois girl was gone. She was replaced by Sister Domenique. It appeared to me that she was severely beaten. She was calling to me. Begging me for help." He cradled his face in his hands and began to sob. "Sweet Lord, why have you forsaken me? Why have you shown me so many visions throughout my life and yet refuse to allow me to save her?"

"Stay with me, Father," Piedmont said, afraid he would lose him to another attack. "Calm down."

"I'll be fine," Xavier said, wiping tears from his eyes.

"Now, let's talk about Domenique," Piedmont said. "You claimed that you were supposed to have met with her and she never showed up. Why is that?"

Xavier's face looked pained and he squeezed his head.

"What's wrong?" Piedmont asked.

"She's angry with me. I told her I'd be there at four o'clock, but I was late. Something has happened to her. I know it. Something awful."

"How do you know?"

"It's happened to me before," Xavier said, his face contorting, his eyes glassy. "I've seen things."

"What things?" Piedmont asked, once again shifting his eyes to Roget.

"You've got to save her," Xavier said, tugging at Piedmont's sleeve. "You're her only hope. She's being held against her will."

"Where is she?"

"In hell!" Xavier screamed. "Satan has her!" His eyes rolled back and his face became pale.

"Goddammit!" Piedmont yelled. "Jacques, get the doctor!

185

I think he's having one of those seizures, but I'm not getting close enough to find out. He might be possessed."

An hour later, Xavier was still out cold. Though the timing was uncanny, the situation couldn't be altered. It appeared that the interrogation would have to take a back seat once again. This angered Inspector Piedmont, but there was no other alternative but to wait.

"I guess we're done here for today," Piedmont said, exiting the monastery and looking up at the old building. "It doesn't look like he's going to wake up any time soon."

"I agree," Roget said. "What are you looking at?"

"Father Xavier's window. I think we're being watched. I saw someone's shadow and the curtains just moved."

"It's probably just the wind."

"I guess you're right, Jacques. Let's get the hell out of this cursed place. It gives me the creeps."

Nothing had gone right. It was supposed to have been a day of proclamation, but instead turned out to be another big waste of time. Answers to the stacks of unresolved questions remained shrouded in a collage of twisted words and the whole predicament stunk of bias. Piedmont knew that the only way he would ever triumph over the hurdles of misfortune was to stay steadfast to his convictions. He knew that life was a game of chance and only the best players won. He'd come to this realization long ago and wouldn't allow any circumstance to influence the outcome. He was determined to wait indefinitely for the solutions to the complicated puzzles of murder and mayhem. Without looking back toward the building, he put on his sunglasses, hopped into the squad car, and sped off the property. It was nearly four-thirty.

"My gut tells me it was Xavier in the window," Piedmont said, gripping the wheel.

"I don't agree," Roget said. "He's too sick. Hadn't you better slow down?"

"Sick, my ass. He knows something. I feel it."

"Maybe he does, but we'll have to handle him with kid gloves if we want to get any information out of him. Now, break, man, you're scaring me."

"And that André," Piedmont continued, pushing harder on the gas pedal. "He's such a cocky bastard. What's his story?"

"I don't know, but I'd like to live to find out. Please, Norbert, slow down!"

"If only Doctor Petrie hadn't interfered," Piedmont said, banging his fist against the wheel, ignoring Roget's pleas. "I would've gotten more out of Xavier. I know he knows where the nun is."

"Personally, I think you were pretty hard on him."

"On who?"

"Doctor Petrie. He seemed like a nice man to me. If you think about it, he only had Father Xavier's welfare in mind. Now, please slow down."

187

"All right," Piedmont grunted, easing up on the gas. "That's your opinion."

Roget smirked, but didn't utter another word.

"Yeah, yeah, I know what you're thinking, Jacques. We all have opinions."

CHAPTER 30

During the weeks following Father Xavier's collapse, Inspector Piedmont and his team of investigators scoured the region for clues. They continued their search for anyone who might have had even the slightest possible connection to the cases, though the odds were against them. Doctor Cartier had been laid to rest and it appeared that if the investigation continued on its current course, it would suffer the same fate.

Throughout this time, Sister Domenique had been suffering her own hellish torment. Mild delirium had set in and she was at the point where time was of no consequence. Her already frail physique had wilted like an unwatered flower, and her muscles, which once ached, were now numb. The chosen one stripped away more of her innocence on his daily visit as a prerequisite to her scant meal, always ending the ordeal with a series of prayers and Latin chants.

On one particular visit, he did something totally out of character. He removed her blindfold. But it didn't help. She couldn't see. The soft glow of the lantern sent a searing pain through her head. And though she strained to focus, she could only make out a clouded silhouette. The vague image of his being appeared to pulsate and she thought his body was manifesting repulsive signs of deterioration. His eyes seemed to glow an off shade of vermillion and within seconds, his flesh disintegrated from his skeleton, during which a godless chant resounded.

Was it reality or a nightmare? She wracked her brain for a logical explanation, but nothing surfaced. The stress was just too great. She concluded that her mind had definitely snapped when she envisioned a demon-like creature, which emerged from his ribcage, splintering his bones to bits. It swelled to an enormous proportion, inundating the tiny chamber. Moments later, it transformed into a grotesque serpentine and hovered high above her bed. It was adorned with leathery wings and had needle-like teeth. As its wings flapped ever-so-slowly, a yellowish-green mucous oozed from its oral cavity, splattering to the floor, piercing holes in the granite like acid. The secretion reeked of burning flesh. Though she witnessed the phenomenon without clarity, her brain took over, filling in the blanks with more gore than any horror story ever written.

"Revel in My beauty," she heard the beast say. "Adore only Me. For I am the Father and you, My servant."

She slowly moved her head in a feeble attempt to focus on Xavier, but only saw him as a shadow. He was kneeling before the beast, adoring it with prayer. He, too, smelled of death. Despite the fact that his face was shrouded in a thick grey mist, his chiseled features stood out.

"My Father," he whispered. "Have I not done all that You have asked of me? Are You not my one true God!"

"My chosen one," the beast boomed. "Look upon yourself, you lowly swine. How can you stand before me unclothed, bathed in defecation. Is this how you honor Me?"

"It was ..."

"Silence! Cleanse yourself and the woman. The time of her purification is at hand. Pillage her no more, for she is with child. My child. The savior."

Its words filled her with instant consternation. Although she desperately tried to comprehend them, her mind remained mystified. It was as though she had been heavily sedated with a hallucinogenic drug and her innards were revolting against a fever. Quaking from head to toe, she listened.

"Woman," the beast bellowed, cocking its horned head to the side and running its razor-sharp talon along the length of her abdomen. "Give thanks for the fact that you were chosen long ago. And that My holy seed has been planted deep within your womb.

It is My gift to you and to the world. Rejoice! From this moment on, it is your duty to care for My fledgling. For when My son is born to this world, he shall rule at My right side over Heaven and Earth. Only then shall My reign of glory commence and if not for you, this would not be possible. For this, I am in your debt." Its words trailed off as Xavier retied the blindfold.

Filled with disgust over what she had just witnessed, her mind churned. She was desperate to hold on to her last threads of sanity, but a sense of impending doom befell her. Relief set in when she heard Xavier's footsteps leave of the room, but unfortunately it was short-lived. Before the hour was up, he returned, untied her bindings, and bathed her.

"Master," he cried aloud, splashing water onto her bare midsection. "I've done all that You've asked. I'm truly honored to be Your vessel."

While lying there, frantic thoughts rushed through her mind. Am I dreaming? Did it really happen? Was it real? Impossible! She resigned herself to the fact that the vision was due to Xavier's strong power of suggestion and believed that if she could remain focused, she would survive. For weeks, she had listened to his fits of rage and fanatical, descriptive exploits. That's it, she thought to herself, suggestive mind manipulation. She discerned that her weakened condition must have been the catalyst.

After rationalizing the bizarre vision, she didn't know

whether or not it would be safe to remove the blindfold. Opting to remain still for fear of another beating, she listened intently to every insane word he muttered until, to her surprise, all went quiet. In time, she was convinced he was either asleep or in some sort of trance. Uncertain of the outcome and with much skepticism, she decided to take off the mask. Her arms were throbbing and her heart beat wildly. With extreme caution, she quickly slipped it over her head and sat upright, all the while holding her breath. Once she felt certain he hadn't heard her movements, she exhaled slowly. I must remain focused, she thought as she kept her eyes trained on his blurry figure, which was slumped on the floor.

Careful not to squeak the bed springs, she massaged her arms and legs until adequate circulation was regained for a safe attempt at escape. With muscles slightly limbered, she lifted herself from the bed and stood perfectly still, praying with all her might that he hadn't noticed. Her heart banged thunderously against her ribcage, so loud that she believed the whole world could hear it, but to her good fortune, he never moved.

She drew in a deep breath and lunged at him, hammering her small fists against his bare back and head. Untold anger discharged from her feverish, meager body, but to her surprise there was no resistance. He just rolled onto his side, seemingly unconscious.

As if God had intervened, she took full advantage of the unexpected Godsend and swiftly wrapped herself in the tattered

193

blanket. Within seconds, she was fumbling her way through the dark, murky tunnels, searching for an exit. "Dear God," she whispered, while wandering about the dreary passages. "Please abort the bastard child I'm carrying and help me to get out of here. I implore you. If you can hear me, please help me!"

She pressed on with no sense of direction, aimlessly weaving through the cobwebs, while feeling her way along the cold passage walls. As she trekked, hopes of finding an end to the maze dwindled. Her pulse raced and her head felt as though it would come unhinged at any given moment. She knew that if she was to survive, she needed to find an exit and quick.

Back in the cell, the chosen one awoke from his hypnotic state, infuriated to find Domenique gone. You bitch, he thought. You'll never play me for a fool again. He realized his downfall. He'd been too soft on her. He swore that when he found her, he'd rectify his mistake. With punishment on his mind, he hurriedly donned his vestments, snatched the map and lantern from the table, and bolted from the cell.

After exploring several paths, he paused briefly to scan the map with hopes of discovering a clue as to which direction she had traveled, but the routes were too intertwined and complex. This is bullshit, he thought, angered by her deceptive behavior. She must

194

be down here somewhere. Determined to be victorious over this latest predicament, he vowed not to allow any more interference with the master plan and expanded his search down the numerous passages.

"Damn!" he cried, stopping once again to glance at the map. "So many routes. This map is useless." He tore it into tiny shreds and threw it into the darkness. "Domenique! Where the hell are you? Without me you are nothing!" He waited for a response, but only heard the echo of a constant drip and the rhythm of his own heart. "Domenique, my angel," he called again. "Please answer me. Come back. It's for your own good." With the scent of defeat in the air, he leaned back against the damp, stone wall and laughed aloud, making his voice ricochet throughout the tunnels. "I don't give a shit if you are God's whore! When I catch you, I'm going to kill you!" As the words left his lips, his master's voice echoed from deep within his brain, compelling him to halt the threatening outburst.

"You puny fool!" the voice said, simultaneously bringing him to his knees with excruciating pain. "You shall do nothing of the sort! If you harm one hair on her head before the child is born, you shall pay with your life! Do you hear Me? Your soul shall burn in My fiery hell for all eternity! Take heed, My chosen one, for I am a most undesirable foe!"

"My Lord," the chosen one said, trying to stand erect, while caressing his stomach with both hands. "I am Your chosen one

195

and I promise that Your will shall be done. Please forgive my transgression."

The chosen one waited to hear more, but the session had ended with an abrupt explosion of spectral splendor. Trillions of light particles flickered through the air and intense heat emitted from a spherical glowing mass. Momentarily blinded by the spectacular event, he teetered from side to side, gripping tightly to his head in a conscious effort to alleviate his growing nausea and disorientation. He believed that the pain was a warning, a prelude to another bout with his master's wrath, but was shocked when his vision cleared. He was elated and immediately impressed with a renewed sense of purpose. Certain once again that the master plan would succeed, he ran off into the obscurity of the underground labyrinth.

From out of the darkness, Domenique heard a male voice calling out to her. It was nonthreatening, unlike the deranged undertones and abrupt outcries she had grown accustomed to in days past. It was different, tender, and for some peculiar reason it made her feel safe. Her instinct was to respond, but common sense dictated that she stop, catch her breath, and wait until she was certain it wasn't the voice of her captor. Filled with unbridled anxiety, she listened.

"Domenique," the distant voice called, amidst the echoes of constant drips. "Are you down here? If you can hear my voice, for God's sake, answer me!"

Her face lit up with renewed optimism and her anxiety peaked. She propped herself against the murky wall, drew in a mouthful of stale air, and made an extreme effort to respond. Though she formed the words, her throat would not cooperate. Refusing to give in to defeat, she made a quick sign of the cross, silently asked God for assistance, and ran blindly through the labyrinth toward what she hoped would be her salvation. On instinct alone, she maneuvered through the dark passages, following the voice to the base of a steep staircase. This is it, she thought, excited by the find. The exit. The path to freedom. The answer to my prayers. Believing that God had heard her pleas, she ascended the stone steps on all fours. When she reached about half way up, she turned a sharp bend and observed a thin stream of light emitting from the bottom of what appeared to be a door. Her adrenalin rushed and her senses heightened. Out of desperation, she attempted to call out again, but her throat remained partially constricted. Only a brief guttural sound escaped.

Feeling lightheaded and sick, she scaled the remaining steps, scraping her knees on the broken granite. Although her heart raced, her legs stung, and her strength was all but spent, her will to survive took presidence. She stood erect and fumbled in the dark for a doorknob, intent on exiting the godless hellhole, which had imprisoned her for so long. But to her horror, the door was actually a stone wall with no handle to grab. Crazed by the maddening predicament, she hurled her haggard body against the rock and was surprised when it shifted, toppling her headfirst onto the floor of an immense wine cellar. Breathing hard, she rolled onto her back and stared up in disbelief.

"Oh, God," she cried, though the words were barely audible. "This can't be!"

Feeling as though her heart would stop at any moment, she watched, eyes pulsating. It was Xavier. He stood over her, exhibiting a strange expression. His face was pale and his mouth hung open.

"N-n-no!" she cried. "No!"

"Domenique?" Xavier asked as he backed into a wine rack. "Is it really you?"

Hellbent on escaping the madman, she immediately scrambled to her feet, lunged back toward the stairs, and fell into Father André's arms.

"I've finally found you," André said, pulling her close. "I knew you couldn't be far off."

"Help me!" she cried, throwing her arms around him. "Xavier's going to kill me! I've been his captive! He's insane! Hurry, get me out of here!"

"Is that so," André said, chuckling. "It's all right now, I'm here." He gave her a gentle squeeze, pushed her aside, and glared at Xavier. "You bastard! What have you done to this poor child?"

"Oh, sweet Lord!" Xavier cried as a puzzled expression shot across his face. "You're behind this, Andr…" Before he finished his statement, his eyes rolled back, and he dropped to the floor.

"Well, Domenique," André said with a smile, "It seems our mutual friend has passed out. Have no fear; I'm here to protect you. No harm shall come to you unless I deem it necessary." He picked up the worn blanket, wrapped it around her, and forced her back through the opening.

"What are you doing?" she asked, panicked by his gesture. "I'm not going back down there!"

"Oh, yes you are! Did you really think you could escape me so easily? You said you were willing to help me see our Lord's plan through to fruition. Did you change your mind, or was it just another lie?"

All at once, the harsh reality of the situation set in, bizarre as it was. It was André all the time. Though fooled into believing she had been held against her will by Xavier, her eyes revealed the truth. Xavier was a victim as well.

"You bastard!" she cried, her voice still hoarse. "You'll never get away with this! Xavier, get up! Call the police!"

"Quiet!" André said, clamping his rugged hand over her mouth. "Or I'll end your life right here and now, along with your precious, Xavier!"

"Like hell!" she screamed, biting down hard on his hand. The bittersweet taste of his blood stung her cracked lips.

"You wretch!" he yelled as he spun her around to face him. "You shall defy me no more!" He punched her square in the face rendering her unconscious. "There, that's better."

She sagged to the floor and lay inert.

"Now, maybe you'll learn to behave," he said, lifting her limp body.

With terrific ease, he flung her over his shoulder and carried her down through the tunnels. Back to her prison cell. Back to the place she had called home for such a long while. It was her hellhole, the domain, which nurtured the conception of her unborn child.

CHAPTER 31

It was well after eight when a long, drawn out moan traveled up through the ancient floorboards, interrupting Father Thomas' habitual evening snack. He swiftly placed his tin of maple cookies down onto the granite counter and stood perfectly still, listening, uncertain as to its origin. As he strained to hear, the constant ticks of the old grandfather clock invaded the silence. It's all in my head, he thought, deducing that the noise was just a figment of his overactive imagination, attributable to self-induced guilt. He had been straying from his diet for some time now and was well aware of the consequences he would face if he were caught binging again. Confident that he'd figured it out, he went back to his cookies. While gulping the last drops of milk from the container, the sound returned, this time more prominent, more pronounced.

"Oh, Lord!" he gasped, shoving a cookie into his mouth and a few more into his pocket. "It's coming from the wine cellar. Someone's down there, trying to steal church property."

He instinctively grabbed a cast-iron frying pan from the drainage rack and cautiously made his way down the rickety steps, wiping the excess crumbs from his mouth, ready for battle with the unknown. Praying for the strength to handle whatever lie ahead, he popped another cookie into his mouth. He stopped on the bottom step and raised the pan over his head.

"Come out with your hands up," he hollered. "The police are on their way."

With hands trembling, he felt along the wall and switched on the light. It was Father Xavier who was causing the ruckus. He was rolling back and forth on the rock floor, babbling gibberish about Sister Domenique and Father André. It was apparent that he was suffering from another one of his spells.

"Sweet Father in heaven!" Father Thomas said, pushing his overweight body back up the stairs, two steps at a time. "I must inform the monsignor. He'll know what to do."

Within minutes, he was standing before the monsignor, explaining most of the circumstances, which led up to his unfortunate finding.

"Not again," Monsignor said, shaking his head. He tossed a manila folder on top of a silver file cabinet and continued, "Well, we just can't leave him down there. Come on, let's get him back to his room."

Once Father Xavier had been safely tucked into bed, the men retreated to the hall.

"What in God's name riled him so?" Monsignor asked. "He's never reacted like this before. And what was he babbling about? Sister Domenique. Father André. What does it all mean?"

"I couldn't tell you, Monsignor," Father Thomas said. "Should I ring for the doctor? Maybe he can shed some light on this. Or should I call for Inspector Piedmont?"

"No!" Monsignor yelled. "For Christ's sake, leave him out of this. Aren't we capable of handling anything on our own anymore? And the Lord knows we don't need any other adverse publicity."

"I'm in total agreement, Monsignor. You're right. Then shouldn't we speak with Father André? Father Xavier did mention him."

"No. Not right now. I believe Father André's in meditation and it would be foolish to disturb him at this time over some ridiculous ravings. I'll speak with him later."

"As you wish, Monsignor," Father Thomas said and scurried back to the kitchen.

CHAPTER 32

On the stroke of midnight, Father Xavier sprung up in bed and focused his attention back to Domenique. He was angry and full of rage. Though in perfect harmony with the situation that had recently unfolded, he still expected her to try and explain away her distasteful actions. Intent on hearing some answers, he searched her pleading, red eyes, but only encountered a pained expression. In time, it was apparent that she was bound to a mysterious code of silence.

"Why, Domenique?" he asked, watching her fuse back into the mist of lonesome shadows. "What do you want of me? Why do you hide? Why do you reject me?" He inched closer to her bed and observed that her angelic features were fading ever so slightly with each passing moment. "No! Domenique, come back! Don't

204

leave me!"

Before he had the chance to grab her arm, he toppled to the floor with a deafening thud and stared blankly up at the ceiling. A clear recollection of his earlier meeting came flooding back to him with all the fervor of a scorpion's sting. She is alive, he thought, convinced that his memory was accurate. It wasn't a dream. I did see her.

With haste, he rose to his feet and quickly donned his vestments. His anxiety was peaked. He didn't know what to do or how to control the sudden rush of emotions which ate up his insides, yet his brain demanded action. Without an exact plan, he sprinted out of the chamber and down to the wine cellar, his eyes piercing through the darkness like a cat.

"Domenique!" he cried, pulling bottles from the racks and smashing them to the floor. "I'm back. I'm here to save you!"

The portrait his mind had conjured up of her standing amidst the wine bottles was smeared, whitewashed by the sweat that spewed from his brow. Though his vision was blurred, his boundless determination ruled his actions. He was resigned to the fact that he would rather die than relinquish the search. With resolve, he proceeded on his rampage. He dashed to the storage room, grabbed a crowbar from atop the workbench, and returned to the racks to pry them loose. Once he had freed a few of the thin planks, he was shocked to see that the entrance was now sealed with cement.

"No!" he cried, digging into the partially dried concrete with his bare hands. "She's down there! I know it!"

"What's the meaning of this?" a voice hollered from behind. "Father Xavier, have you lost your mind?"

Startled by the intrusion, Father Xavier spun around to see Monsignor Valois standing at the base of the stairs with Father André by his side. He wasn't prepared to face off with them and knew Monsignor Valois wouldn't listen to reason if he tried to explain. What nerve, he thought. What guts. How the hell can André stand there with that insolent smirk and self-righteous attitude when he knows Sister Domenique is alive and in some sort of danger?

"Why do you hold your tongue?" Monsignor asked. "Explain yourself!"

"I-i-it's Sister Domenique!" Xavier cried. "She's down there, hidden behind this damned sealed door! We've got to save her!"

"Should I bring him back to his room, Monsignor?" André asked calmly. "He must be in need of another dose of his medication."

"Father André, what the hell are you saying?" Xavier screamed. "You know as well as I, she was here. You held her in your arms. She was screaming for your help. How can you stand there and say nothing about the incident?"

"What is he babbling about?" Monsignor asked.

"I don't know," André replied, moving closer to Xavier. "He's most likely had another one of his hallucinations. Now Xavier, hand over the crowbar like a nice little boy."

Xavier held tight to the piece of cold metal, unsure of what to do next. His brain raced. He was cornered and felt the noose tightening around his neck. On the verge of another fainting spell, he fought to stay alert, continuously shifting his between the two men.

"Come now, Father Xavier," Monsignor said softly. "Take it easy. Put the iron down. Someone could get hurt. Allow us to return you to the warmth of your bed and the comfort of your room. There, we can lay your demons to rest."

"Like hell!" Xavier screamed. "I'm not going anywhere! For God's sake, Monsignor, I'm her only hope. Can't you see what Father André's done? He's manipulated the whole situation. I know I sound mad, but this is his work." He shot a glare at André and raised the bar high above his head. "You did this! Why did you seal this doorway? Where did you take her?"

"Can you make any sense of what he's babbling about, Father André?"

"No, Monsignor, I have no idea," André said. "I never knew such a door existed."

"Liar!" Xavier screamed. "She was naked and beaten. You saw her, too. For God's sake, you comforted her!"

Without warning, André lunged at Xavier and tackled him

207

to the stone floor. Punches flew and screeches of pain resounded. In a matter of minutes, the fight was over. The crowbar was confiscated and Father André was in control of the situation.

"What should I do with him, Monsignor?" André asked, handing him the crowbar. "Maybe a straitjacket is in order."

"Thank God," Monsignor said. "It seems he's fainted. Bring him up to his chamber. If he's no better in the morning, I'll phone for the doctor."

"Very well, Monsignor," André said. "I'll be right back to clean up this mess."

"No, no," Monsignor said. "I'll take care of it. You just see to Father Xavier's needs."

"By the way, Monsignor," André said. "Did you know about this so-called secret doorway?"

"Well, uh, I had heard rumors of its existence many years ago."

"You don't say."

"Yes, but I had dismissed them as old wives' tales. Not in my wildest dreams did I ever expect to find it."

"Interesting," André said. "Is there a possibility Sister Domenique could actually be down there?"

"Impossible," Monsignor said flatly. "It's obvious that this entrance has been hidden away for generations. There's no way anyone would even know about it."

"Then how do you explain the wet cement? Someone must

have known it was here to seal it up. Who do you think did that? Don't you think we should alert the police? There may be something to Father Xavier's story."

"No! For now, let's keep this between the two of us. The last thing this church needs is more bad publicity."

"Ah, that's exactly what I was thinking," André said as he winked. "The fewer people who know about this, the better."

"I'm glad we're in agreement," Monsignor said. "We'll forget this little incident ever happened. Now, bring Father Xavier back to his room."

"As you wish," André replied. "But are you sure you won't need my help to clean up?"

"I'm positive."

"Have it your way," André said, slinging Xavier over his shoulder. Without arguing the point, he carried him up to his room and dropped him onto the bed. "You really are stupid," he said, leaning over Xavier, allowing spittle to drizzle onto his cheek. "My dear Father, you have no clue that I've been pulling all the strings. You could say that I've been the puppet master. And as my Master decrees, I swear there is no way that you, the other, shall ever be permitted to interfere with the divine plans for Domenique."

After a few moments of silence, Father Xavier opened his eyes a slit and watched as Father André reached into his pocket, pulled out a bottle of pills, and shook it in the air. Knowing his only defense was to quell his fears, he quickly closed his eyes and pretended to remain sleeping. He didn't understand what André meant by 'plans', but knew now that he was Domenique's sole hope for salvation.

"Time to see more ghosts," André said, laughing aloud. "It appears the monsignor's book on family medicine has surely come in handy. A few more doses and you'll be out of the picture for good. And you shall be held accountable for all the sins of the past."

Father Xavier was sickened by the salty taste of André's fingers as he shoved the pill into his mouth. His heart rose to his throat and his pulse quickened. A number of memories flickered across his brain and something oddly familiar stabbed at the pit of his stomach. Could this have been predestined? Is my existence so trivial that I'm to surrender my life to this madman? No! I won't allow this to happen to me. I must regain my sanity. I must compose myself. I can overcome this. He focused on his inner strength and calmed himself, slowing his pulse rate.

"Fine, little Father," André said, massaging Xavier's throat. "Swallow your medicine like a good little boy." After some minutes had passed and a few Latin words had been spoken, he left the room, slamming the door.

Xavier remained lethargic until André's footsteps faded into the distance. He sat up, spit the partially dissolved pill into his hand, and stared blankly at it. Alas, he was privy to the truth. He couldn't remember the last time he thought with such clarity. Everything made sense. Father André was the cause of his attacks and he was the kidnapper.

"But why?" he whispered, wracking his brain for a logical answer. "Why would he do this? What the hell could be his motive?"

Feeling a bit groggy, he rose from the bed and pushed the unanswered questions aside. He slipped the pill into his pocket, forged down the flight of stairs, and prayed with every step that he wouldn't be detected. He knew he would pay dearly if caught, and at this point, no one would have believed his story. The realization that he was alone was maddening. Now, all he needed was the evidence to support his claim. He knew his only chance for survival was to convince Inspector Piedmont that he was sane and that Father André was behind Sister Domenique's disappearance.

Ready to set his plan into motion, he entered the monsignor's office. He leaned back against the door and breathed in a deep sigh of relief. Confident he'd managed to avert detection, he said a quick prayer of thanks, secured the latch, and dialed the phone.

"Grand Cache R.C.M.P.," a woman's voice said on the other end of the line.

"I need to speak with Inspector Piedmont," Xavier said, watching shadows dance around the room. "It's urgent!"

"I'm sorry, but he's off duty until tomorrow at seven a. m.

Could anyone else help you?"

"No. It has to be him. Is there any way I can reach him this evening? A number I could call?"

"One moment, please. I'll connect you to his voice mail."

Before he had the chance to reply, he was listening to a recording, telling him to leave a message after the beep.

"Inspector," he whispered, holding tight to the receiver. "It's Father Xavier from Saint Michael's. I must speak with you as soon as possible. It pertains to Sister Domenique. I know where she is. I pray you'll come at once!"

CHAPTER 33

The sun's rays could barely be seen along the horizon as Inspector Piedmont pulled his vehicle through the monastery gates and sounded his horn. His patience was dwindling with each passing second. Though he should have been jumping for joy over the possibility of finally obtaining Father Xavier's written confession and learning the whereabouts of Sister Domenique Rondeau, something just didn't feel right. He couldn't put his finger on it, but he knew that even though he wanted to, he'd have a difficult time believing Xavier's claim. In his estimation, Father Xavier was certifiable and his delusions would only hinder his credibility. Weighing the odds and anxious to find the underlying reason for the cryptic phone message, he slammed on his brakes, skidded into a parking slot, flew into the building, and stormed right through to the monsignor's office.

"Where the hell is he?" Inspector Piedmont yelled, glaring at the monsignor.

"Oh, Inspector," Monsignor answered, rattling his cup and saucer. "You scared the life out of me. What in heaven has you so riled up this morning?"

"I'm not here for small talk. Where is he?"

"Where is who?" Monsignor said.

"Father Xavier."

"Well, given the time, I imagine he's still asleep. Why would you need to speak with him again? He hasn't been feeling well and I don't believe he's up to it."

Without offering a response, Inspector Piedmont bolted from the office, flew up the stairs to Xavier's room, and barged in. The room was in semi-darkness. Father Xavier stood by the opened window.

"Where's Sister Domenique?" Inspector Piedmont yelled, grabbing on to the bedpost. "Where have you been keeping her?"

"Oh, Inspector," Xavier said, turning away from the window. "Thank God you've finally arrived. I didn't know how much longer I'd be able to keep up this charade. I've been pretending to be asleep all morning."

"What the hell are you talking about? If you're playing some sick game, I'll see that you're put away forever."

"No games, Inspector. I have definite proof that Sister

Domenique is still alive. She's being kept somewhere in the monastery."

"Just wait one minute. Let me see if I have this straight. You're not confessing to her kidnapping?"

"No. What would ever give you that idea?"

"Your message," Inspector Piedmont said, feeling for his gun. "You said you had Sister Domenique."

"You're mistaken. I said I know where she is. If you don't believe me, go back and listen to your personal voicemail."

"Okay, so where is she?"

"Here in the monastery."

"Where in the monastery?" Piedmont asked with skepticism.

"Somewhere in the basement. Father André has her."

"André? What the hell are you implying?"

"Yes, I saw her. He definitely has her. And I think the monsignor's covering for him."

"Wait a goddamned minute," Piedmont said, squeezing the bedpost. "Let's see if I've got this right. You're claiming that Sister Domenique is somewhere in the cellar, Father André is holding her captive, and the monsignor is an accomplice to this whole crazy scenario?"

"That's exactly what I'm saying."

"Stop the bull," Piedmont said, wracking his brain for logic. "I know the monsignor and I haven't seen eye to eye since my daughter died, but I have a hard time believing that the asshole's involved in a kidnapping. He's a pompous jerk, but...."

"I know it all sounds bizarre, Inspector, but I saw her with my own eyes. She was with Father André, naked, and the monsignor's on his side. He doesn't believe me."

"I have a hard time believing you too. Maybe you were having another one of your delusional spells, like at the funeral."

"No. You've got to believe me. Sister Domenique's life depends on it."

"Okay, it's against my better judgment, but I'll give you one shot," Inspector Piedmont said, theorizing the possibilities. "André, eh? Naked? Maybe I was right all along. Maybe they do have a thing for each other. There's always the possibility you stumbled onto their little love nest during one of their kinky sex games. These kinds of things are common amongst you repressed religious types, right?"

"For God's sake, listen to me! She was frightened and had marks, bruises all over her body."

"Maybe she likes it rough."

"You're not hearing me, Inspector," Xavier screamed, rushing to the doorway. "Time is not on our side. She's in danger! Are you going to help her or not?"

"Bring me to her," Piedmont said and followed him down to the wine cellar. He stood in the center of the room and looked around. "Well, where is she?"

216

"Over there," Xavier said, pointing to the far wall. It's an entrance to an old, forgotten tunnel system. That's where I saw her last."

"Hmmm," Piedmont mumbled as he walked up to the wall and rubbed his hands along the surface. "It appears that someone's sealed it up."

"My guess, it was Father André, in a feeble attempt to cover his tracks."

"Is this all you've got?" Piedmont said as a stout figure emerged from out of a dark corner.

"Don't be frightened, Inspector," the monsignor said, walking into the light. "It's only me."

"What the hell are you doing down here, Monsignor?" Piedmont exclaimed, angered by the intrusion. "Do you make it a habit of creeping up on people?"

"Oh, Inspector," Monsignor said. "I truly am sorry. My intention was never to frighten you. However, I overheard your conversation with Father Xavier. I certainly apologize for eavesdropping, but as you must know, this is clearly Church business. And as you can see, Sister Domenique is not here. It's too bad you've trekked all the way out here only to discover that Father Xavier has experienced more of his delusions. You can't imagine how embarrassing this is."

Inspector Piedmont's confusion hindered his ability to think like the detective he'd been trained to be. He honestly believed that by coming to the monastery this time, he'd obtain the answers to the mystery surrounding Sister Domenique's disappearance. But it appeared fate had other plans for him. He wouldn't gain any new information and it seemed as though, for the moment, his professional back had been broken. Once again, he was in the same position he'd been in so many times before, dealing with the insanity spawned from the godless monastery. Completely dispirited, he shifted his eyes around the room in a last attempt to make sense of Father Xavier's bizarre claims before succumbing to defeat. As he did so, he noted a pile of dismantled wine racks stacked in the corner. With a resurgence of hope, he clicked on his flashlight, walked up to the barren wall, and felt along the line of new cement.

"What do we have here?" Piedmont asked, encouraged at the finding. "Could Father Xavier have been right all along? What the hell are you hiding behind this sealed wall?"

"For heaven's sake, Inspector," Monsignor said, beads of sweat forming on his brow. "It's nothing."

"Nothing?" Piedmont said, shining his light into the monsignor's eyes, watching his pupils contract. "It obviously was a portal of some kind."

"Now that I think of it," Monsignor said with a nervous laughter in his voice. "You're correct. If memory serves me, it was an old entrance to an obsolete portion of the monastery. It was used long ago by the monks as a sanctuary of sorts, before the

Roman Catholic Church purchased the property."

"My, my," Father André said, startling the group as he emerged from the storage room. "It appears that even the Catholic Church has ancient skeletons hidden in its closets."

"Father André?" Piedmont exclaimed. "How long have you been spying on us?"

"Long enough," Father André replied.

"How many more of you priests are going to crawl out of the woodwork before the day is through?" Piedmont shouted. "This damn place is infested."

"I resent your remark," Father André said. "Your comparison of priests to rats is highly offensive."

"I'm not surprised to see him," Father Xavier said. "He's always lurking in the shadows."

"How droll, my dear Father Xavier," Father André said. "You really ought to pursue a career as a mystery writer. I mean, that line about lurking in shadows. Your use of prose is unmatched."

"Keep up the smug attitude," Xavier said. "I promise it'll be your downfall."

"Oh, Father Xavier," André said, smoothing his cassock. "Although it's always a pleasure to have these petty arguments, you'll have to excuse my abstinence today. I have more pressing business to attend to."

"You didn't answer my question, André," Piedmont said,

attempting to hold back his temper. "What the hell are you doing down here?"

"I'm here on the monsignor's orders," André said, flashing a cocky smile. "He asked me to refill the fonts in the chapel."

"This isn't the chapel," Piedmont said. "Did you get lost?"

"How observant, Inspector," André replied, laughing aloud. "You've really earned your title. You're absolutely correct. This is not the chapel. However, you have not done your homework. The holy water is stored down here in the storage room. It makes perfect sense if you think about it."

"Asshole!" Piedmont said. He turned back to the wall and scrutinized the outline of the doorway once again. "Why has this been recently sealed, Monsignor?"

"Ah, this should be quite entertaining," André said, backing up against the storage room door. "Yes, Monsignor, do enlighten us."

Monsignor Valois shot him an icy glare and sat down on the bottom step, which audibly protested under his weight. He twisted the hem of his cassock around his chubby fingers and cleared his throat, but never uttered a word.

"Come on, Inspector," Xavier said. "This is taking too long. Domenique could be dying down there!"

"He's right," Piedmont said, disbelieving that he'd actually agreed with Father Xavier. "I don't have all day. Start talking."

"There's a simple explanation," Monsignor began. "Last

night, Father Thomas found Father Xavier down here on the floor in an incoherent state, muttering something about Sister Domenique and Father André. Well, like usual, I brushed it off as just another seizure and told Father Thomas to bring him back to his room. When they left, I felt a cool breeze coming from behind the wine rack and noticed that the wall was slightly ajar. Naturally, I sealed it up for fear one of the elderly brethren would stumble through and fall to their death."

"Don't listen to him," Xavier screamed. "He's lying! He's hiding something! André knows she's down there. He has some kind of master plan for her." He turned and faced André. "You didn't think I'd remember, did you?"

"I don't know what you're talking about," André exclaimed. "I'm new here and know nothing about secret doors, passages, or sinister master plans."

"You're a damned liar!" Xavier screamed. "You'll rot in hell for this!"

"He's insane!" André said, turning his back to the men and heading toward the stairs. "I'm not going to stand here and listen to this garbage!"

"You're not going anywhere!" Piedmont shouted, not wanting to let any of them out of his sight until he had a firm handle on the peculiar scene unfolding before his eyes. "You'll stay put until we get to the bottom of this."

"Whatever you say, Inspector," André said, leaning against

221

the wooden handrail. "You're the boss, I guess."

"For Christ's sake, Monsignor," Piedmont said, his words brimming with anger. "Why the hell didn't you inform me of this passageway before?"

"You didn't ask, Inspector," Monsignor replied.

"You stupid son-of-a-bitch! I could hold you accountable for obstruction. If the nun's down there, I'll throw the book at you. Why does everything around here have to be such a goddamned secret?"

"It wasn't a secret," Monsignor said, eyeing him innocently. "I really didn't think anyone was aware of its existence besides me. And no harm's been done."

"If you knew about this, why the hell didn't you check out Xavier's accusations? You know how difficult the investigation has been. Don't you care if she's found?"

"Now you sound as ridiculous as Father Xavier," Monsignor said. "Of course I care. And there's no mystery here. I believe Father Xavier accidentally stumbled upon the passageway and his mind conjured up a cloak and dagger story. As you are well aware, he's been known to do that."

"There's nothing wrong with my mind!" Xavier shouted. "I researched this monastery in the Catholic Archives before I transferred here. The information was easy to find. After stumbling on some notes regarding a vast tunnel system beneath this building, the enigma surrounding it intrigued me. I started to explore the layout as soon as I arrived. If you recall, Monsignor, I attempted to discuss it with you on numerous occasions, but you refused to take me seriously."

"Is this true, Monsignor?" Piedmont posed. "Did he inform you of his finding?"

"Dear me," Monsignor said. "How could I possibly remember anything so insignificant? He might have. There's just no way to be sure."

Inspector Piedmont observed their faces, hoping to detect some sign of guilt. For the first time, he saw Xavier as a strong man with a definite purpose. The monsignor appeared nervous and out of character, his combative disposition fading with the color in his face. Finally, he shifted his gaze to André. He was the same as he had been on his previous visits, smug and astute.

"I want this wall opened up," Piedmont demanded before radioing Roget for backup. "We'll soon see who's lying and who's not. And if I find anything that even resembles foul play, I'll shut this place down permanently and lock you all up for life."

"Have mercy, Inspector," Monsignor said, holding up his rosary beads. "What will become of the monastery's reputation if something is found? Is there no way to keep a lid on this? The adverse publicity would be detrimental to our existence in the community."

"I wouldn't even try," Piedmont said, itching to thrash all of them. "You bastards will finally get what you deserve. I hope your God is watching out for you, because you're going to need him."

"You really are a cold, heartless man, aren't you?" Monsignor said, walking to the center of the room with visible signs of renewed energy. "You're doing this out of spite. You'd do anything to bring down the church if it meant I'd go down with it. You never could forgive me for not rushing to your side when they found your beloved Jacqueline's body, could you? Well, Norbert, life doesn't revolve around you. I'm a man, a priest, not God. What in heaven's name could I have done for the child anyway? She was already dead."

"You insensitive bastard!" Piedmont screamed. "We needed you, but you were too busy, too consumed with grandeur to fulfill your priestly duties."

"I'm sorry," Monsignor said. "I had a commitment at Saint Bartholomew's. It was unavoidable. You see, I was standing in for the bishop, preparing young adults for the Sacrament of Confirmation. Do you know how many priests would have given their eyeteeth to do that? It was an honor bestowed only on me. Me, Inspector. No one else but me."

"You're right," Piedmont said, eyes filled. "It's all you ever think about. Yourself and your goddamned church." He walked to the base of the stairs and continued through clenched teeth, "You really are a lame excuse for a human being."

"Well, I've never been so insulted in all my life,"

Monsignor said. "If you're finished abusing me, I'd like to get back to my office."

"Inspector," Xavier interrupted. "I just remembered. I know of another entrance to the tunnels."

"Another entrance?" Piedmont said. "Where's that one hidden, in the attic?"

"Don't look at me," Monsignor said, raising his hands. "I know nothing about it. I'd assumed this was the only one."

"It's around back," Xavier continued. "I'll show you, but let me get my map first."

"Map?" Piedmont said. "What map?"

"When I discovered the tunnel system, I did my best to map out the vast area. It's incomplete, but it's a good start. I'll be right back." Without waiting to be dismissed, he left.

"This is utterly asinine," André quipped. "I feel like I'm in the middle of a three-ring circus."

"Monsignor," Piedmont said, disregarding André's constant complaints and watching Xavier scale the stairs. "You can go back to your office now, but stay there. Unfortunately, we're not done. I'll need to speak with you later. And André, you stay right here where I can keep my eyes on you."

"Well, it's about time," Monsignor said, huffing as he stormed up the stairs.

Moments later, Xavier returned with a disappointed expression displayed on his face. His hands were empty. He faced

André and gritted his teeth.

"It's gone!" Xavier said. "Someone's stolen it!" "I swear, by our Lord above, if you've harmed one hair on Sister Domenique's head, I'll kill you!"

"Go straight to hell!" André yelled and charged up the stairs before Piedmont had the chance to stop him.

"Don't leave the premises, André," Piedmont yelled and turned his attention back to Xavier. "Okay, Xavier, it looks like it's just you and me. I hope I won't live to regret this, but show me the other entrance."

"Before we leave, Inspector, take this," he said, handing him the pill from his pocket. "This is what André's been giving me. I think he's been substituting it for my regular medication. Can you have it analyzed and tell me what it is?"

"How do I know where this came from?" Piedmont asked, eyeing him suspiciously. "You could have found this anywhere."

"I appeal to you, Inspector. If my hunch is correct, that pill is the cause of my recent odd behavior."

"Okay, I'll take care of it," Piedmont said, placing the pill in his inner pocket. "But for now, let's go. I want to see this other entrance before my men arrive."

CHAPTER 34

In a shadowed alcove, Father André stood silent, patiently waiting for the monsignor to arrive. He knew he would eventually have to return to his office in accordance with the inspector's earlier orders if he was to keep up the charade. As far as the game plan, he was uncertain. Before he could contemplate further, he was distracted by the distinct sound of the monsignor's cork clogs as they tapped down the hall. He's so close, he thought, his hands growing clammy. I could simply reach out and end his miserable existence right here and now if I choose. But what fun would that be?

Stimulated by power over life and death, he watched him unlock the door and rush into his office like a starving mouse heading unknowingly toward the cheese on a trap. His first instinct

227

was to follow, but as a precautionary measure, he waited a full two minutes before leaving the cover of darkness. On cat's paws, he edged to the door and opened it just wide enough for one eye to peer in. Resting his face comfortably against the cold wood, he silently watched as the monsignor fumbled through his cassock pocket, hands trembling.

"Now!" his master whispered. "André, enter now!"

He strolled into the office on cue, posture perfect, lines well rehearsed. He sat in one of the Victorian chairs, crossed his legs, and grinned, all the while eyeing his prey. The day of truth had finally arrived and excitement coursed through his veins. He relished the idea of control.

"Father André?" Monsignor said, his voice quavering. "Why are you here?"

"Aren't you glad to see me, Monsignor?" he asked. "Is something troubling you?"

"Well, of course something's troubling me. Not only do I have a seriously afflicted priest on my hands, but I also have to contend with the unpleasantness of an inconvenient police investigation. Oh, Father, do you realize how detrimental this could be for the monastery if this story leaks out to the press? We will be in ruin and the spoils divided amongst other parishes."

"The horror!" André said, his eyes narrowing into two tiny slits.

"How could you be so insolent at a time like this? Have

you no loyalty?"

"What a joke. The only thing you're loyal to is profit."

"How can you say such words. Yes, I'm concerned about losing benefactors, but I'm also concerned about humanity, including the brethren I've grown to love and think of as my own sons."

"All of humanity, eh?" André said. "If you'll pardon my frankness, I beg to differ. I don't believe you care about anyone but yourself."

"Bah! Utter nonsense."

"Okay, then why didn't you want me to telephone the police last night when Father Xavier was tearing apart the wine cellar? Why did you lie to them? What are you trying to hide? If you recall, Father Xavier did scream something about seeing Sister Domenique. Are you so filled with guilt that the welfare of your own daughter is less important than your reputation?"

"Daughter?" Monsignor said, his eyes wide.

"Yes," André said, shifting in his seat while changing the position of his legs. He placed his hand on his chin and continued, "Aren't we all your children? We are God's offspring and you, Monsignor, are the head of this church. So, in reality we are your sons and daughters. You said as much only seconds ago."

"Oh, of course. Yes, I guess I am. It's a big responsibility, you know."

"You didn't answer my questions. Why all the deception?"

"Father André, have you realized how much I've depended upon you since your arrival? It may not be fair to you, but I count on your strength and loyalty to me and the monastery. I was impressed when you took it upon yourself to handle Father Xavier's welfare in the absence of Doctor Cartier. It appears you always know what to do. You're always putting another person's needs before your own. And for that, I commend you."

"Excellent monologue, Monsignor," Father André said, applauding with slow claps. "But my question referring to the incident in the wine cellar has not yet been addressed. What are you hiding? What's down there?"

"D-d-didn't I already explain that to the police? Weren't you listening?"

"Not good enough, Monsignor. I don't believe that lame story for one second. If there was even a remote possibility that Sister Domenique could be down there, you wouldn't have stopped me from calling Inspector Piedmont unless you had something to hide. Now what is it?"

"I'm shocked at you, Father André. I thought you were different, but it seems I was dead wrong. You are as impertinent as the inspector and as insane as Father Xavier. Do you have no heart? Is it your intention to harm the monastery, the very institution that supports you?" He stood and banged his hands on the desk. "Listen here, you insolent antagonist. I've worked long and hard to attain my position here and will not allow insinuation or fact to get in the way of my becoming the next bishop. Have I made myself clear?"

"Perfectly," André said, complacent, his head cocked to the side. "Do you hear that?"

"Hear what?"

"It's the chime of the old grandfather clock. It's already noon."

"What's that supposed to mean?"

"Listen carefully to its rhythmic beat, Monsignor. With each stroke of the pendulum, so pass the minutes that bring your secrets ever nearer to revelation. As we speak, they're searching throughout the tunnels for what they believe will be the recovery of Sister Domenique. But we know differently, don't we, Monsignor? With each minute that expires, the closer they are to exposing something big. Real big." After a bout of hearty laughter, he left.

CHAPTER 35

Domenique inhaled sharply when she thought she heard male voices coming from the other side of the sealed door. Am I dreaming again? Am I still hearing things? Is it Xavier? Is he here to free me? How will he ever forgive me? She screamed through the gag in a desperate attempt to bring attention to herself, but only released a muffled choke. Frantic that she couldn't be heard, she moved her gaunt figure from side to side, yet the bed didn't squeak.

"This one's also locked," she heard a strong, male voice say.

"That makes fifty," another man said. "Come on, let's check down there."

Her prospect for freedom retreated as their voices faded

away. Why are they leaving? I'm in here! Please, come back! Suddenly, a sharp, stabbing pang traveled through her abdomen, causing her small frame to convulse uncontrollably. It was the developing fetus and she knew it. Instantly, her mind invented the frightening image of André straddling her again, raping her repeatedly. Agonized by the thought, she moaned, wishing with all her might that André and his wicked offspring would die. As another pain traveled through her stomach, her mind shifted back to the present. They'll be back, she thought. Xavier will find me. He will. He has to.

CHAPTER 36

"It's almost noontime," Piedmont said, casting the glow of his flashlight down another tunnel. "Do you really think she's down here? I mean, so many routes."

"There's always that possibility," Roget said, bringing up the rear. "But if she is, it could take months to find her. Every path looks the same."

"Goddamn it!" Piedmont said, wiping perspiration from his face. "We don't have months. If we're to believe Xavier, and unfortunately he's our only lead, she's trapped somewhere down here."

"Okay, what do we do now?" Roget asked.

"I guess we'll have to form some sort of system to eliminate confusion."

"How do we do that?"

"The process of elimination."

"I don't get it."

"We'll chalk an 'X' on each door once the room's been checked out. After we've cleared each passage, we'll mark the walls. That way, we won't be reinvestigating the same tunnels over and over."

"Excellent idea, Inspector. Do you think they've broken through the wine cellar yet?"

"Most likely, but for the moment, let's rally the men into the sitting room and I'll set the plan into motion."

"Yeah, and I'll round up a few thousand cases of chalk," Roget said.

"Right," Piedmont said, straining to see down the long, dark passage. "We'll need quite a bit. We'll also require high-intensity lamps."

"I'll have the monsignor see what he can do." Once in the sitting room, Roget asked, "Isn't Father Xavier still down in the catacombs?"

"No," Piedmont answered. "I sent him back up quite a while ago. He gives me the willies and I didn't want him hanging over my shoulder while we were working."

"I can understand that," Roget said. "I'll go gather the men while you speak with the monsignor."

"Okay, let's get to work."

CHAPTER 37

The midday sun played hide-and-seek with the clouds,
which moved gently over the mountaintops as Father Xavier
glimpsed a shadow darting across the courtyard. It seemed to head
toward the corner of the building. Wanting to see more, he pushed
his window up and stuck his head out.

"It's André," he said under his breath. "It must be."

Suddenly, an eerie stillness replaced the soft, westerly
wind. The temperature plummeted. He jerked back, bumped his
head on the sash, slammed the window down, and rubbed his
hands briskly on his upper arms to alleviate the chill. Through the
pane of glass, he gazed in awe at the landscape. It was as if he was
examining a newly painted canvas for the first time with colors so
vibrant, he half expected them to run. He looked past the courtyard

to the old, iron gate where he was to have met with Domenique some time ago. He sensed her calling to him.

"I must find her," he said, moving swiftly to the dresser. "Time is running out." He stared down at the silver tray André had left behind, picked up the pill, and laughed aloud. "He must think I'm a real lamebrain if he believes that I'd ever take one of these again." Disgusted by the thought, he tossed the pill into the trashcan and looked up at the ceiling. "Domenique, my friend, I'll find you if it's the last thing I ever do. I promise."

After reciting a short prayer, he stepped to the door, pressed his ear against the splintered oak, and listened. No noise came from the other side. He hesitantly turned the latch and peered out into the hall, expecting to find the guard, who had been stationed there earlier, feet up, reading a newspaper. To his surprise, the guard was face down on the floor. The wooden chair lay on its side and the newspaper, stained a deep crimson, covered his head. A pair of stainless steel scissors was planted in his back.

"Holy Christ!" Xavier whispered, bending down to feel for a pulse. "Who could have done this?"

Instinctively, he dislodged the weapon, dropped it to the floor, and wiped the blood from his hands onto his robe. He searched the hall with apprehension, but only heard the ticking of the old grandfather clock. Each stroke brought back a memory. The time when he was supposed to have met with Domenique. The time he had heard the vicious, life-threatening words spew

237

from André's mouth. The time when he saw André with Domenique in the wine cellar. André. André. He just couldn't get his name out of his mind.

"I can't concern myself with André right now," he said aloud. "Domenique is all that matters. She's alive and I'm the only one who can save her."

With a definite purpose, he dashed down the back stairway.

CHAPTER 38

"Okay, men," André heard the inspector say, while listening near the sitting room door. "You're to take this chalk and mark off each and every room and tunnel that you inspect. Have I made myself clear?"

"What about the locked chambers?" a male voice said. "We've already found at least fifty of those. Who knows how many more we'll find."

"Blow down every goddamned door that won't open with a simple turn of the knob," Piedmont said.

On hearing those words, André had heard enough. With his pockets filled, he covertly left his post, snuck down to the tunnels, and unlocked a vacant room not far from Domenique's. It's a good thing I followed him that day, he thought as he walked over to a small dresser. On its top sat a framed photograph. He picked it up, examined the picture, and revisited his recurring dream.

The young boy peeks through the chained door with tear-filled eyes, but this time the baby's cry from an unseen room is more exaggerated.

"I expel you, Satan," God screams. "Release the handmaiden, Vivian, from your clutch."

"No, Daniel!" the woman cries.

God holds up a large crucifix and strikes the woman repeatedly.

The red is blinding.

"Alas, do you repent for your sins of the flesh?" God yells thunderously. "Are you remorseful for your copulation with the priest?"

The woman slumps over and speaks no more.

The vision fades.

André wiped tears from his eyes and gently replaced the photograph. For some strange reason, he was moved by the memory. Recalling his mission, he emptied his pockets into the drawer, wiped the handle with his handkerchief, and exited the room. As he relocked the door, his God told him to forget the past and only dwell on the future. He knew he must now devote all thoughts and energy to the master plan if it was to succeed.

Brimming with new enthusiasm, he tiptoed down the

narrow tunnel, unlocked Domenique's cell, and slipped inside. He lit the lamp and sat next to her on the bed. Though the light flickered, he could plainly see that her form was worn. It appeared that her fight had vanished. He ran his fingernail along her abdomen.

"My, my," he said, his voice cracking. "You've become quite a celebrity these days. As God is my witness, no one will find you until my Father's needs have been met." In a guttural tone, he continued, "Did you know that in Greek Mythology, a labyrinth such as this one, was built by Daedalus for King Minos of Crete, devised to imprison a monster known as the Minotaur. Annually, the Minotaur devoured maidens, offered in tribute to the Gods. The irony foretold in myth has subsequently become your reality. You, Domenique, once the child is born, will be my offering. For I am the Minotaur and you are the key to my salvation."

CHAP†ER 39

By late afternoon, the officers had resumed their search through the underground maze, equipped with all tools required to carry out their objective. One group started at the entrance in the wine cellar and another from the door behind the building. As ordered by Inspector Piedmont, they cleared each room and marked an 'X' in white chalk on the doors and passages. It was thought by many that with so many routes, the possibility of reaching Sister Domenique anytime soon was improbable.

"At this rate," Piedmont said, hours into the search, "it'll take weeks. I didn't know so many rooms and passages could exist in one location. These priests have a veritable fortress here."

"Inspector," Roget asked. "Do you think we'll ever find her?"

"Don't know," Piedmont said, resting his hand on the cold, murky, rock wall. "But I honestly believe we have a good chance."

He drew an 'X' on the wall and headed down the next dark passage to another door. This handle wouldn't budge either. He gave Roget the order to break it down and watched as he set the charges.

"Fire in the hole!" Roget yelled.

They dashed for cover, held their ears, in anticipation of the blast. Within seconds, the explosion reverberated through the halls. Large chunks of rock and splintered metal flew through the stagnant air. The strong stench of sulfur imbued the already stale oxygen and thick dust lingered in the dampness.

"I hate that sound," Piedmont said, his ears ringing.

"There's no other way, Inspector," Roget said. "Monsignor said he had no keys to any of these doors. So, our only alternative is to blow them up."

"Guess you're right," Piedmont said. "But I still hate that goddamned noise."

With careful steps, he hopped over the rubble, holding tight to the lantern. He entered the room and gasped. To his astonishment, the room was immaculate, free of dust and grime. It housed an antique, canopy bed with aged silk bedding. A chipped, enamel wash basin sat on a wooden pedestal, and a timeworn vanity with an oversized, cracked mirror butted the far wall. Resting on the vanity was a polished, framed photograph, an antique hairbrush, and an assortment of colorful, perfume aspirators.

"What's that smell?" Roget asked with a scowl.

"Disinfectant, I think," Piedmont said, scrutinizing every aspect of the unusual room. "Either that or those perfumes over there have turned rancid. In any case, the odor is foul."

"How peculiar," Roget said, walking up to the vanity. "It appears that this room has been cleaned recently. Notice the brush strokes on the floor. And if this place has been sealed up for as long as the others, wouldn't this perfume have dried up by now? It doesn't take long for alcohol to evaporate."

"Good assumption, Roget. But what makes this room so special?"

"That's what we have to find out, Sir."

Piedmont donned a pair of thin, latex gloves, intent on figuring out the mystery of the locked room. Careful not to disturb the other items on the vanity, he picked up the photo. On close examination, a funny feeling played in his stomach. His eye twitched and his hands shook.

"What's wrong, Inspector?" Roget asked, eyeing his commander.

"Take a gander at this," he said, holding up the picture. "See anything familiar?"

"Well, if that isn't a tic on the ass of a monkey, I don't know what is!" Roget said, reflecting his light on the shiny frame.

"There's definitely something strange going on around here."

"I agree," Piedmont said, opening the top drawer of the vanity. "I think we've just unburied a coffin of dark secrets." He began fishing through the contents and stopped short. "Holy, Christ!"

"What is it?" Roget asked, leaning over his shoulder. "What have you got?"

"This can't be possible!" Piedmont said, holding a gold locket up to the light. "No!"

"What's wrong?"

"I-I-It's Jacqueline's," Piedmont answered, choking back a sob. "I gave it to her on her last birthday." With hands trembling, he unclasped the tiny hook and opened it. Inside was a picture of Claudine, Jacqueline, and him. "I'll kill them! One of those goddamned bastards killed my baby!"

"Calm down, Norbert," Roget said, placing his hand on his shoulder. "It'll be all right. Don't lose it now. We're so close. Soon, we'll have this asshole in custody where he belongs. But I can't believe you were right. The church is involved."

"I'll lock them all away and throw away the key," Piedmont said. "If I don't pummel them to death first." He wiped his eyes and gently placed the locket and the other articles into a plastic bag. "Let's finish up, so we can get the hell out of here."

"Okay, what do we have?"

"There are thirteen items in all. It's reasonable to believe that there's an item from every victim, seeing one of the items belonged to my daughter. Weren't we told that Joline was wearing pink, satin ribbons on the day she disappeared?"

"Yeah, I think you're right."

"Well, this looks pink enough to me," Piedmont said, pointing to the ribbon in the bag.

"We need forensics down here right away to dust this room for prints. With any luck, we'll get a clean one."

"This whole place is under arrest," Piedmont said, his jaw tight. "I want to personally fingerprint each and every one of those Jesus freaks!" He grabbed the photo and stormed from the cell, bumping into Father Xavier in his haste.

"Oh, excuse me, Inspector," Xavier said.

"What the hell are you doing down here?" Piedmont screamed, grabbing the priest by his collar. "Didn't I tell you to stay in your room?"

"I couldn't, Inspector," Xavier said, his voice rattling. "I wanted to search for her, too."

"Do you know anything about this room?" Piedmont asked.

"Why?" Xavier said. "What did you find?" He pushed his weight against him. "Is Domenique in there? Let me pass. I must see her."

"Hold on!" Roget said, stepping between the two men and shoving Father Xavier up to the wall. "How did you get past the guard at your door? I personally posted him there and ordered him not to move."

"He's dead," Xavier said. "I don't know what happened, but he was murdered."

"What?" Piedmont exclaimed, his eyes bloodshot. "You goddamned liar! You're behind all of this, aren't you? You've had me going for some time. Roget, get him out of my face before I kill him. Lock him in a room and then check out his story. If his fingerprints are found anywhere near my man, book him. And make sure you tell forensics to get down here on the double! I'll be in the monsignor's office."

"Will do, Inspector," Roget said, shoving Xavier down the dark passage.

CHAPTER 40

André shielded himself with Domenique's body, ready to plunge his dagger into her back if she made a sound, but eased his grip when he heard the policemen's voices trail off. "You did very well," he whispered close to her ear. He took in a cleansing breath, refastened her to the bed, double checked his knots, and tiptoed over to the door. With caution, he leaned forward and listened for a time. Once certain they were gone, he quickly unlocked the door, chalked an 'X' on it, and settled safely back into the room and onto the bed.

Seconds later, the doorknob rattled. "This passage is all clear," he heard a man say. "It's already been marked. Let's try the one down there on the left."

His heart leapt in his throat, choking off the oxygen,

causing his lungs to ache. If not for his split-second timing, the master plan would have failed. Thankful that he hadn't been seen when he marked the 'X' on the door, he snuggled next to her.

"You're safe now, Domenique," he whispered softly, his nerves nearly back to normal. "They're gone for good. They won't be back to interfere with my Master's plan." He dabbed her tears and smoothed back her stringy, dirty hair. "Don't cry my angel. You're not alone, I'm here with you." Careful not to make any noise, he picked up the Bible from the table and began reading from the book of *Revelations* 20:5,6,7:

> *"But the rest of the dead lived not again until the thousand years were finished. This is the first resurrection.*
> *Blessed and holy is he that hath part in the first resurrection; on such the second death hath no power, but they shall be priests of God and of Christ, and shall reign with him a thousand years.*
> *And when the thousand years are expired, Satan shall be loosed out of his prison."*

"Wasn't that enlightening?" he whispered, closing the book and returning it to the table. "My Master's time to reign is nearly upon us!"

Enthralled with a sudden feeling of euphoria, he stood and chanted in Latin over the unborn child. Blasphemies and Anti-

Christian phrases flowed viciously from his lips. His contemptuous cursing rivaled the one, true God. He also condemned her for who she was and as quickly as it had all begun, the sacrilegious session ended.

"Sweet dreams, my angel," he said, tucking the blanket around her midsection. "Keep warm." He picked up the medical bag, walked to the doorway, turned, and blew her a kiss. "Au revoir. Until the next time."

CHAPTER 41

"Get to it men," Piedmont said, nodding to the other officers. "Fingerprint everyone. I don't care if it takes all night. Roget, you stay with me. I may need a witness." He gave the monsignor a tissue and added, "Now, what were you saying, Monsignor?"

"It was the black hand of death," Monsignor said, wiping the ink from his fingertips. "It's reached out and stolen another soul from this world. It's not the first time, you know? It's brought bad tidings before. It all began years ago. And now with the deaths of God's innocent children, it has broadened its horizons to include others." He faced Piedmont with a forlorn expression, his eyes moist and bloodshot. "I'm truly regretful for the recent fatality of your officer, but I'm confident he's entered the Kingdom

251

of God."

"Enough of this bullshit!" Piedmont said, pushing Roget aside and slamming the door. He walked slowly back to the desk, deep lines forming on his brow. "You said you haven't left this office since we'd spoken in the wine cellar. How do I know you didn't sneak out of here, take the back stairway to the second floor, and murder him?"

"That's absurd!" Monsignor said, pivoting around and lowering the window a bit. "Why in God's name would I do that? What motive could I possibly have?"

"He's got a point, Inspector," Roget said. "What would be his motive?"

"Time will tell," Piedmont said, sitting in the wingback chair, fidgeting with the end of his mustache, and staring into the monsignor's eyes. "Could be that you want to kill us off one by one. You knew we'd eventually stumble onto something in the tunnels and you were afraid of that, eh?"

"What are you jabbering about?" Monsignor asked. "I have nothing to hide."

"Well, how do you explain this?" Piedmont said, throwing the evidence bag onto the desk.

"What's this?" Monsignor asked. "What does this have to do with me?"

"We have reason to believe these articles belonged to the thirteen children slaughtered across Canada," Roget said solemnly.

"What does this have to do with me?" Monsignor asked.

"They were found on your property," Piedmont said, never releasing his stare.

"Where did you find them?" Monsignor asked, his voice quavering. "How did they get here?"

"Stop the innocent act, Monsignor," Piedmont said, opening his briefcase. "You know, as well as I, where we found them." He pulled out another larger, plastic bag and held it up. "Look familiar?"

"Sweet Mother of God," Monsignor exclaimed. "How did you get that?"

"That's what we want to know," Piedmont said. Before he could continue his interrogation, a soft tap sounded and the door opened.

"Come in, Reverend Mother," Roget said. "Glad you could make it." He escorted her to a chair and continued, "We regret having to interrupt your supper, but under the circumstances, it was necessary."

"What is she doing here?" Monsignor asked, standing and teetering from side to side. "What will you gain by this, Inspector? No good shall come of it. How many people must you hurt for the sake of your own pain?"

"What is this about?" Reverend Mother asked. "Why have you summoned me here at this hour? Have you found Sister Domenique? Do you have a lead as to her whereabouts?"

"I'm sorry Mother," Piedmont said. "Not yet." He gently placed the antique, picture frame into her trembling hands and watched her reaction. To his surprise, she pressed it close to her bosom and sobbed. "Mother, can you identify the woman in the photograph?" He immediately shifted his eyes from her to the monsignor and waited for her response.

"It's Vivian," she answered softly, sitting erect and staring blankly into space.

"Vivian?" Piedmont exclaimed. "Who the hell is Vivian?"

"Why in God's name couldn't you have left it alone, Inspector?" Monsignor muttered, lowering his head and cupping his hands over his face.

"Yes, Vivian," Mother continued. "She was my sister."

"Your sister?" Roget asked. "You mean your blood sister? Or are you referring to another nun?"

"She was the youngest," Mother said softly. "She left home at seventeen." She paused and ran her finger along the image. "It's amazing."

"What's amazing," Piedmont asked.

"Christ!" Monsignor screamed. "Can't you leave this alone?"

"Shut up, Monsignor!" Piedmont shouted. "You had your chance. Allow her to continue. Now, Mother, what's so amazing?"

"It's her daughter. She bears a remarkable resemblance to

her. May I ask you where you got this?"

Monsignor flew around the desk and tore the picture from her hands. "No!" he cried, glaring at Piedmont. "You should have left this buried in the past. You really are an insensitive bastard! Are you getting your kicks from the pain you're causing?"

"Hold on for one goddamned minute," Roget said, backing up against the bookcase. "I'm confused. Let's start at the beginning. Reverend Mother, are you saying this is a photograph of the monsignor and Vivian? Your sister? Sister Domenique's mother?"

"Yes," Mother said softly. "You have it correct."

"Where is Vivian now?" Piedmont asked.

"She's dead," Mother said. "The last time I saw her was twenty-five years ago on a rainy, August night. She came to me terrified for herself and for the life of her newborn child. Her husband had gone mad. He had learned that another man sired Domenique, though she never said who it was. I insisted she take refuge in the abbey, but she refused. She left Domenique in my care and made me promise to protect her until she returned. But she never did. Years later, I found out that she had been murdered. I had no idea she even knew the monsignor."

"Okay," Piedmont said, pacing back and forth across the highly polished, tiled floor. "What's your role in this soap opera, Monsignor? Who was she to you?"

"It's a long story," Monsignor said, clutching the photo,

255

tears streaming down his cheeks.

"We've got time," Piedmont said.

"I-I-I loved her," Monsignor said. "My God, how I loved her. But I only added to her already miserable life."

"What do you mean?" Piedmont asked.

"It was a lifetime ago," Monsignor said. "Vivian had come to me for confession. She'd told me of her wild youth, her abusive relationship with her husband, Daniel, and of a son born out of wedlock."

"Son?" Mother exclaimed. "She never told me I had a nephew. Where is he? What's become of him?"

"I honestly don't know, Mother," Monsignor said somberly. "I've only seen him once. He must have been around one or two years old at the time."

"What was his name?" Piedmont asked

"I can't remember."

"Interesting background information," Piedmont said, shifting his weight from one foot to the other. "But you haven't answered my question. What misery did you cause Vivian?"

"If you give me a moment to collect my thoughts, I'll explain."

"Take your time," Piedmont said. "We're not going anywhere."

"She came to me twice a week for nearly a year, sometimes badly bruised," Monsignor said. "I tried to convince her that the only chance at a new life would be to report Daniel to the police, but she wouldn't hear of it. She was terrified he would harm her son, and for that reason, she remained his hostage until her death."

"Why is it you never mentioned you knew her?" Mother asked. "For heaven's sake, we've been friends for years. How could something so important have slipped your mind?"

"You must believe me, Mother. I honestly didn't know she was your sister. She'd told me that she had no family and I had no reason not to believe her."

"Do you really expect us to believe this bullshit?" Piedmont asked.

"I suppose I can't expect you to believe anything, Inspector. However, during that time, we'd become extremely close. A forbidden love had formed. When she told me she was pregnant with my child, I panicked. I insisted she get an abortion. Though it was a sin, I had a career in the church to worry about. She refused and I never saw or heard from her again. I assumed she just went back to Daniel."

"Are you saying you didn't know Domenique was your daughter?" Mother asked, glaring at him. "Didn't you see her picture plastered in the *Gazette*? My Lord, she's the spitting image of Vivian!"

"As God is my witness, no," Monsignor said, dabbing the corners of his swollen eyes. "I rarely read the news and I never put two and two together. Please, Inspector, find my daughter. I don't care about the repercussions anymore."

"A little late for that," Piedmont said, snickering at the remark. "It appears you have quite a neat little package here. A moment ago, we had a pompous asshole for a monsignor, a man with a 'holier than thou' attitude. Now we have the bereaved father before us. I suppose you'll play the part of the scorned lover next. Hey, Roget, who do you think will play the role of the villain?"

"Inspector," Monsignor said angrily, "I've confessed to having an immoral affair with Vivian. I've embarrassed the church and myself. For God's sake, what else do you want from me?"

"Answers," Piedmont yelled, pointing to the plastic bag. "How do you explain these thirteen items? Did you murder the children and keep these belongings as a sick reminder of your deeds? Did you kill my daughter?"

"No," Monsignor said emphatically. "I've never seen them before. How can you insinuate that I'd participate in such a horrible act? My God, even though we've never seen eye to eye, you can't possibly believe I'm a murderer."

"I don't know anything of the sort," Piedmont said flatly.

"I can prove my innocence," Monsignor said. "I'm guilty of many things, but this charge I'll fight to the end and win. As I told you on your previous visit, some priests do not belong in the church, but that does not make them killers. I have committed no crime against humanity, only against God. I keep a daily log of all of my activities and have a legitimate alibi for every time one of the poor souls was murdered. You can check for yourself."

"Does your log include the day you were screwing Domenique's mother?" Piedmont asked.

"I'm only a man, Inspector," Monsignor said. "Just a weak man, made up of flesh and blood. It's all I'm guilty of."

"You're a bastard!" Mother screamed. "You knew Vivian was in danger and took advantage of the situation!"

"I did nothing of the sort," Monsignor said. "As you well know, I'm a priest. It was not my place to inform the authorities without her consent."

"A priest?" Mother exclaimed with an expression of disgust on her face. "You're not a priest, you're a pig! You're not a man, you're an animal!"

"Think of me as you may," Monsignor said, folding his arms across his chest. "But I'll go to my grave knowing I truly loved her."

"If I find that you had anything to do with my daughter's murder, you'll be going to your grave sooner rather than later," Piedmont said. "Roget, read him his rights."

"On what grounds, Inspector?" Roget asked.

"Murder," Piedmont said. "He's a major suspect at this point and that's good enough for me."

"But we have nothing concrete to tie him to the children, Domenique, or to the dead officer upstairs," Roget said. "At least not until the results of the fingerprints are in."

"What do you call this?" Piedmont said, grabbing the plastic bag from the desk and holding it up. "Are you a goddamned fool? We found this evidence in his personal shrine downstairs."

"I don't want to burst your bubble, Inspector," Monsignor said. "But that's not proof. Any one of the brethren could have followed me down to that room and planted it there. I'm certain you're well aware I'm not loved by everyone. In my position, it's easy to make enemies. You, Inspector, would know that first hand. I suppose you'll have to arrest us all. I certainly hope your cells can accommodate nearly two hundred men."

"He's right, Inspector," Roget said. "I believe the only sensible thing to do at this moment is to allow forensics to continue their work." He turned to the monsignor and shook his fist. "And if they come up with anything connecting you to the killings, I'll personally erase that cocky smile from your face."

"I suppose we all have our jobs to do," Monsignor said.

"That's right," Mother said. She stood and leaned over the desk, outstretched her rosary beads, and continued, "As God is my witness, I'll strangle you to death if you've harmed Domenique. That's a promise. You'd better pack your bags because I'm reporting your actions to the archbishop." With those words, she stormed from the office.

"Seems you've made another enemy," Piedmont said,

winking at the monsignor. "It appears your church is crumbling from its base."

"You'd like that, wouldn't you, Inspector?" Monsignor said, his eyes narrow. "You're a Godless man."

"And you're still an asshole," Piedmont said, walking to the door. "This monastery is under house arrest. No one is to leave. Roget, let's go talk with Xavier again and leave this bastard to pack. His reign is nearing an end."

Chapter 42

In the courtyard, André leaned against the cold bricks until he was certain the officers had left the monsignor's office. *I must find out what the other knows,* he thought. Just as he was about to step away from the window, he heard the crackling of dried leaves. He quickly ducked back into the shadows and waited.

Within seconds, two beams of light passed dangerously close to his hiding place. His heart raced and he attempted to become one with the wall. Though he couldn't see their faces, he knew there were two of them.

"Let's check over there," one man said.

"Okay, Joe," another replied. "Maybe we'll have better luck."

He watched the flickering lights bob along the ground until

they disappeared into the blackness and his way was clear. He knew it was risky, but he had to make it up to his room without being detected. With the courage of a bear, he scaled the ivy-covered trellis and slipped in. After regaining his footing, he tiptoed over to his chamber door and listened. The guards were still in the hall. Though he strained to make out their conversation, their words were muffled.

"Those fools," he whispered, walking to the bed. "Who do they think they are? They can't keep me bottled up like this. My Father won't allow it!" He sat quietly for a while, going over all the new information he'd gathered and tried to piece it all together. "So, Monsignor Valois has finally admitted to his adulterous act with mother, eh? Now, with the evidence in place, he shall soon pay for destroying my family."

Before he could rationalize further, the inner voice broke his concentration. "My chosen one," the voice said. "I am proud. However, there is still much work to be done. You must dispose of the false priest and cleanse My sacred house. Then, the way shall be clear for you to prepare the handmaiden for the birth of My son, the savior. Finally, have all paths lead to the other."

Upon accepting the tasks, André stripped and stood naked by the window, allowing the moonlight to silhouette his muscular body. It felt good to have the cool, night air caress his shimmering skin. With a sense of self-control, he watched the thin, black tops of the evergreens calmly sway from side to side while reviewing

263

his mission. It had been a long, hard road, but finally the end was in sight.

"Guide me, Lord," he whispered into the night. "Give me strength to carry out Your will. Aid me in conquering all of the obstacles, which shall hinder the eventual culmination of Your plan. As You are my Witness, my God, my Father, Your will shall be done."

Consumed with love for his Father, he slipped out onto the ledge and felt the rough stone under his bare feet. Like a cat, he sprinted along the ledge to the other's window and nestled back against the thick greenery, wondering where it would all lead. Before he had the chance to peer in, he heard the inspector's voice.

"You're either a lucky man, Xavier," Piedmont said. "Or a victim of terrible circumstances."

"What do you mean, Inspector?" Xavier asked.

"For starters, the scissors that killed Corporal Gray are clean, and your prints weren't found in the underground cell."

"For God's sake, Inspector, maybe now you'll believe me. I've been trying to tell you all day that this is André's work. He has Domenique and I don't feel safe around him. He's killing people!"

"We have no proof," Roget said. "But we can place you in the areas of concern. The murdered officer was stationed right outside your door. You were the one who informed us of the underground tunnel system where we found other evidence and you're the one who has the blackouts."

"No," Xavier cried. "It wasn't my epilepsy. He was drugging me. Haven't you had the pill examined yet?"

"Oh, I'd totally forgotten about it," Piedmont said. "Thank you for reminding me. I'll have it analyzed first thing in the morning. With all that's happened today, my mind is a little scattered."

"Thank you, Inspector," Xavier said. "I believe that once the pill is analyzed, it will clear up most of the confusion surrounding my so-called seizures."

"Okay, Xavier," Piedmont said. "Let's get back to the matter at hand. You claim that your life is in danger. Is this correct?"

"Yes. I do."

"Then why the hell didn't André murder you after he supposedly killed my officer? Wouldn't it have made more sense? He would have had the perfect opportunity."

"No. I mean yes. Oh, Inspector, I can't imagine what he has planned. But I do have a feeling that it will be horrible. The last time he tried to administer the medication to me, he talked strangely, almost guttural. It was as if his personality had split in two. He referred to me as 'the other' and claimed to have some sort of master plan for Sister Domenique. It was all so cryptic."

"Yes," Piedmont said. "You mentioned that before. Do you have any ideas as to what it means?"

"I don't know, Inspector. I wish I did. But what bothers me most is the way he acted. It was as if he was possessed by demons. I couldn't see his face because my eyes were closed, but his voice had changed. It sounded bizarre, something out of a horror story. He said that he was the puppet master and I its puppet. I know it sounds crazy, but I felt as though some demonic force was channeling through him. Something strong."

"Hold it right there," Piedmont said. "Let me see if I have this right. We have demonic possession, a master plan, and puppet masters. All this bullshit story needs now is the wicked witch of the west and Satan, himself."

"I know how ridiculous this sounds," Xavier said. "But you have to believe me. André isn't who he claims to be. I know it. It'll be difficult to prove, but I insist the answers to this shrouded insanity will be found here at the monastery. I believe in you, Inspector. I believe in your keen capability to put an end to all this madness. I'm willing to stake my life on it."

André smirked, knowing what he had to do next. If the master plan was to work, he must sort out the many details. He waited until the conversation turned boring and stealthily made his way back to his room. Once in the safety of his cool sheets, he began to outline his agenda.

CHAPTER 43

During the night, Piedmont slipped out of bed, dressed, and sped back to his office. Something about yesterday's events nagged at him and he needed answers. He flipped on the overhead light, brewed a pot of strong, Columbian coffee and began sifting through the pile of evidence. He knew it would take some digging, but he was confident he'd locate something he'd missed on his previous exploration.

Hours into his work, dawn crept in and bit his backside. The station buzzed with activity. By now, his concentration was broken. His attention was instantly shifted to his forehead and the ache that now plagued his eyes. He popped two aspirin into his mouth, guzzled the last of the cold brew, and once again began shuffling through the file cabinet.

"How long have you been here?" Roget asked, bursting into

the office.

"Jesus Christ!" Piedmont said. "Don't you know how to knock?"

"Touchy, eh?" Roget said. "Due to a lack of sleep, I presume."

"Whatever. I guess I got here around twelve-thirty or so."

"What the hell were you doing here all night?"

"Just following up on some hunches."

"Did you find anything?"

"Not a thing."

"So, what's on the agenda for today?" Roget asked, playing with the end of a manila envelope. "Another trip to the monastery?"

"Yeah, unfortunately," Piedmont said, closing the file drawer. "I'm not looking forward to another round with those nuts, but unfortunately we have no other choice."

"I hear you," Roget said. "It's as if they were all abducted by little, green men and replaced with alien life-forms."

"I guess that would explain the puppet business, eh?" Piedmont joked.

"Yeah maybe, but what do you really think is going on out there? I'm so confused. We've finally found our first pieces of concrete evidence and as luck threw it at us, there's no one to connect them to. This whole thing stinks."

"I know just what you're saying," Piedmont said, reseating

himself behind his desk. "We must have missed something. We had to. My nose tells me that there's a connection here somewhere. The task is to find it."

"Where do we start?"

"Has the report on Xavier's pill come back yet?"

"It's right here," Roget said, tossing the envelope onto the desk. "I gave it to Simmons last night and told him not to leave until it was analyzed. He wasn't very happy about it, but it seems he came through. It's always good to have someone around who owes you a big one. I hope it's what we need."

"It says here that it's levodopa," Piedmont said, thumbing through the report. "It's a common drug usually taken to treat Parkinson's disease."

"Parkinson's!" Roget said. "That's not what the doctor said he's being treated for. How the hell did he get his hands on that?"

"He told me that this is one of the pills André had been giving him. If we're to believe him, it may be a medication for one of the other priests."

"I suppose it would be easy for André to get his hands on it, given the fact that the doctor must prescribe dozens of prescriptions to the brethren. I'll have to check with the doctor to find out who this medication is prescribed for. Once we know that, we can make the case to connect André, Father Xavier, and the drug. Does the report say what the side-effects are?"

"Yes," Piedmont said. "They include the loss of appetite, nausea, vomiting, dizziness, faintness, palpitations, involuntary tongue, jaw or neck movements, abdominal pain, mental disturbances, and insomnia. This pill, combined with epilepsy, could account for Xavier's frequent seizures."

"Yeah," Roget said. "If in fact, it was administered by André as he claims. But who's to say he's telling the truth?"

"You're right, Jacques. This case is a mess. I don't know who to believe."

"Allow me to play the devil's advocate for a moment. Let's say, for the sake of argument, Xavier's telling the truth. What facts do we have and how would they all add up if this were true?"

"Okay, I'll humor you," Piedmont said, resting his feet on the desk. "Xavier did inform me of the secret passageways. If he were the one who murdered the children, why the hell would he lead us to the evidence? That would be suicide. He would only incriminate himself. What would he have to gain by that kind of gesture?"

"Well, it's a known fact that some psychos subconsciously feel the need to be caught for their crimes in order to receive their just credit and fame."

"If that were the case, why the hell would he accuse André of having Domenique? It wouldn't help his cause. It would shift the credit to André and he'd lose the fame."

"Okay, Inspector, you're right. I'm not an analyst. I'm just a dumb police officer."

"Don't sell yourself short, Jacques. You might be on to something. Let's keep up this devil's advocate bit for a little while longer."

"It's your show, Inspector. What other evidence do we have pertaining to Xavier?"

"He's the one who gave us this pill and insisted on its analysis. Why?"

"Because it would implicate André?"

"You're absolutely right. Now, let's put it together. What do those two have against each other? And why?"

"Don't know. Their background files haven't arrived yet. We should have them by this afternoon. It'll be interesting to see what light they shed."

"Patience, my friend," Piedmont said, swiveling around and twisting the blinds open. "It'll all come together in due time."

"I'm certainly glad to see you're back to your old self again, Norbert. You had me scared for a while. I seriously believed you were going off the deep end."

"See? All that worrying for nothing. Didn't I tell you I was fine? You should have believed me. It took me a while to screw my head on straight, but I did it. Now, I have one purpose in life. To find my daughter's killer." Before he could continue with his analysis, a young woman dressed in a smart-looking, gray suit and sensible, black penny loafers barged into the room.

"He's here, Inspector," she said, smiling at the men. "Should I have him wait in the lobby or show him into your office now?"

"By all means, Eloise, show him in," Piedmont said, rising to his feet to greet the gentleman she escorted into the office. "Good day, Bishop LaVallee. I appreciate you making the trip on such short notice. I'm Inspector Norbert Piedmont and this is Sergeant Major Jacques Roget. Please be seated."

"Nice to meet you both," Bishop LaVallee said, seating himself opposite the desk. "I left as quickly as possible. When I received your phone call yesterday, I was totally taken aback by the information you relayed. Is Father Xavier all right?"

"I suppose," Piedmont said. "Under the circumstances. When was the last time you saw him?"

"Well, let me see," Bishop LaVallee said. He looked toward the ceiling and rubbed his chin. "I believe it was several months ago, back at Saint Alban's. When he requested a sabbatical to Saint Michael's Monastery, I saw no harm in it as I was well aware of his heavy workload. And after taking his illness into consideration, I thought it best to grant it."

"Wait a minute, Your Holiness," Roget said. "If you'll pardon my intrusion, it doesn't make any sense."

"Good heavens, why?" Bishop LaVallee asked.

"Father Xavier told us you were the one who had ordered

his sabbatical," Roget said. "He said he had no choice in the matter. Can you explain this?"

"I can't understand why he'd say such a thing," the bishop said. "It doesn't sound like Father Xavier at all. He's not known for lying or exaggerating upon facts."

"Really?" Piedmont said, raising his eyebrows. "I thought it was one of his many attributes."

"Are you certain we're speaking of the same person?" Bishop LaVallee asked. "He's well known and loved in his parish and this doesn't sound anything like him."

"Can you identify the man in this picture?" Piedmont asked, handing him a photograph.

"Why, yes. It's Father Xavier. He looks a tad thinner, but it's definitely him."

"At least we know we're speaking about the same person," Piedmont said, handing him another photo. "Can you identify this person?"

"Well, there's something familiar about him, but I can't put my finger on it. I believe I've seen this face before."

"Think, Bishop," Piedmont said. "It's extremely important."

"I'm trying, Inspector. Bear with me."

"But you're positive you've seen him in the past?" Roget asked in a hopeful tone.

"Yes," Bishop LaVallee said, handing the pictures back to

Piedmont. "There's a good possibility. I've met a great many people in my lifetime and it would be almost impossible to place everyone. Who is he?"

"His name is Father André Jeneau," Roget said. "Does the name ring any bells?"

"No," Bishop LaVallee said. "I'm sorry. The name is unfamiliar to me."

"That's too bad," Piedmont said, his mind switching gears. "So, are you certain Xavier requested the leave?"

"Yes," Bishop LaVallee said, fishing through his brown, leather briefcase. "I can prove it. I have his request right here."

"May I keep this?" Piedmont said, examining the signed document.

"You may. I have another copy in my office."

"Thank you, Bishop," Piedmont said. "It may prove helpful. Have you made your arrangements to stay at the monastery yet?"

"Yes, my secretary has handled all the details early this morning. I plan to stay as long as it takes for me to get Father Xavier back home safely."

"You could be here for quite some time," Piedmont said. "Everyone residing at the monastery is under house arrest. Are you sure you can be away for that long?"

"Inspector," Bishop LaVallee said, walking to the door. "I don't know all the details or what's happening around here, but I won't believe for one moment Father Xavier is involved in anything sordid. As I said before, I feel it's a privilege to work with him and I am optimistic about his future. There is some confusion as to this letter, but I am certain that Father Xavier will be able to clear it up when we speak. I have total faith in him and I'm positive you'll feel the same way in time."

"You priests really do believe in miracles," Piedmont said.

"Of course," Bishop LaVallee said. "Our faith is based on them. Good day, Inspector. You know where I'll be if you need me."

CHAPTER 44

Domenique shivered beneath the moth-eaten, wool blanket, her ragged body experiencing metabolic insufficiencies. She could barely withstand the excruciating pain ricocheting between her temples, and her empty stomach cried with hunger pangs. Gastric juices climbed her throat in search of food to digest, burning as it traveled up and down her esophagus with relentless fury.

Why would André do this to me? Why does he hate me so? Trying desperately to maintain her sanity through the grievous ordeal, her tortured mind wrestled with a slew of unanswered questions. She was skirting dangerously close to mental shutdown and physical collapse. As she tried to concentrate, her midsection started to convulse. Strong waves of nausea ebbed and flowed. Fearful she would vomit from the constant motion, she twisted her body to alleviate the sensation only to encounter a sharp stab to the side. This time, the pain was external. She continued to shift her weight around in a slow fashion until she identified a cool metal. Oh my Lord, it's the scissors, she thought as excitement replaced her woes. André forgot the scissors!

It appeared that the sudden rush of euphoria was too great for her mind to handle, prompting it to shutdown. Reality ceased to exist. As if falling from a great ship into the abysmal depths of an uncharted sea, she sank like lead to the stony bottom. Resigned to permit the currents of resolution decide her fate, she lay inert until carried off to a distant port. It was an innocent place locked away within her subconscious.

Chapter 45

After probing through his belongings for most of the morning, André finally found it. He'd almost forgotten that he'd hidden them behind the false back in the armoire, but was relieved when alas he remembered. Without delay, he shoved the keepsakes into his medical bag and crawled out onto the long, narrow ledge. He shimmied along the shelf and stopped at Father Xavier's window. He noted a pair of worn jeans lying on the bed beside a red and white, checkered flannel shirt. On the floor sat a relatively new pair of tennis shoes. He scanned the room for movement, however nobody was around.

"Going somewhere, Xavier?" he said to himself. "A person could get the wrong idea. Someone may think that you are attempting to leave the scene of the crime. Now we can't have that, can we?"

André ducked into the room and stopped short when he heard the sound of running water coming from the bathroom. He tiptoed over to the door and peeked in. The light was on and he assumed Xavier was in the shower. Without making a peep, he closed the door and dashed across the room to the closet. Just as he placed the medical bag on the floor, the water stopped. The silence was deafening. Instant fear rushed through his body. His heart thumped hard and his throat became dry. Nerves nearing panic, he closed the closet door and exited through the open window. He caught his breath and then slithered along the ledge back to the safety of his own room. Besieged by the jitters, he shed his clothes, jumped into bed, and prayed for the strength needed to carry out the master plan in its entirety. Uncertain as to whether or not he had the will to succeed as the chosen one, he begged the Lord to eliminate the guilt, which riddled his mind.

"My chosen one," the inner voice said. "I damn you for the guilt that plagues you. For these emotions shall bring forth your demise if you allow them to reside in your thoughts. You must rid yourself of them and realize that all your actions have been necessary for victory. You should rejoice in the knowledge that the other shall pay for the sins of the past. I have waited centuries for this time to come, so you must devote your life to My final coming. You must remain faithful only to Me."

The last phrase was repeated several times before leaving

André revitalized. He felt a regained alliance with his God, and his natural proclivity for confidence and arrogance replaced his guilt. His moment of conscience had vanished and his mind was clear. He now understood his position and would not allow anything to hinder his Master's original plan. With everything set back on its original course, he jumped out of bed and went forth with his daily rituals.

CHAPTER 46

The afternoon sun smoldered through the pines as
Piedmont and Roget made their way up the steep, gravel road to
the monastery. As usual, Piedmont shifted the jeep into four-wheel
drive and threw the lever into low gear. This time, the engine
raced and the transmission whirred. Though he pushed his foot
down hard on the accelerator, the vehicle only crept up the rutted,
dirt road. Rocks flew from under the tires and the smell of burning
rubber filled the air.

"I don't want to tax this old engine anymore than I have
to," he said to Roget.

"Yeah, it sounds like this baby needs a major overhaul."

When they finally reached the iron gates, they were
surprised to find them open and unmanned. Though highly

unusual, it was a relief that they wouldn't have to wait for one of the aged priests to admit them onto the grounds. Before entering the compound, they toured the perimeter a few times, hoping to catch a glimpse of either André or Xavier. It didn't matter who was found so long as answers were given to the questions that the recent evidence had produced. After realizing that they must be inside, he parked the vehicle at the main door and proceeded up to Xavier's chamber.

"Ready to talk, Xavier?" Piedmont asked, entering the room and seating himself by the open window.

"Of course," Xavier said, not appearing surprised in the least by his abrupt entrance. "I'll help in any way I can."

Piedmont eyed him from head to toe, surmising that he was either sincerely happy to see him or he'd been given another dose of bad medicine. He opted to believe the latter. Because no one in their right mind, especially under these morbid circumstances, would walk around with a silly-assed grin on their face unless drugs were involved.

"Are you all right, Inspector?" Xavier said. "You seem out of sorts."

"I'm fine."

"Did you have the pill analyzed?"

"I did."

"I'm relieved to hear that, but shouldn't Sergeant Major Roget be here when you give me the results?"

"Not necessary. He's downstairs questioning one of the other priests. But that's not important."

"Okay, Inspector," Xavier said, sitting on the window seat. "Please, tell me what it is. I've been out of my mind, waiting for some shred of concrete proof to materialize."

"Maybe we have it, maybe we don't," Piedmont said. "The pill is called levodopa. It's used to treat Parkinson's disease. Have you ever heard of this medication?"

"No," Xavier answered. "But it's a well-known fact that Father Augustus is afflicted with Parkinson's. The medication is probably his. Now it's starting to make sense."

"It does? Enlighten me."

"It's André. He must have been the one who stole Doctor Cartier's medical bag. It was common knowledge that the doctor carried extra dosages of our medications with him for cases of emergency, and it would have been easy for André to get his hands on them. For some unknown reason, the doctor trusted him."

"Interesting scenario, but who's to say you weren't the one who took the doctor's bag? It would have been just as easy for you to have taken the pills and then blamed it on André."

"How insane. Why would I do that? What would I have to gain by making myself ill?"

"It would be a great cover."

"Cover?"

"Yes, cover. Who's to say that you didn't murder the

283

children and then decide to hide out here? My sources tell me Montreal was your home base, which is where the murderous rampage began. In fact, you were a resident there for years before transferring to Winnipeg."

"True. I entered the seminary in Quebec, but they needed me in Winnipeg. You can check for yourself with the bishop. It's a fact that not many men are ordained these days, and it was necessary for me to relocate to Saint Alban's. We're always shifted from place to place. It's a common practice."

"Okay," Piedmont said. "Then I'm sure you'd have no objections to a thorough search of your room. I don't have a warrant, but can get one if needed."

"No, I don't mind at all. But what about André? Have you found any background information on him? He's your man, Inspector. If you'll recall, he was the one in Doctor Cartier's confidence, not I."

"The information's on its way. Trust me, we'll know everything there is to know about him in due time."

Piedmont put on a pair of latex gloves, radioed for Roget to come upstairs, and within minutes, they were tearing apart the chamber. They removed the dresser drawers without care and flung articles of clothing in every direction. Once they had emptied the nightstand, they tossed it on its side and moved on to the closet. Sitting on the floor was a worn, black leather bag.

"Well, well, what do we have here?" Piedmont asked,

picking up the medical bag. "It appears the good doctor's belongings have been found." He held it up and glared at Xavier. "How do you explain this?"

"I don't understand it," Xavier said, shock written all over his face. "It's impossible. That wasn't there yesterday."

"Then how did it get here?" Piedmont asked. "Was it carried in by angels?"

"I-I-I don't know where it came from," Xavier said, lowering his head. "This makes no sense."

"Here's my theory," Piedmont said. "When Doctor Cartier came in to check on you, he realized you were faking the severity of your illness. You were afraid he'd report it to us, so you killed him."

"You're wrong, Inspector!" Xavier screamed. "André's behind this! He's the one who put it here! He's responsible for my blackouts and he has Domenique!"

"André! André! André!" Piedmont yelled. "You're always yapping about André. He must be some fantastic magician. I mean, to be able to plant incriminating evidence in a room guarded from the outside and occupied at the same time. He's definitely a man of many talents."

"If your theory's true, Inspector," Roget said, "Why would Xavier leave the case behind for us to find? Wouldn't logic demand that in time we'd search his room?"

"You're absolutely right, Sergeant," Piedmont said, keeping

his eyes trained on Xavier. "That's the part of his plan that went awry. He had no way to dispose of the case because a guard has been posted in front of his door for some time. He murdered Corporal Gray and most likely would have done in Maxwell if the opportunity had arisen."

"It isn't true," Xavier said indignantly. "I've never murdered anyone, nor have I ever planned to do such a horrible deed. You're calling me the monster. The killer. My God, think for a minute! Listen to your own words. This is exactly what André has planned. It all makes sense. He is the puppet master pulling at all the strings. We are all his puppets!"

"Let it go, Xavier," Piedmont said. "You're accusations won't work anymore. Give it up while you still have the chance. You know, I almost fell for your story in the beginning. I started to believe you. I actually thought that you might have been just another victim. You're pretty good. I'll give you that. You even have Bishop LaVallee fooled. But not me. I won't fall for your lame acting ever again."

"I haven't lied about anything!" Xavier screamed. "I've done nothing! For God's sake, please, listen to reason."

"All right, Xavier," Piedmont said, jotting down the information. "How can you explain that we found the missing medical bag in your room? With a guard at the door, it would have been impossible for anyone to have entered unnoticed. If you're claiming it was André, how did he get in here? Did he fly in through the window on the wings of a dove or was it on the back of a fairy?"

"I haven't a clue, Inspector. I can't explain it. But I believe the truth has to surface eventually."

"Then who the hell killed my Corporal? If you're not to blame, who was it? Was it a demon, a ghost, or was that André, too?"

"It was André," Xavier said stammering. "He's guilty. I know he is."

"How do you know?" Roget asked. "Did you see him?"

"No," Xavier said. "I just know. That's all there is to it."

"Not good enough, Xavier," Piedmont said angrily. "No court in the land will convict a person on supposition alone. Why is it you're the only one who has ever claimed to have seen Domenique? With all of the priests around here, wouldn't that be almost impossible? Wouldn't someone else have witnessed her miraculous appearance also?"

"I'm not the only one who has seen her. André has, too. He's taken her somewhere. I have no proof, but I know it!"

"So you've said," Piedmont stated flatly. "But as you know, we've combed the tunnels and searched through every one of those goddamned rooms. There was no sign of her. You really had us going in circles for a while."

"She has to be down there," Xavier cried. "You must have overlooked something. A room. A passage."

"I overlooked nothing," Piedmont stated emphatically. "I pride myself on my thoroughness as an investigator." With a quick jerk, he threw the medical bag onto the chair and began examining its contents. "My, my! We have all kinds of goodies here." He proceeded to pull out some rolled gauze, bottles of prescription medications, and an assortment of medical tools. As he reached for the remaining articles, he turned and stared at Xavier once again.

"What is it, Inspector?" Xavier asked. "What in God's name have you found?"

"I don't believe these belonged to the doctor," Piedmont said, holding up a bra, a small pair of panties, and a nun's wimple. "Are you going to tell me that these are André's also?"

Xavier gasped. His eyes blinked rapidly and it appeared as though he would faint at any second. His lips moved, but no words escaped.

"Speak up," Roget said. "We didn't hear you."

"Yeah, Xavier," Piedmont said. "What kind of rabbit will you pull out of your robe this time?"

"I-I-I know this looks bad, Inspector, but you must believe me. I would never harm Domenique. She's my friend."

"Who said anything about harming Domenique?" Piedmont asked, stepping closer to him. "Why? Did you kill her, too? Is she dead? Where did you dispose of the body? Did you bury her on the grounds? Come now, Xavier, spit it out. Let's put an end to this hell you've created."

"No!" Xavier cried, grabbing his head. "You're twisting my words. Domenique is alive!"

"Then where the hell is she?" Piedmont screamed. "Spit it out, man!"

"I've already told you, André has her."

"André, André, André," Piedmont said, disgusted with the outcome of the interrogation. "That's all you can come up with. Cuff him, Roget, and read him his rights."

"What are the charges?" Xavier asked, backing away, sweat dripping from his forehead.

"For starters," Piedmont said, holding up the nun's headdress and shaking it. "You're charged with the kidnapping and possible murder of Sister Domenique Rondeau, the murder of Corporal Gray, the murder of Doctor Cartier, and whatever else I can throw at you!"

"No!" Xavier cried as the bedroom door flew open.

"What's going on here?" Bishop LaVallee said, stepping into the room. "I could hear your voices all the way down the corridor."

"It seems you've arrived at just the right time, Bishop," Piedmont said, grinning at the priest. "We've found evidence to convict Xavier. It appears as though he actually did see Sister Domenique, right down to the flesh." He held up the bra and smiled. "See what I mean?"

"Bishop," Xavier pleaded. "The evidence they speak of was planted here. They don't believe me! They're accusing me of murder!"

"Ridiculous!" Bishop LaVallee said. "There must be some logical explanation."

"Okay, Bishop," Piedmont said. "You can live with your blinders on if it'll make things easier for you." He pulled out a sheet of paper from an inner pocket of his jacket and handed it to Xavier. "Look familiar? You told us the bishop ordered you to come here for a mandatory rest, yet this document claims otherwise."

"Wait a minute," Xavier said, examining the paper. "I never sent this request. I didn't write this. Something's terribly wrong here." He grabbed his Bible and pulled out a similar document. "This is the letter I received from the bishop demanding my mandatory sabbatical. He requested my leave, not I."

"Let me see that," Bishop LaVallee said and grabbed it from his hands. "This isn't my signature." He faced Piedmont and continued, "Who could have done this? It has the church's seal, but it doesn't belong to my diocese."

"You priests are really good," Piedmont said, laughing aloud. "When it comes down to the wire, you stick by each other through thick and thin. You'll even go as far as to produce conflicting evidence out of thin air. It doesn't matter who is hurt or killed in the process. Did you concoct this plan when you talked earlier? My God, how far will you go to save your own necks?"

"Enough of these insults and accusations, Inspector," Bishop LaVallee said, his face red. "I insist that you evaluate these documents immediately. You'll be smiling through your backside once you've found out that they are forged."

"Okay, Bishop," Piedmont said. "I'll play along. But this is the last time." He proceeded to have them sign their names five times on a blank piece of paper, and then compared the signatures to the documents.

"Well, Inspector," Bishop LaVallee said. "They're not alike, are they?"

"The two letters were definitely written by the same person," Piedmont said. "But it's obvious that neither yours nor Xavier's signatures match."

"Maybe now you'll believe me, Inspector," Xavier said. "This new evidence proves that I was sent here under false pretenses. André was correct in saying he had a master plan. But why me? Why Sister Domenique?"

With all leads veiled in hidden truths and the results ensnared in a vicious circle, Piedmont paced the room, not knowing what or who to believe anymore. Could Xavier have been right all along, he thought. Could that cocky bastard, André, really be capable of pulling off such horror? Such deceit? Is it feasible that the true culprit had disguised himself so well that he threw us off track? Xavier had stuck to his story from the beginning. His versions never faltered. Is it possible Jacqueline's death could have blinded me to the facts?

"Are you okay, Inspector?" Roget asked, patting him on the shoulder. "You look ill."

"I believe it's only his guilt," Bishop LaVallee said. "He feels terrible about the trouble he's caused Father Xavier and now he can't take back his vicious words."

"Not fair, Bishop," Xavier said. "Inspector Piedmont was only doing his job. You have no idea what we've been up against. André must have calculated this plot for a very long time. Up to this point, he's been able to manipulate everyone involved. Only now, the tables have turned."

"I apologize, Inspector," Bishop LaVallee said. "Under the circumstances, I reacted as a scorned fool rather than a man of the cloth. Your harsh words were extremely offensive, but that doesn't excuse my rudeness. Please forgive me." He stepped over a pile of clothes, stood by Xavier, and continued, "Who is this André character? I haven't met him yet. What would drive a man like him to such drastic lengths?"

"Well, Bishop," Piedmont said. "That's what we'd like to find out. Roget, call Eloise and see if his background file has arrived yet. If it has, have her send it over immediately. Then, and only then, will we be able to address the question and act accordingly. We'll have to compare his signature to the documents as well."

"I'll get right on it, Inspector," Roget said and swiftly exited the chamber.

"Bishop," Piedmont said, placing the lingerie back into the bag. "Could you please stay here with Father Xavier? Don't let him out of your sight. If what he says is true, his life may be in danger."

"Do you really think so?" Bishop LaVallee asked.

"I do. If André feels as though we're on to him, any one of us could be his next target. Therefore, as a precautionary measure, I'd like you to stand guard. And you should also pray that your God is strong enough to protect you."

"Thank you, Inspector," Xavier said. "I appreciate your belief in me. But how do we locate Sister Domenique?"

"Leave everything to me," Piedmont said, offering a half smile. "If she's alive, we'll find her."

"I pray you're right," Xavier said. "I'm certain you'll do everything in your power to resolve this dilemma."

"I'm afraid it'll take more than prayers," Piedmont said, walking to the door. "It'll take good judgment and quick actions to trap him. Like you said, he's been pulling all the strings and now it's time to sever them. Good day, gentlemen."

CHAPTER 47

"I'm not going anywhere," Monsignor Valois said to his reflection in the bathroom mirror. "It'll take more than hearsay to finish me off. When I speak with Cardinal Sanchez about the Vivian business, I'll just fib a little. To err is human; to survive is all that matters."

"Fib, Monsignor?" a voice said from behind. "Does that sound like the actions of someone who heads the church?"

"Sweet, Jesus!" Monsignor said, swinging around, his heart palpitating. "Father André, what's the meaning of this? What are you doing in my room? How did you get in here?"

"My, my, Monsignor," André said, resting his arm against the doorjamb, blocking his path. "*Sed liberia nos a malo. Libera nos, quasumus!*"

"Deliver us from what evil?" Monsignor asked, confused by the strange words. "What are you babbling about?"

"The perpetual evil of Christ's whores! The perpetual evil of the church and everything it stands for! Deceit and fallen priests fill My Lord's house! My Father told me years ago that the name Valois would be stricken from *The Book of Life* and that glorious day has arrived."

"What is this gibberish about?" Monsignor asked, backing into the sink and wiping the shaving cream from his face with a hand towel. "Have you gone mad?"

"You must pay for the sins of the past," André said, his voice changing pitch. "For I, the Father, shall inherit the earth."

"Are you threatening me?"

"No," André answered. Instantly, his eyes rolled back and his face contorted as if in excruciating pain. His color paled and beads of perspiration formed in the creases of his brow. "It is I, the Master of heaven and earth." He cocked his head and pointed his finger at him. "You, Monsignor Valois, shall suffer the consequences of your past. You, alone, destroyed the family of Daniel, one of my chosen disciples. You, alone, corrupted my plan! However, the corrections shall ensue. The chosen one shall bring forth your demise."

"Get the hell out of here!" Monsignor cried as panic swept over him. A tingling sensation traveled through his veins to his extremities, nearly taking control of his actions. Needing to disarm the crippling effect and regain some sort of hold on the situation, he grabbed the straightedge razor from the vanity, shoved his way into the bedroom, and circled the bed. "Get out or I'll call for Inspector Piedmont!"

"You think so?" André said. He sauntered to the door and placed his hand on the knob. "You shall be squashed like an insect under my feet, Valois. Be warned, by the time the clock chimes midnight, the deed shall be done. Use the remaining hours to repent." Without saying anything more, he exited, slamming the door behind him.

Father André's schizophrenic behavior flabbergasted the monsignor. His insides rattled. He dropped the razor to the Oriental rug, wobbled to the door, and bolted it. What am I to do? I couldn't possibly ask Inspector Piedmont for help. He'd never believe me. I've been through a lot over the years and have always managed to redeem myself. What shall I do now?

Instantly, distant memories gushed to the surface and gnawed at his mind. He saw Vivian standing alone in the cobblestone courtyard. Recent scars marred her creamy complexion. She'd been crying and a little boy stood by her side.

"Daniel knows about you and the pregnancy," she said, tears rolling off her cheeks. "What should I do? I'm fearful for my life and the life of my son. He'll kill us!"

"Abort it, you fool," he heard himself say. "For God's sake, I'm a priest. If word gets out about this, they will excommunicate me. Vivian, I beg you. Please, find it in your heart to spare me the embarrassment. You are young and have your whole life ahead of you. I, on the other hand, only have the church. I lack the strength to survive in the outside world. I'm a coward. Forgive me."

"Never!" she screamed. "How could you ask such a thing of me? Abortion is a sin against God! You helped to create this child. Listen to yourself. We can go away. We can start a life together. You'll never be alone."

"Absolutely not! I won't allow anything to come between the church and myself. Not even you. Abort the fetus while you still can. Go back to Daniel."

"This is unbelievable! But I suppose I shouldn't be surprised. You're no different. You're like every other man, cruel, self-centered, and insensitive. I know now what I must do. I'll keep your damned secret. But when our child is born, Xavier and I will leave Canada. You'll never see or hear from us again. Xavier, Xavier, Xavier. . . ."

"Is it possible he's the same Xavier?" Monsignor said as the memory faded. "Could Father Xavier be Vivian's child? No, he can't be. Can he?" He sat in an overstuffed chair by the window and contemplated the disturbing thoughts until mental exhaustion muted his brain.

CHAPTER 48

It was early evening when Inspector Piedmont received André's background report. He'd been anxiously waiting for answers and hoped that the information would shed light on the situation. Without regards to the messenger, he swiftly scanned the documents. Something had to glue all the pieces together and he'd find it.

"Finally!" Piedmont said. "The proof we've been waiting for."

"Yeah," Roget said. "It sure ties up some loose ends, eh? So, what's next on the agenda?"

"I guess there's no time like the present for a good lynching, eh, Roget?" Piedmont said, folding the documents in half and placing them under his arm. "I figure if we give him enough rope, he'll hang himself."

"It appears Father Xavier was telling the truth all along," Roget said.

"Looks that way," Piedmont said. "This report definitely gives strength to his story. Who would have figured that a man like Xavier would end up being on the level?"

"Just goes to show you that you can't judge a priest by his cassock."

"You're right, Jacques," Piedmont said, chuckling. "I think we can safely say Father André Jeneau is our man."

"Yeah, he really has quite a history."

"He's probably upstairs right now, pacing back and forth like a caged tiger, trying to figure his way out of this one."

"Don't we have enough evidence to make an arrest?" Roget asked. "What are we waiting for?"

"Come on, Jacques. You're not thinking like a detective. You're thinking like a street officer. A good investigator has to be creative and able to adapt to rapidly changing situations."

"You're absolutely right," Roget said. "What do you have planned?"

"Let's snare him in his own web," Piedmont said. "Follow me. This could get interesting. Besides, he's the only person alive who can lead us to Sister Domenique." They left the sitting room, scaled the stairs, and rushed up to the officer posted in the hall."

"Long day, Inspector, eh?" the officer said. He stood and

stretched. "I thought you'd be gone by now."

"No, not yet, Corporal," Piedmont said. "Is Father André still in his room?"

"He should be," the officer answered.

"Should be?" Piedmont said. "Isn't it your job to know?"

"Uh, y-y-yes, Inspector. What I meant to say was that I've only left my post twice this afternoon. Both times to use the bathroom. I wasn't gone long, though. So, I assume he's still pent up in there."

"You stupid bastard!" Piedmont said, shaking a fist in the air. "Couldn't you have held your water? My God, your shift is only two hours long. Don't you realize that one of these priests is a killer? Why do you think you've been stationed here?"

"Sorry, Inspector," the officer said, stepping out of his way. "But it's been murder on me. I've been suffering with kidney stones for the past week, and I've had to drink gallons of water."

"Sorry doesn't cut it," Piedmont said. "What am I running here? A hospital for bladder control or a crime scene?" Without waiting to hear more of his excuses, he added, "Get out of my sight! You're relieved of duty and don't return until you can hold your water. Oh, and on your way out, inform Corporal Jones that he's to be your replacement until further notice."

"Yes, Sir," the officer said, hurrying down the hall. "I'll relay your order immediately."

"Can you believe that idiot?" Piedmont said. "What the

hell do I have to do to get competent help around here?"

"I know what you're saying, Inspector," Roget said. "But I kind of understand what he's going through. I've had kidney stones before and it hurts like a bitch. It's like pissing bullets."

"I sympathize," Piedmont said. "But I don't have time to listen to personal pissing problems. I've got a killer to catch." He huffed and stormed into André's chamber. "Hey, André, what's up?"

"What's the meaning of this intrusion?" André asked, fastening a button on his cassock. "Don't you have anything better to do than to barge into my room uninvited? Is privacy too much to ask for? Good God, your presence has upset the monastery all day. It's nearly seven o'clock. Shouldn't you be home preparing for dinner or out chasing car thieves?"

"Settle down, Father," Piedmont said. "Don't get your undies in a bunch. I have more questions to ask and I'm not leaving until I get answers. Sergeant Major Roget will be noting your replies."

"Questions?" André said. "Haven't we gone through all this before? I can't imagine I could possibly have any more information for you."

"I hope you're wrong," Piedmont said, eyeing him keenly. "Some new information has surfaced pertaining to Father Xavier and I believe you are the person who could clear up some of the confusion."

301

"Xavier?" André said, sitting down on his window seat. "Now that's a fascinating topic. So, you've finally retrieved some damaging evidence against him. I knew it wouldn't take long. Something had to surface eventually. I believe he's a menace to society. Neither women nor children are safe around him. In my estimation, you should lock him in a jail cell and throw away the key." He paused and added, "Of course, that's only my opinion."

"Aren't you being a bit harsh on him?" Piedmont asked, never losing eye contact. "Don't like him much, eh? Why is that?"

"Inspector, haven't you ever met someone and felt uneasy from the first moment? That's the way our initial meeting began. I never trusted him. He could never look you straight in the eyes. His eyes seem to be hiding something, something evil."

"I agree, he is a strange man," Piedmont said, sitting at the edge of the bed. "When did you meet him? Was it when you lived in Montreal, Winnipeg, Edmonton, or was it when you arrived here from Saint Camille's?"

"I met him here," André said matter-of-factly, shifting his position and folding his arms across his chest. "I've already told you I've never been to Edmonton or Winnipeg and I have never heard of Saint Camille's. This is all too ridiculous, but I'll repeat myself at the risk of being redundant. My last place of residence was Saint Clementine's. Get the facts straight, Inspector, if you're going to bother to ask questions that you already know the answers to."

"Ah, yes, Saint Clementine's," Piedmont said, ignoring the snide remark. "Does old Father Ferrer still reside there?"

"I'm not sure. Why do you ask?"

"I'd mentioned to my wife that you were from Saint Clementine's and she was ecstatic," Piedmont began. "She reminded me that her cousin Mildred was married by Father Ferrer some time ago. It brought back some pleasant memories. And she asked me to ask you how he was doing." He kept his eyes locked on André, searching for some subtle sign of guilt, but only encountered a cynical glare. "Is he still the great donut eater he always was?"

"Of course," André said, releasing a sigh. "He's as big as a barn. Some of the brethren used to refer to him as the donut pusher. I suppose it's better than drugs."

"Thank you. I'll let my wife know that some things never change."

"But what does this have to do with Father Xavier or myself?" André asked.

"Oh, forgive me, I got sidetracked. It appears your perception of Father Xavier has been correct all along."

"Really?" André said, rubbing his hands together. "Do tell."

"Yes," Piedmont said. "We approached him this morning with some newfound evidence. We believe he was the one who murdered Doctor Cartier and is possibly the one who abducted Sister Domenique."

"Murdered Doctor Cartier? Why?"

"We think the doctor found out that he was lying about his attacks and was going to inform us, but was killed before he had the chance."

"How could you know that?" André asked. "This is interesting, but total speculation."

"Not really," Piedmont said. "We found the doctor's medical bag in Xavier's closet. Inside the bag were some articles of clothing, and they're being examined as we speak. If we're correct, they'll prove to be Sister Domenique's."

"Ah, what terrible luck for my Father, Xavier," André said. "Have you arrested him yet? Did he tell you where Sister Domenique is?"

"No," Piedmont said, searching his eyes. "This is where you come in."

"Inspector," André said, eyebrows raised. "How could I possibly know where she is? What do you want from me?"

"Don't bring your water to a boil, Father," Piedmont said. "Calm down. We were just hoping you would know where Father Xavier would hide. He ran off after we approached him with the evidence."

"Oh, now I understand. He must be running amok like a scared rabbit, eh?"

"I suppose you could say that," Piedmont said. "Can you help us?"

"I really think Monsignor Valois might be better suited to help you locate him."

"Well, Inspector," Roget said. "Seems like we've hit another dead end."

"Yeah," Piedmont said. "I guess I was wrong. I guess Father André won't be able to help us track him down after all."

"What do you mean?" André said. "Why would you assume that I would know where to find Father Xavier? You know I can't even tolerate being in the man's company."

"Strange," Piedmont said, looking around the room.

"Why do you say that, Inspector?" André asked. "Our distaste for one another is no secret."

"Well, for starters, you always knew his whereabouts when it came time to administer his medication. You must have been friendly enough to do that."

"Your entirely wrong," André said, writing invisible words on the windowpane. "Father Xavier and I are not friends. The reason Doctor Cartier chose me to administer his medication only happened by chance. On a few occasions, I was nearby when he was attempting to calm him. Being that Xavier was excessively violent and the doctor extremely old, he asked me to help restrain him. He also feared that Xavier would harm himself or someone else. As a precautionary measure, he asked me to watch over him in his absence. I'm a light sleeper and as you know, our rooms are adjacent to one another. If he were to take a fit through the night, I'd hear it and be able to act accordingly. You see, Inspector, it had nothing to do with friendship."

"You must have been invaluable to Doctor Cartier," Roget said, writing in his notebook. "I mean, for him to have entrusted you with dispensing such a lethal medication."

"I am invaluable," André said, facing the men with a look of pride. "I've been chosen for many important tasks. I suppose it all began when I was a mere boy, predestined to serve my Father in numerous ways. He has a master plan for us, you know. Only those who walk around without strings shall lead. I, Inspector, am a leader and Doctor Cartier saw that."

"I can relate," Piedmont said. "Sometimes I feel as though I'm being led around by the nose, not knowing which way to proceed next. Like a puppet you might say."

"That's where we differ as human beings," André said, his eyes glazed. "I am led only by my desire to serve my Lord." He returned his gaze to the window and continued, "So, Xavier's actions have proven his guilt, eh?"

"Yes," Roget said. "It appears he's guilty."

"Did you see him earlier today?" Piedmont asked.

"No, Inspector. As you know, I haven't had the privilege of leaving my chamber. But now that you've discovered Domenique's undergarments in Father Xavier's room, I'll finally be free to come and go as I please."

"In time, Father," Piedmont said, shifting his eyes to Roget and giving a slight nod of his head.

"I'm growing weary of this tedious question and answer session, Inspector," André said. "I regret that I couldn't have been of more help to you. Now that Father Xavier is your primary target, would you mind terribly if we ended this boring tête-à-tête? I have work to catch up on and I've already lost too much time."

"I'm sorry, Father," Roget said. "We understand this has been a great inconvenience to you. If you would please sign this statement, we'll be on our way."

"What's this?" André asked, taking the paper from Roget.

"It's routine," Roget said. "It'll release you as a suspect and states that you've been truthful with all of your answers."

"Gladly," André said. "I'll sign anything if it will rid me of your constant prodding." He signed the document and handed it to Piedmont. "Good day, gentlemen. My sincerest wish is that I find Father Xavier before you do."

"Why?" Piedmont said, walking to the door.

"Because all those who do evil deeds shall be punished. And those same persons shall be stricken from *The Book of Life*."

"What the hell does that mean?" Roget asked.

"My dear gentlemen," André said. "Please don't look at me that way. You're taking it all wrong. What I'm trying to say is that if I see Father Xavier, I'll report directly to you. Anyone who

307

could have done the horrible things you say he did deserves great punishment. Of course, in the end, the Father will decide what that shall be."

"Just leave the justice to us," Piedmont said. "The law will decide who gets punished and how. You could say that we play God. Good afternoon." Without further ado, they exited to the hall.

"Caught in his own web of deceit," Piedmont whispered. "We never mentioned what articles of clothing were found in the medical bag, yet he referred to them as underwear. And I have to say that Father Ferrer story was genius."

"What do you mean," Roget asked. "Who is this Father Ferrer?"

"That's where my hunches came in," Piedmont said. "I made him up and he fell for it. I thought I had lost him there for a moment, but he admitted to knowing him and stuck to his story about coming from Saint Clementine's. You read his background report. He never resided there."

"Very clever, Inspector. Now he thinks we're after Xavier."

"Exactly what I want him to believe."

"Aren't we placing Father Xavier's life in danger? What if he murders him next?"

"Don't worry, Jacques. We'll keep Xavier concealed. He'll be safe as long as he stays out of sight, but we're going to have to keep our eyes on André. That son-of-a-bitch is a murderer and he's holding the nun for God knows what. And we don't want any more deaths on our hands. I realize I'm taking a major risk here, but I don't believe I have any other options."

"Do you think it's wise to proceed with this charade without informing the solicitor general?" Roget asked. "If anything goes wrong, it'll be our heads."

"For now, we'll keep it under our hats," Piedmont said.

"I hope you know what you're doing."

"Me, too."

"Are we just going to allow André to continue pretending he's a real priest?"

"Of course," Piedmont said. "We know the truth. And as long as he isn't aware of that fact, we have the upper hand." He reexamined the signed document and went on, "Let's get this to the station and get it analyzed. If my assumption is correct, his signature matches the two forged letters."

"Sounds like a plan," Roget said. "But where are we going to hide Xavier?"

"At the abbey, of course," Piedmont said. "Can you think of a better place to conceal the whereabouts of a priest?"

"No, I suppose not."

"You round up Father Xavier and Bishop LaVallee," Piedmont said. "And I'll handle this document."

"Won't André think something's fishy if the bishop

disappears as well?"

"No. I don't even know if he realizes he's here. Just to be safe though, we'll spread it around that he flew back to his parish on some high-level emergency. Now get moving, we have work to do. We'll meet at Saint Bartholomew's in about an hour."

"Okay, Inspector. I hope this plan works."

"Me, too, Jacques. Me, too."

CHAPTER 49

André woke to the lonesome cry of an owl, which was roosted on a branch outside his window. How could I have slept so long? he thought as he sprung from his bed. He wiped the sleep from his eyes, moved through the darkness to the window seat, and listened to the symphony of crickets chirp in the moonlit courtyard below. Entranced by the reverberation of night, he gazed up at the full moon, outstretched his arms, and prayed.

"The time has come, Father. Your will shall be done. Amen."

He drew in the thick, damp air, held it as long as he could, and exhaled ever so slowly. He could almost feel the oxygen bursting in his head. It was refreshing to clear his mind. Absorbed with a regained arsenal of perception and wit, he slipped out of the dimly lit chamber and into the pitch blackness of the hall.

Cautiously, he slipped past the sleeping guard, guided only by the slivers of light, which crept from beneath the row of doors. On reaching the staircase, he stopped short and listened to sounds coming from the first floor. His trepidation mounted. He quickly panned the flight of stairs, expecting to see one of the brethren ascending, but no one was there. After a while, he asserted that it was just his overactive mind playing tricks on him. Certain that he'd figured it out, he continued in the darkness toward his destination.

Once at the monsignor's door, he stopped, waited for the old, grandfather clock to strike ten, and slowly turned the marble knob. Without wanting to be heard, he opened the door just enough for his head to poke through. Elongated shadows painted the planked floor and the suffocating scent of polished wood filled his nostrils. He tiptoed over to the large, four-poster bed, but to his misfortune, it was vacant.

Suddenly, familiar voices came from the hall, inciting instant panic. He dashed into the closet and nestled back into the rack of clothes. His heart beat thunderously, so hard that he believed the entire household could hear. It's maddening to be experiencing discomfort on such a glorious night, he thought. Elation is what I should be feeling. Consumed by his will to survive, he summoned the strength he'd possessed during the purification of the children's souls. It was fascinating and all consuming, exactly what was needed at this moment in time.

CHAPTER 50

After returning from the abbey, Piedmont slipped beneath his cool sheets, shop-worn from the day's ordeals. Now that Father Xavier was safely tucked away and out of André's reach, he could breathe a little easier. He gave Claudine a peck on the cheek and then did something he hadn't done for a very long time. In fact, not since his daughter's death. Though he'd promised himself never to do it again, he prayed. He prayed hard, asking God for the strength required to triumph over her killer. Before he recited the last verse of *The Lord's Prayer*, he drifted into a deep sleep.

His body tossed and turned while his mind wrestled with horrific dreamscapes of torture and pain. Savage gremlins feasted on the murdered children and Jacqueline cried out for help. André appeared and hovered in mid-air over a flaming pit, shouting

313

vulgarities in the name of the beast. The two scenes blended into an appalling mix of utter torment.

Suddenly, out of the dark recesses of his subconscious mind, came a soothing voice. "These visions," the voice said calmly, "are a precursor of things to come. For the climax is at hand. Beware the false priest, for Satan leads him. You must remove him from this world in order to restore your peace. Do this in my name."

Like a child plagued by goblins and bogeymen, he bolted up in bed, beads of sweat dripping down his face. His heart raced and his head ached. It was only a dream, he thought, attempting to shake off the uneasy feeling. It wasn't real. Subconsciously, he knew he'd come face to face with André. The killer. The bastard who had butchered his only child and so many other innocents.

Unable to go back to sleep, he rolled over, hugged his wife, and tried to rationalize his growing fears. Dear God, he thought, give me strength. Don't let me screw up. I must find a way to end this hellish nightmare. I can't bring back the dead, but I still have a good chance to save Sister Domenique. Finding her will help me avenge my daughter's death. Amen."

He lay there for a while contemplating his next course of action, confident he had made the right decision to protect Father Xavier. He wasn't sure how he came to believe in him, but his nose dictated that he was on the correct path, the path that could lead to more destruction if he wasn't careful. Having found the inner strength needed to triumph over the evil, which had hung over the area like a shroud of darkness for what seemed an eternity, he eventually fell into a peaceful sleep.

CHAPTER 51

André pressed against the closet's cool, cracked wall and listened to the conversation between Monsignor Valois and Father Beaumont. "We've been friends for many years, Father," he heard the monsignor say, his tone sad. "But I have no other choice."

"Are you certain you're making the right decision, Monsignor?" Father Beaumont said.

"Yes. I know it may sound drastic, but I've asked to be transferred to Florida. Down there, the Catholic Church is still considered a mission. I'm to head a small parish in Lakeland."

"Don't you feel as though you're stepping down? Can you be happy there? It's so terribly far away."

"It's not a question of happiness or resignation, but that of survival."

"I don't understand, Monsignor."

"Good gracious, don't look at me that way. I didn't mean my survival. I meant the survival of the church. Now, if you'll excuse me, I've booked an early flight and must get some sleep. Good night, Father Beaumont."

How interesting, André thought, rubbing his hands together. He intends to flee his homeland the same as Xavier did. But unfortunately, my dear Monsignor, that won't be possible. My Lord has other plans for you. Soon, very soon, you shall meet Him. For your time of atonement is near.

He inched closer to the door, opened it a crack, and waited. Once certain the monsignor was asleep, he slipped from his hiding place and melded into the darkness of the room. By now, his adrenaline soared. Peaked with fury, he rushed to the bed and covered the older priest's mouth with his hand.   The monsignor's large body thrashed from side to side. His muffled cries resembled that of a wounded moose. His arms flailed wildly, and his thick legs kicked hard beneath the tight bedding. Though his body jumped and jerked, his feeble attempts at freedom were no match for the strong arms that bound him.

"What could be going through your mind, Monsignor?" he whispered into his ear. "Is it the fear of losing your life or are you afraid your secrets will be revealed before you have the chance to run? Who is in control of the situation now?" He removed the bedding and lifted him to his feet. "It's time, Monsignor. Soon, my Father's wish shall be fulfilled and you shall pay for the sins of the past."

"N-n-no, André," Monsignor whispered. "Come to your senses. I've already informed Inspector Piedmont of your threats. If something happens to me, he'll know who to track down. He'll find and arrest you. He'll lock you away. You'll never see the light of day again!"

"Hush, you decrepit fool!" André said. "Do you really believe I'd fall for more of your lies? Damn Inspector Piedmont! Damn you! Damn your miserable life!"

He grabbed a pillow, tore off its oversized covering, and tied it over his mouth. He then shoved him face down onto the bed, yanked the cord from the lamp, and bound his hands. With great ease, he picked him up, forced him out into the dark hall, and closed the bedroom door. Halfway down the hall, he stopped.

"Come now, Monsignor," he whispered harshly. "Time is of the essence. Move your goddamned ass! There's someone you must meet before the midnight hour arrives." He placed his mouth closer to his ear. "Listen, Monsignor. Do you hear that? It's the old grandfather clock. Pay close attention to the simple rhythmicity of its ticks. For at the strike of twelve, you shall be sitting before the Father. Then you shall finally atone for your past indiscretions. Now, move it!"

The ancient floorboards creaked as he pushed him down the back stairway to the tunnels below. The path was covered with

318

rubble and debris. Though difficult, he guided him safely through the network of passages to the heavy, metal door. He opened it, shoved him into the room, and proceeded to light the lantern as he'd always done. But this time, he had a new guest.

"Monsignor," he said, keeping his eyes trained on the aged priest's face. "I'd like you to meet your daughter." He shifted his gaze between the two as he held the lantern high above his head, casting shadows across the room. "Isn't she an angel?"

The monsignor's eyes grew wide. His complexion paled. He began to show signs of fatigue and he gasped for breath. Like an overripe apple, falling from a limb, he dropped to his knees with a loud thud.

"Watch closely, Domenique," André said, removing her gag. "Watch as I tear the evil from him. Once I'm finished with his cleansing, it'll be time for a revelation."

CHAPTER 52

"This had better be good," Inspector Piedmont said, glancing at his alarm clock. "It's nearly eleven o'clock."

"Inspector," Roget's voice boomed through the receiver. "I apologize for calling at such a late hour, but I know you'll forgive me once I've given you the latest news."

"Wait a minute," Piedmont said, making certain Claudine was still asleep. He carried the phone into the bathroom and whispered, "What is it, Jacques?"

"You were right. André's definitely our man. The documents match, but there's much more. Are you sitting down?"

"No, I'm not. I'm in the bathroom, freezing my ass off. Now make it quick."

"It seems André's past is more complicated than we'd first

320

thought. He was born Anthony Jemille, son of Daniel and Rebecca Jemille of Edmonton. The same Daniel, I might add, that the Monsignor mentioned. However, here is where it gets confusing. It appears that this Daniel fellow murdered Rebecca when André was still a child, but they never had enough evidence to convict him. Several years later, Daniel married Vivian, Reverend Mother's sister. Vivian and Daniel had a male child. When Daniel found out his wife was screwing around with a priest and was pregnant, he must have snapped."

"Monsignor Valois being the priest, I presume," Piedmont said, holding the receiver closer to his ear.

"Correct. And Sister Domenique being their offspring. It was a long time ago, but the pieces to this bizarre puzzle are finally fitting together. When Vivian approached Valois regarding the pregnancy, Daniel must have found out. Remember Reverend Mother saying that Vivian feared for her life? Well, it appears she had good reason. After Domenique was born and was under the protection of Reverend Mother, Daniel must have had one hell of a time punishing Vivian for her affair. She was found in a shallow grave behind Daniel's home. She'd been savagely butchered, almost unrecognizable. If it weren't for her dental record, they never would have identified the body."

"How were the authorities tipped off?"

"By chance. Daniel tried to sell their son to a poor farming family in the area. That was the turning point. Thank God some of

321

the neighbors got wind of it and informed the officials. In addition, they claimed to have heard André brag that his father was God's chosen disciple and that he would rid the world of whores, including his stepmother. One day, while showing off to neighboring children, he went as far as to unearth the body to prove his father's greatness and strength. In the end, neighbors admitted hearing Daniel rant and rave through all hours of the night. They said he was always preaching some kind of weird God shit. As a result, he was arrested and sentenced to life in prison. A few months later, he was found hanging in his cell."

"Jesus!" Piedmont said, sitting on the toilet seat. "This is crazy. No wonder André's a nut. He must have been filling his head for years. But what became of Daniel and Vivian's son?"

"Believe it or not, he's right here under our noses.

"What?"

"It's Xavier."

"How can that be possible? Wouldn't he have known about his half brother, André?"

"I seriously doubt it. André was pushed through the system and lived all over the country. He had lots of problems and numerous foster parents. Xavier, on the other hand, was adopted by an older couple and then sent off to a Catholic orphanage."

"Anything else?"

"Yes," Roget said. "This story gets more interesting by the minute. Are you sitting yet?"

"Yeah."

"Years ago, Xavier's adoptive parents were slain by an unknown assailant. In the beginning, they had believed Xavier was responsible for the gruesome deed. He had had a motive, being that the parents were abusive, but the hair and fibers didn't match. And the fingerprints ascertained from the revolver weren't his. He was cleared of the charges and sent to the orphanage. Years later, he entered the priesthood in Quebec, and we know the rest."

"Are you telling me Sister Domenique is Xavier's half sister? And Xavier is André's half brother? Is Reverend Mother aware of this soap opera?"

"No," Roget said. "Not yet. Wait. There's more."

"You've got to be kidding!"

"It appears André has had quite a few aliases. Years back, he was arrested for child abuse in Winnipeg under the name of Alex Jansen, but all charges were miraculously dropped. He has also worn many hats. He has paraded the countryside as a professor of Theology, a shopkeeper, a private investigator, and now a priest. And we can place him at eight of the thirteen locations where the murdered girls were found."

"Keep talking."

"We lifted his fingerprints from the phony document he signed and you'll never believe what we discovered. They match the prints found at the crime scene in Xavier's childhood home."

"Are you telling me he's the bastard who killed my

323

daughter?"

"I'm sorry, Inspector. It looks that way. So, you want us to pick him up?"

"No!" Piedmont said, pulling open the pink mini-blinds. "If we tip him off, he may run and endanger our chances of recovering Sister Domenique. Let's be rational. We'll begin by breaking the news to Reverend Mother and Xavier that they are long-lost relatives."

"At this hour?"

"Yes. It can't wait until morning. God knows what André has planned. As a precautionary measure, we'll inform them now. And tighten the security around the monastery. If André is seen out of his room, have him followed."

"It's your call, Inspector. I'll pick you up in ten minutes."

Piedmont hung up the phone and tried to grasp the meaning of what he had just heard. It was beyond his belief. Too much to comprehend. He exited the bathroom, returned the phone to the nightstand, redressed, and gently kissed his wife on his way out of the room.

"I hope this new information doesn't send Xavier over the edge," he said, rushing down the stairs to wait for Roget. "I never thought I'd say it, but I truly feel for him."

CHAPTER 53

"No!" Domenique cried in a rasp, feeling the scissors' cold steel beneath her back, wishing she were free to stab him. "You're lying."

"Believe me," André said with a chuckle. "I was as surprised as you." He kicked the monsignor in the face and continued in a calm tone, "I had no idea that you were the evil offspring of Vivian and the monsignor. What do you think of your father? Pretty impressive, eh? It must be an honor to be the child of the church and of a high-ranking priest. I suppose that was the reason my Father chose you to be the mother of the savior."

Domenique's tears burned. Through clouded vision, she saw the monsignor slumped on the dirt floor, fresh wounds on his chest, his face bloody. The white cloth tied around his mouth was

325

stained a deep crimson, and his nightclothes were ripped to shreds. She laid back, eyes wide.

"What's the matter, Domenique?" André said. "Is this too much for you? Behold, for this day is the day of revelation."

The monsignor groaned a few times. He threw the lamp cord to the ground, ripped the gag from his face, and stumbled to his feet. He let out a wild scream and hurled his beaten body at André. As he wrestled him to the floor, clouds of dust enveloped them.

Domenique was confused, angered, and in pain. Visions of good and evil raced through her head. She thrashed her haggard body from side to side, trying desperately to free herself from the binding straps, but could make no leeway. All she could do was look on in horror. In no time at all, André had pinned the monsignor back to the floor and restrained his arms with a purple sash.

"That should hold you," he said calmly. "Now, don't move a muscle or I'll slice your throat before it's time."

"André!" she screamed. "For God's sake, let him go! You're an animal! You're no man of God!"

In a majestic manner, André stood. He brushed the earth from his cassock and delicately wiped the beads of sweat from his face with a handkerchief. A wild expression flashed across his face as he stepped to the center of the room.

"It appears, Monsignor," he said. "You and Domenique

definitely have the same barbaric blood flowing through your veins." He pivoted around and faced Domenique. "Doesn't this wonderful revelation lift your heart, your spirit, my angel? You should be delighted that I have reunited you with your father, though your reunion shall be short lived."

"You're wrong, André," she said, lifting her head. "This isn't possible. Your mind is playing tricks on you. You can't tell the difference between truth and fantasy."

"Tell her, Monsignor," André said. "Enlighten her with your damned secret. Do this in dear Vivian's memory."

"Forgive me, my child," Monsignor said, resting his head against the rock wall. "Please, forgive me."

"Is it true, Monsignor?" she asked, tears forming again. "Is this a warped figment of his imagination or is it true? You must tell me!"

"Yes," Monsignor said in a whisper. "I am your father. But you must believe me, I've only recently learned of this myself. Nevertheless, you must understand the circumstances that surrounded your birth. I had no choice. I couldn't claim you as my own. It wasn't possible at the time. The church."

"The circumstances?" André scoffed. "Which set of circumstances are you referring to? Do you mean your adulterous sin or the fact that you wanted my dear stepmother to abort her? Maybe you are speaking of the pain you caused my beloved Father, Daniel. A wolf in sheep's clothing is how he referred to you. And know this, he has never forgiven you for the ruination of his holy family."

"Stepmother?" Monsignor said. "What are you saying?"

"That's correct. I'm Daniel's first born son, born of the love between him and my mother, Rebecca."

"You. You're Daniel's son?"

"Don't ever speak his name!" André screamed, rushing over and landing a solid slap across his face. "If you want to live long enough to finish this chapter of *The Book of Life*, keep your blasphemous mouth shut!"

"No!" Domenique cried, disbelieving the painful words. "None of this is true! I have no family."

"Domenique," the monsignor whispered. "I had no idea that you've always been this close. Your aunt and I have known each other for years, but I was not aware that she was Vivian's sister. Maybe had I known, I would have found the courage to approach you. Things could have turned out differently. Forgive me."

"Aunt?" she said, feeling nauseous. "What aunt? What are you saying? Why are you spewing these lies? André, just kill me and get it over with!"

"In time, my dear," André said, sitting next to her and gently caressing her abdomen. "I'll grant your wish in time. After the savior's birth, there shall be no further need for you. You will then join the Father, Vivian, the thirteen, the monsignor, and in the end, your half brother, Xavier. Your aunt, the esteemed Reverend Mother, shall pay as well. But not with her life. She is predestined to walk the earth alone without any living family members. The same as I, she shall know what it's like to lose those she loves. Soon, I shall fulfill my Master's plan. I will have cleansed the world and conquered the evil. Upon execution of my Master's plan, the reign of the true savior shall commence and the false god, who rules the heavens, shall bow at His feet. It shall be the beginning of the New World Order and I shall reap my just rewards."

CHAPTER 54

"What?" Xavier exclaimed, pacing back and forth between the windows in Reverend Mother's office. "You must be mistaken, Inspector. There is no way André could be my brother. It's all too far fetched. If this is true, why would he try to kill me?"

"Don't know, Xavier," Piedmont said solemnly. "It seems life has dealt your family some nasty cards, but all is not lost."

"How can you say that?" Reverend Mother asked. "I've already lost my dear Vivian to that madman, Daniel, and now, God knows what his insane son has done with my niece. Why can't you do something?"

"Hold it right there," Piedmont said, raising his arms. "You're not the only one who has lost someone. He killed my daughter and who knows how many others."

330

"I'm sorry, Inspector," she said. "That was callous of me."

"Damn right."

"Do go on, Inspector," she said.

"Let's start with the good news," Roget said. "You and Xavier are finally reunited. And Xavier, you should feel lucky to be alive. If you hadn't given us that pill, there's a good possibility your aunt would be visiting your grave and none of this information would have surfaced."

"Domenique is my sister," Xavier said repeatedly. "I have a sister. I can't believe it."

"That's right," Piedmont said. "And we're going to find her if it's the last thing we do."

"He's right, Xavier," Reverend Mother said, embracing him with a firm hug. "We've found each other at last, and I'm positive Domenique will join us soon."

"But you still haven't answered my question, Inspector," Xavier said, pushing her away. "Why would André do this to us? Why would he murder my adoptive parents? Why has he sent me here? Why has he taken Domenique?"

"I have no answers," Piedmont said, scratching his head. "His motives aren't clear yet. What we do know is ten years ago he spent some time in the Roveau's Institute for the Mentally Insane and was released with a clean bill of health."

"Obviously, Inspector, the treatment didn't work," Mother said. "He's murdered all those innocent children, including your daughter. If you know this, why haven't you arrested him? How many more people must die before this all ends?"

"It must seem our methods are strange," Roget said. "But if we're to save Sister Domenique, we can't allow André to realize we're on to him. He's the only one who can lead us to her."

"I don't care about police protocol!" Xavier screamed. "I don't want to hear about some chancy scheme to nab him either. Just find her! Beat it out of him if you have to."

"That's not the way it works, Xavier," Piedmont said. "Though I'd love to beat him to death."

"He's right," Roget said. "If we pull him down to the station and get hard on him, he'd probably clam up. We'd never find her. He has to believe that this master plan of his is working. We're counting on his arrogance and overconfidence, like when he was a child and gave away his mother's resting place. That will be his downfall."

"You'd better be right, Inspector," Mother said, glaring at him. "Or I'll hold you personally responsible."

"Understood, Mother," Piedmont said, picking up his briefcase. "But you must also understand that patience is a must if our plan is to work."

"What plan?" Xavier asked.

"Well, André already believes you're our prime suspect," Piedmont said. "We fed him that line on purpose. We know, through our conversations with him, that he definitely wanted to pin Domenique's disappearance and most likely her murder on you. But as long as you're in our custody and he doesn't know where you are, we believe she'll remain safe. I don't know for how long, but at least it gives us a little more time."

"Are you insane?" Xavier screamed. "You can't play with her life like that!"

"Calm down, Father," Roget said. "The inspector has everything under control. We have men positioned throughout the monastery. They're watching his every move. We'll get him." He motioned to the inspector and continued, "Haven't we bothered these good people long enough? Let's allow them to get back to sleep. We still have a lot of work to do."

"Sleep?" Reverend Mother said. "I don't think I'll be able to sleep for a long, long time."

"Have faith, Mother," Piedmont said. "Isn't that what you people preach everyday? Well, it's time to practice it. Have faith in our abilities as investigators to put an end to this nightmare. Never forget that hatred drives me, and I will not rest until justice is served. He murdered my Jacqueline and I'll personally see to it that he pays!"

"Forgive my tactlessness, Inspector," Mother said. "I realize that his evil has touched your family as well. Do what you must." She escorted them to the door and stopped as the clock chimed twelve. "Inspector, do you really believe that she's still alive?"

"Yes," he said. Before he could reassure her, Xavier rushed up to them, panting and gasping for breath. His face was peaked.

"She's at the monastery," Xavier said. "She's frightened and calling for help." He fell to his knees and broke down, sobs interrupting his speech. "She's calling for me."

"Sweet Mother Mary!" Mother said, her face paling. She pulled at the lace of her flowered nightgown. "He's just like her! He is Vivian's child!"

"Is he having another spell?" Roget asked, backing into the curtains. "I thought this was all behind him. André hasn't been able to feed him the pills. Inspector, his eyes are rolling back. Should I call for an ambulance?"

"I-I-I'm all right," Xavier said, his words slurred. "It's André. She's afraid of André. Her heart is pounding hard. Her breath is short. She needs me."

"Mother," Piedmont said. "What did you mean by saying he's definitely Vivian's son?"

"It was quite a long time ago," Mother said, sitting in a prim fashion by the window. "But I remember it as if it were only yesterday. Vivian and I were children. Early one summer morning, I'd gone off into the woods to pick flowers for the dining room table. She was supposed to have accompanied me, but I didn't have the heart to wake her. Therefore, I ventured out alone. As I walked deeper and deeper into the forest, I lost my sense of direction, but the only thing on my mind was to fill my basket with

334

the most beautiful posies I could find. I figured that if I kept moving, I'd eventually run into Papa's old hunting lodge."

"Excuse me, Mother," Piedmont said, eyeing Xavier. "But what does this have to do with him?"

"The morning turned into afternoon and then evening. I was frightened, cold, and absolutely lost. I remember the scary sounds coming from the woods around me. The dark evergreens seemed to come alive. I felt as though the branches would wrap themselves around me and the blackness would swallow me up. When I believed all was lost, I huddled under some bushes and began to pray. Suddenly, out of the darkness, I heard a familiar voice calling to me. Tears clouded my vision, but I could make out the silhouette of a child. As it neared me, I could tell that it was Vivian, but at the same time, it wasn't. It was her aura or ghost. It didn't make any sense. She wasn't dead. She was home with Mama and Papa, probably worried sick about me. In any case, the figure guided me out of the woods, safely back to my house, and then disappeared into the thick fog. A fog as thick as tonight's. Elated that I'd arrived safely, I dashed into my house only to find that Vivian had contracted scarlet fever. She'd been under the doctor's care all day. I went to her bedside. She was sweating profusely and mumbling in almost a whisper. I placed my ear to her lips and what I heard stunned me. She said that she was glad she'd found me in the woods and was able to lead me home. Upon saying the words, her fever broke, but she never recalled the

335

incident."

"Quite a story, Mother," Piedmont said, massaging his temples. "But I still don't see the relevance."

"Xavier must have the same gift," Mother said. "His brain must be linked to Domenique's in the same way that Vivian's was to mine. I believe him, Inspector. Domenique is alive."

"A few months ago," Piedmont said, "I would have thought that the bunch of you needed serious medical attention, but now nothing seems impossible."

"If this is true, Inspector," Roget said. "Maybe Xavier can help us locate Domenique. He seems to be in tune with her and he does know a little more about the tunnel system than we do."

"André has her," Xavier said, standing and wiping his eyes. "Inspector, we must find her tonight. Time is running short. Please allow me to assist in the search. I know I can find my sister if given the chance."

"Okay, Xavier," Piedmont said. "I owe you that much, but it could be dangerous. Can you handle a gun?"

"No," Xavier said flatly. "God is the only weapon I'll need. I'm not concerned for my life, only for Domenique's."

"How gallant," Piedmont said, exiting.

"Let's get over to the monastery," Roget said. "If he's right, we haven't much time."

"May God be with you," Mother said, standing in the doorway.

CHAPTER 55

"Tick-tock," André said, kicking some earth into the monsignor's bloodied face and looking back at Domenique. It took all the energy he could muster to hold back the laughter on the tip of his tongue. His insides were bursting. He wanted to share his excitement with his captive audience, but opted to keep his feelings to himself. "Tick-tock. It's midnight!"

"What do you plan to do to us?" Domenique asked.

"Us?" André said in a mocking tone. "No, Domenique. Not us. My Father's plan for this evening does not include you. This is Monsignor Valois' allotted time. His hour of atonement has arrived."

Monsignor Valois stirred in the corner. He moaned, but never spoke. He wrestled for a short time with his bindings and then settled back to the floor. He was badly bruised and in obvious pain.

"It's no use, Monsignor," André said, dragging him by the collar to the door. "The family reunion is over. We're going back to the place where it all began."

"Where are you taking him?" Domenique screamed. "Think about what you're doing, André. Please, stop this!"

"Think?" he exclaimed. "That's all I've done for years."

Before leaving the room, he turned and smiled at her. He then carried him off to the chamber where he had hidden his prized artifacts. Inside the room, he hurled him onto the four-poster bed, lit one of the burned down candles, and reached into his cassock pocket for a dagger. He climbed atop him and held the weapon high.

"It is time to pay for the sins of the past," André shrieked. He plunged the knife deep into the monsignor's right eye, spraying blood in all directions. "For the evil and the wrongful acts of the flesh, I cleanse you!"

Monsignor groaned, let out a deep sigh, and lay quiet. Blood gushed from the wound. His tense muscles relaxed and his arms fell by his sides. His fight was gone.

"Don't stare at me that way," André hissed, stabbing the other eye. "That fateful day is forever burned in my memory. The day my father ordered me to follow her. I saw you straddle her and inject your evilness. You dirtied his angel! You destroyed our holy family! When she came home, she was different, soiled by lust. You bastard! Vivian was the only one who ever loved me and you made her go away!" He stabbed him repeatedly, butchering his body, cutting holes into his flesh. "You destroyed my only chance at happiness! You destroyed Father!" Once finished with the cleansing, he wiped the dagger on his cassock and sauntered to the door, dripping with blood. "You're in His hands now. His will is done."

CHAPTER 56

Fog had rolled in and visibility was near zero when Piedmont and the others exited their vehicles in the center of the monastery's courtyard. The sea of gray mist hovered only inches above the cobblestones and the statue of Christ was barely discernible. The building loomed high amidst the dreary nighttime elements, emitting subtle hints of ancient mysticism. At that moment, visions of vampires and ghouls crossed Piedmont's mind. I'm being ridiculous, he thought, stepping back to sum up the monstrous edifice, which was shrouded in a ghostly cloud. It just looks different at night.

"This place looks like something out of a horror novel," Piedmont said. "It makes my skin crawl. All we need now is a freak electrical storm to develop overhead."

"Knock it off, Inspector," Roget said. "You're scaring me. Let's just keep our minds on the business at hand."

"You're right, Jacques," Piedmont said, anxiety building in the pit of his stomach. "I won't allow this goddamned shitty weather to obscure my objective. I want to get that son-of-a-bitch!" He brushed past Father Xavier and called out to one of his officers, but no one responded. "Where the hell is Evans?"

"He's probably patrolling the other side of the property," Roget answered. "And there's no way we'd see him through this pea soup fog."

"That doesn't make sense," Piedmont said, rubbing his hands along his upper arms in a brisk fashion to alleviate the chills. "The fog wouldn't stop him from hearing me."

"You're right, Inspector," Father Xavier said. "Something is amiss. I can feel it."

"Stop the hocus pocus shit, Father," Piedmont said, flicking on his flashlight. "Keep your damned premonitions to yourself or at least wait until we're inside."

As Piedmont's men flashed their lights around the yard searching for Officer Evans, an unsettling silence consumed the night air. It generated gooseflesh, which traveled Piedmont's arms and hovered overhead like a mantle of gloom. Having no luck, he radioed the station in hopes that Evans had reported in, but as of yet, he hadn't. It appeared the officer was nowhere to be found.

"Maybe he's inside," Roget said with a note of optimism.

"Did you see that, Roget?" Piedmont said, cocking his head back, staring up at the building.

"See what?"

"Up there," Piedmont said, pointing to a circular room in the far corner. "It was quick, but I thought I saw someone holding a lamp in the window. I could have sworn it flickered."

"I don't see anything," Roget said. "I can't even make out the window. Maybe the fog's playing tricks with your eyes."

"No," Piedmont said emphatically. "Father Xavier, who belongs to that room?"

"Monsignor Valois," Xavier said.

"Why would he be up at this hour of the morning?" Piedmont asked. "I can't believe he's getting a jump on his spring cleaning. What do you suppose he's up to?"

"This is odd," Xavier said. "Normally, the entire household is sleeping by eleven, but with everything that's happened lately, anything is possible. I'm certain the monsignor was either reading or reviewing his homily for morning mass."

"By moonlight?" Piedmont said. "Highly unlikely. In any case, I'm glad he's awake. I want to speak with him before we tackle André."

"I'll show you the way to his room," Xavier said, leading them to the monsignor's bedroom. He tapped lightly on the door and stepped aside.

"Thank you, Father," Piedmont said. "I'll take it from here."

Without further warning, he blasted through the doorway and aimed his flashlight on the monsignor's bed. The comforter and linens were strewn on the floor, but the monsignor was nowhere to be found. He walked over to the nightstand and felt the lamp. It was still hot.

"Where the hell is he?" Piedmont asked.

"I'm not surprised," Xavier said from the doorway. "I told you that something wasn't right. Evil has invaded the monastery and time is running out."

"Would you shut the hell up!" Piedmont yelled, pushing Xavier aside and exiting the room. "Xavier, you wait here. Come on, Roget, let's round up André."

Guns readied and expectations high, they dashed through the corridors toward André's chamber. For some strange reason, Piedmont's heart leapt and his body quaked as he slowly turned the knob. With extreme caution, he opened the door a crack and nosed his gun into the room.

"Get up, André!" he yelled, his heart hammering in his chest. "Get your ass out of bed with your hands up."

They waited for movement in the room, but all remained quiet.

"Give it up, André," Piedmont called again, holding tight to the trigger, ready to fire if necessary.

Still, no movement.

"I said, get up!" he repeated, rushing to the bed. He could make out André's body under the blankets and pointed the revolver at his head. "Move your ass!"

"You heard the man, André," Roget said. He gave the lamp a click, but the room remained dark. He tried again, but still nothing happened. Aiming his flashlight and gun on the bed, he yelled, "Get the hell up!"

"I'll give you one more chance," Piedmont said, his barrel flush with André's temple. "The only thing holding my bullet back is this sheet. My final advice to you is, get up or I'll shoot!"

André didn't move.

With hands trembling and sweat dripping from every pore, Piedmont tore away the blankets and jumped back. It was Corporal Evans. He was dead, but still warm. His body had been severely beaten, flesh cut to shreds, eyes missing. A bloody impression of the crucifix was imbedded in his forehead.

"Holy Christ!" Roget yelled. "We're too late. He's killed again."

"That bastard!" Piedmont said, instinctively throwing the covers back over the officer. He flashed his light around the room and gasped when it illuminated some words written on the wall. "It's blood."

"What's happened here?" Xavier asked, stepping into the room. "I heard some yelling." Without waiting, he walked over and examined the writings. "It's Latin. *Facilis descensus Averno.*"

"What does it mean?" Roget asked.

"The descent to hell is easy," Xavier answered. "As I said before, evil is afoot. We must hurry if we're to locate Domenique in time. I know she's got to be somewhere down in those tunnels."

"Damn!" Piedmont said, clicking his handset. "The battery's too low. Roget, find a goddamned telephone. Call for backup, and you'd better have forensics get over here right *toute suite*. I'll have Xavier lead me to the tunnels."

"I think you'd better take this, Xavier," Roget said, handing him his gun. "You may need it."

"It's totally against my beliefs," Xavier said. "But I suppose it's better to be safe than sorry."

"Do you know how to use it?" Roget asked.

Xavier smirked, aimed the gun at the open window, and fired.

"Guess you'll do fine," Roget said before exiting the room.

"Come on, Father," Piedmont said. "We don't have much time. Lead the way."

CHAPTER 57

Covered in blood, André fell to his knees at the foot of Domenique's bed and let out an ear-splitting shriek. His mission was nearly accomplished. He'd conquered the evil that he'd been chasing for many years and corrected many wrongs, but the battlefield was still outlined in red. He knew what was required to gain immortality and believed that he was almost there.

"Have I not done well, my Father?" he prayed. "Have I not avenged You?"

"Yes, My son," his Father's voice echoed through the chamber. "You have carried out My divine plan to perfection. Thus far, you have cleansed this world of much sin, proving that you are My chosen one. However, there is more work to be done. If you are to attain true immortality, you must end the life of the other. For he shall be the one who will fight to release the handmaiden. If this scenario plays out, you shall spend eternity burning in My perpetual flames."

"I understand, my Father," André said.

"Cleanse the mother of My child," the Father said. "Wash away the filth that surrounds her. For her body must be kept healthy and her mind imprisoned until the savior's birth."

"André," Domenique said in a strained whisper. "What have you done with the monsignor?"

"How dare you interrupt me when I'm consulting with my Father." He stood, neared the bed, and looked down at her. "Not that it matters, but the dear monsignor is gone. He's with my Father. He's finally paid for his sins with his life."

"No," she cried. "Fight the voices. I can help you. I swear, I can. There are doctors who can rid you of your demons."

André let out a strange cackle. He spun in circles and spread his arms wide. His face distorted and he felt as though he was being stretched on an invisible rack. To alleviate the discomfort, he spun faster.

"You're mad!" she cried. "You need psychiatric help!"

"How dare you dictate to the chosen one!" he said, cocking his head to the side. "You are a lowly descendant of lust. The product of adultery! Hold your tongue or lose it. Keep your twisted thoughts to yourself."

"André, what's happening to you?"

"I am the true master of heaven and earth. I rule the living and the dead. Vivian betrayed Daniel and My church. Xavier betrayed My chosen one. You shall correct the wrongs by giving birth to My son, the savior."

"Oh, my God, I am heartily sorry for having offended thee," she prayed aloud.

"Quiet!" he screamed and smacked her across the face. "Your false prayers cannot help you. Lift up your heart to the one, true Lord. Accept Me as your God!"

"Y-y-yes, André. Please forgive my weakness. Don't harm me." She shut her watery eyes and sobbed. "Please, remember the child."

Content with his show of superiority, he gave her a gentle pat on the head and stormed from the room. He returned a few minutes later with a bucket of fresh water and proceeded to unleash her arms and legs. Oozing bedsores had formed on her side. With ginger strokes, he cleansed and dressed the open lesions.

"I certainly hope this is not contagious," he said. "This definitely changes everything. Under the circumstances, I'm not sure if I should grant you the honor of bathing me in the same water. I will not have any disease crawling around on my body. Besides, I'm not really certain you can be trusted."

"Oh, André," she said, sitting up. "Let me show you that I am trustworthy. If I'm to carry your child, you should at least trust me. You are merciful and I am grateful for this chance to prove myself."

"You are the handmaiden," he said, brushing the moist hair from her forehead. "Finally, you've come to realize your true calling." He quickly shed his clothing and stood naked before her. "Gaze upon my beauty. Sanctify my body in the name of the Father. Consecrate me, for our union is holy." He placed his hands on her slightly swollen belly, chanted in Latin to the unborn child, and giggled. "Can you hear him? He is already quite witty and intelligent. Our son shall rule nations."

Suddenly, he pulled his hands back as if they'd encountered burning coals. Disoriented by the excruciating pain, he wobbled to the center of the room. He fell to his knees and once again began to pray. As he did so, the walls began to shake.

CHAP†ER 58

Piedmont's light bobbed nervously along the walls and floor as he and Xavier traveled through the black, stone corridors of the underground labyrinth. With careful steps, they traveled deeper and deeper into the twisted maze, passing the numerous marked doors, some open and some closed. Even though they encountered many forks on their path, they advanced with high hopes of locating Sister Domenique. They knew she had to be somewhere down here. But whether she was alive or not, remained to be seen.

"Where the hell are we?" Piedmont asked, flashing his light on Xavier's face. "It seems we've hit another dead end."

"Let me think," Xavier said. "Maybe if I concentrate, I can connect with her again."

"What are you doing?" Piedmont said, watching with skepticism as Xavier gently placed his hands on the rock walls. Do you really expect the wall to speak to you? Come on, we don't have time for this shit."

"Quiet, please," Xavier said. "I'm getting something."

"Sure," Piedmont said, resting against the damp rock. "Probably arthritis."

"She's nearby. Her aura is strong. She's stressed and filled with fear." He closed his eyes and called out her name. "Come, Inspector. We must head west."

"Where the hell is west? We can't see a goddamned thing in front of us. And you want us to head west?"

Before he had the chance to argue further, the earthen floor trembled slightly. A light coating of dust fell from the ceiling and an almost indiscernible rumble echoed in the distance. The density of the air changed and it became harder to breath.

"Did you feel that?" Piedmont asked, flashing his light from ceiling to floor, watching small pieces of wall crumble down.

"It's a warning of things to come," Xavier said.

"Bullshit! It's the start of a goddamned earthquake." He aimed his light upward and studied the ceiling, following a thin crack down to the floor. "Hope this place holds."

"It will, but we must hurry. If we travel west, we'll find her."

"There you go with that west again," Piedmont said, following with extreme caution. "You'd better be right. I don't want to end up buried alive down here, north or west."

"Neither do I, Inspector," Xavier said, holding a handkerchief to his mouth. "Neither do I."

CHAPTER 59

Domenique gripped the scissors with both hands, rose from the mattress, and stood on the rippling, dirt floor. Her mind raced with fear and her legs were weak, but she knew this would be her last opportunity. She shivered from head to toe, raised the scissors high, and cautiously stepped toward André's bare back. As she approached, the tremors grew stronger and his strange Latin chants exaggerated to an extraordinarily high pitch. The combination of sounds unnerved her, but she kept telling herself that if she wanted the torturous nightmare to end, she must remain steadfast and strong by her convictions.

"May God forgive me," she cried, plunging the steel deep between his shoulder blades.

He screamed ferociously, scrambled to his feet, and blocked her only exit. "You goddamned bitch!" he hollered, trying

353

to free the weapon. "I don't care about my Master's plan. You shall die!" He lunged forward, knocked her back onto the bed, and tightened his hands around her neck, cutting off her umbilical cord to life.

She felt her face swell red and her eyes bulge from their sockets. Her lungs begged for air. She tried kicking and punching her way to freedom, but realized the inevitable. In the end, she would have to succumb to his morbid desires.

"Die!" he screamed against the constant rumbling of the ground. "Die!"

Just as she was about to lose consciousness, she heard a man's voice. They've come for me, she thought, rejuvenated by the possibility. Consumed with new hope, she dug deep inside her meager form, found some hidden strength, and brought her knee up to his groin in a last ditch effort to escape.

"Damn you!" he yelled, releasing his hold on her. He backed away and massaged his crotch. "What the hell was I thinking? It's your fault. You want me to destroy my child. My own flesh and blood. The savior." He looked toward the ceiling and raised his arms. "Daniel was right about you. You are the angel of man's destruction and must be destroyed after the birth."

She choked, automatically sucked in a deep breath, and let out a blood-curdling scream. A scream so loud, it echoed for what seemed minutes. Almost immediately, her prayers were answered. She heard a man's voice call out her name. It was then she made the connection. The voice belonged to Xavier. He had finally come to rescue her. Now she would finally have the chance to make it up to him, if she could only come out of this alive. She knew he would forgive her for believing that he was her captor. All she needed was a chance to explain.

"Get up, you lowly urchin!" André hissed, breaking her concentration. He snatched his dagger from the table and pulled her to her feet. "I promise, they'll not take you away from me again." He held her in front of him and stumbled to the doorway.

Simultaneously, the ground's upper crust convulsed. The topsoil danced in advance of the earth's next belch and a cloud of dirt billowed. A strange crunching sound commenced. The walls shook.

"You'll pay for this," he said, pushing her out into the trembling passageway. "I swear it!"

Three minutes into their trek down the cloudy corridor, the walls started to buckle. The ceiling displayed visible signs of imminent collapse and a barrage of small rocks came showering down. The tunnel's stress level was at its maximum capacity. It was obvious that it wouldn't hold much longer.

"Help!" she screamed through the heavy dust. "Xavier, save me!"

"Shut the hell up!" he warned, placing the knife dangerously close to her neck. "My Father's wrath is upon us. It appears that your would-be rescuers are too late."

CHAPTER 60

Mother Earth discharged another angry jolt. Sizable chasms formed with jagged rocks jutting upward from the perimeters of the new holes. A storm of painful debris pelted Inspector Piedmont and Father Xavier, clouding their vision. All in all, the path was treacherous.

"She's down there," Piedmont hollered, dodging the onslaught of flying rock. "Her voice came from that direction."

"I told you she was alive, Inspector," Xavier yelled. "And I knew she'd be to the west. We're linked together like twins. Two minds, one thought."

"Yeah, right," Piedmont replied, jumping over large stones, attempting to maintain his balance. "All along, I thought you were just plain crazy. Now I have to admit I was wrong."

"I never thought the day would come when I'd hear such words from your mouth."

"Enjoy it," Piedmont said. "You'll probably never hear it again." He took the lead and turned a bend in the passage. In the distance he saw a shadowy figure dart into the blackness. He stopped short and aimed his gun. "Stop right there, André, or I'll shoot." He waited with his index finger set on the trigger, ready to unload the full clip if threatened.

"Go right ahead," André's voice called from the shadows. "You can't harm me. For my Father, the Almighty One, shall triumph and all those who defy His plan shall perish amidst the rubble."

"He must have Domenique with him," Xavier whispered. "I found a room back there just before the bend. It had to be the place he'd been keeping her all this time. It reeked of defecation and the floor was covered in blood. And I also found some restraints still tied to the bedposts."

"Let the nun go!" Piedmont shouted angrily as the ground began to shudder violently once more. "The game's over!"

"She'll never be taken from me again," André said, pulling her into the distorted beam of Piedmont's flashlight. "Never! For I am the chosen one!"

"Domenique!" Xavier cried out. "We're here to save you."

"How wonderful, Inspector," André said in a quieter tone. "You're not alone. You've brought the other to me. You've made the grueling task of locating my ignorant brother most convenient. I thank you."

"Shut up, André!" Piedmont called out. "Or is it Anthony? Anthony Jemille."

"Anthony?" André said. "Anthony's dead. He died long ago, a pathetic shadow of a human being. I, on the other hand, am André Jeneau, the curator of souls, son of the Almighty."

"Release the nun, you sick bastard!" Piedmont hollered. "This is between you and me. Let's end this madness right here in this hell hole."

"Not in this lifetime, Inspector," André said. "For you are not part of the master plan. Just leave Xavier and Domenique to me and get out while you still have the chance. By the looks of it, my Father's temper is erupting."

"You okay, Sister?" Piedmont yelled over the compressional waves. "Domenique? Are you okay?"

"I-I-I'm all right," she said. She hesitated a few moments and then continued, "Do what he says or he'll kill me."

"You heard her," André said. "It would be a pity if I have to slice her throat just because you aren't man enough to take orders. It's your call, Inspector."

Perspiration poured from Inspector Piedmont's forehead, temporarily blinding his view as he mulled over his options. With hands trembling, he wiped the sweat from his eyes and made a decision. He knew if she was to survive, he must drive a wedge between them. The question was, how?

"So, what's the verdict, Inspector?" André asked. "It's all up to you. You can either leave now or witness their executions. What will it be?"

Piedmont had to react quickly if he wanted to gain control of the escalating situation. He realized it was chancy, but he had to try. He dropped his flashlight to the ground, let out a horrific scream, rushed forward, and fired his gun repeatedly at the crumbling ceiling, hoping to confuse André and buy the time needed to confront him head on. Sparks flashed in the dust-laden darkness and groans erupted as he approached them.

"Stop, Inspector," Xavier screamed. "You might kill her!"

Three more shots rang out, echoing throughout the tunnels.

"Stop shooting!" Domenique cried out. "André's not here. He's run off." Her voice then trailed off to a moan.

Piedmont ceased firing and proceeded toward her, tripping over the rubble in his haste. Before he had the chance to adjust his eyes to the darkness, Xavier approached from behind and handed him his flashlight. He shined his light onto her and gasped.

"Good God!" Xavier cried, falling to his knees.

She was lying on the ground, naked, covered with dirt and fragments of rock. A bullet had grazed her forearm and only indistinguishable groans escaped her lips. It was apparent she was pregnant, abused, and suffering from acute malnutrition. Her face was skeletal and her eyes, sunken in.

Piedmont stared at her, shocked, disbelieving his eyes. He yearned for instant closure to the madness, which had overtaken his life these past months, yet knew it wasn't finished. Realizing that her well-being came first, he instinctively brushed away the debris, removed his jacket, and covered her.

"You'll be all right, Sister," he said, placing her into Xavier's arms. "I'm sorry we didn't get here sooner."

"Thank you," she whispered. "But you mustn't worry about me. Go after André! He's murdered Monsignor Valois and God knows who else."

"I must have wounded him," Piedmont said, flashing his light down to a trail of blood.

"No," she said. "I tried to kill him. I stabbed him in the back with a pair of scissors, but I didn't have the strength."

"Well, it didn't seem to slow him down," Xavier said.

"What if he comes back for the baby?" she cried. "What will happen if he comes back for me?"

"Don't worry, Domenique," Xavier said, wiping away her tears. "The inspector will capture him."

"Keep the faith, Xavier," Piedmont said and smiled. "Keep it for both of us. That bastard has eluded us for a long time. He killed my daughter and countless others. But it will finally end here. He won't get away this time."

Without warning, the earth grumbled with another foreshock and the ground wheezed. The craggy walls sighed under the strain, buckled, and cracked wide open. Stone projectiles blew out of the crevasses and mixed with thick smoke, engulfing the tunnel. The air was getting thin.

"I have to get her out of here before this place collapses," Xavier yelled, shielding his head from the flying debris.

"Okay, Xavier," Piedmont hollered. "But when you get out, tell Roget to get his ass down here quick. I'm going to need him."

"All right, Inspector," Xavier said. "Watch your backside. André's a dangerous man."

"Rest assured," Piedmont said, holding the light up to his face, trying to stand steady. "I know how dangerous he is, but he's only a big man when it comes to defenseless nuns and little girls. Let us see how he reacts when I stick my hand up his ass and pull out his heart. Let's see if he's so big and bad then."

"Good luck, Inspector," Xavier said, toting Domenique away. "May God be with you. See you topside."

Gun cocked, Piedmont wasted no time in following the blood trail he knew belonged to André. The killer. The monster that had plagued Canada for almost two years and had taken his daughter from him. With a vengeful heart, he traveled carefully up one path and down another. His adrenalin raced, sending tingles to his extremities as he swiftly made his way deeper into the bowels of the seemingly endless tunnels.

Sweaty, dirty, and nearly an hour later, he caught a glimpse of André's sleek silhouette standing at a distance of about thirty-five meters. He was naked, leaning crooked against the wall. He was blocking his face from the light. It appeared he was writing something on the wall.

"Stop right there, Jemille!" Piedmont yelled, trying to catch his breath, holding fast to the trigger. "If you move another centimeter, I'll shoot."

"Do not come any closer," André said gutturally, placing one hand in the air. "For if you do, hundreds of my minions and fanged trolls shall climb out of the cracks and bare their razor-sharp teeth into your human flesh. They'll feast on your heart like starved rats."

A cold chill traveled Piedmont's spine as he gripped tight to the trigger, ready to shoot if prompted. He knew that it wouldn't take much to end this bastard's life, but he had to remain cool in order to maintain his authority and dictate a successful outcome. It was time to be the professional that he had been trained to be. To pass this crucial test, he could not allow his personal motives to cloud his judgment.

At that moment, another tremor shook the tunnel, this time more violent than the last. He fell against the crumbling wall, but quickly regained his footing. With his light still bobbing on André,

362

he cautiously inched his way over the rubble. André never looked as large as he did now. His rippled muscles glistened from sweat and it appeared that, even in his condition, he would be a most formidable foe.

"You won't get away this time," Piedmont said, gritting his teeth and swallowing hard. "You'll spend the rest of your worthless life behind bars, you goddamned Satan worshiping bastard!"

André let out a horrendous screech and flapped his arms wildly. The bizarre actions brought Piedmont's heart to his throat. For a split-second, his mind envisioned André in his true evil form, a beast with leathery wings, hoofed feet, and spiny teeth. He slammed his watery eyes shut and fired blindly until his clip was empty.

"To hell with protocol!" he screamed. "This is for Jacqueline! Die, you bastard!"

When the dust cleared, he saw André wobble from side to side and then fall into the chasm created by the most recent quake. He reloaded his gun and rushed to the jagged edge, but he was too late. André was gone. The only sound was that of his limp body wracking against the rocks as it tumbled to the bottom. Without remorse, he peered down into the seemingly bottomless black hole, spit, and watched as his saliva was swallowed by the denseness.

"Hell is too good for you!" he yelled into the pit.

He believed that he should have felt either satisfaction or relief, but to his surprise, he only encountered a strange numbness. He felt no enjoyment from his act of vengeance, no comfort, no peace of mind. He now realized that revenge was not all it was fired up to be. It was highly overrated. With mixed emotions, he retreated from the deteriorating tunnel system for the safety of daylight.

CHAPTER 61

The brethren were in a turbulent state over the frequency of the earth tremors. They knew that with the eruptions coming from the proximity of the wine cellar, it placed the monastery in an extremely volatile position. With the entire household in such a frenzied panic, they didn't seem to notice Xavier as he carried Domenique into the empty sitting room.

"Here we are, Domenique," Xavier said, gently placing her onto the divan. He covered her with a crocheted afghan and smiled. "You're safe now."

"Thank you for rescuing me," Domenique said.

He walked to the window, opened the drapes, and promptly returned to her side. He was astounded to see that her forehead was branded with the impression of a crucifix. Instantly, gooseflesh covered his body. He couldn't even begin to imagine the ordeal she'd gone through.

"What did that monster do to you?" he asked, his voice quavering.

"Not now," Domenique said, pushing him away, her eyes filling with tears. "Please don't ask. I can't talk about it."

"I understand," he replied sympathetically. "Everything will be fine. The ambulance will be here soon and we can talk later."

He was amazed to see how much she'd changed. She was merely a shadow of her former self. Faint whispers escaped her dried, cracked lips, and her energetic personality was gone. It was obvious her spirit had been broken, maybe even destroyed beyond repair. It was heart-wrenching to witness the disintegration of this dehydrated woman sitting before him, this tormented shell of a person who vaguely responded to the name, Domenique.

"I stabbed him," she muttered, tears rolling down her cheeks. "I don't know how he could have survived, but he did. He's possessed. Demons drive him. Did you see him? Did you see the lifelessness in his eyes?"

"Yes, I did," he said, trying to hold back his own tears of anguish. "But don't worry, André will be apprehended. Inspector Piedmont will catch him and make him pay for all he's done to you."

"Not for what he's done to me," she replied, a dazed expression on her face. "For what he did to him."

"To whom?"

"Monsignor Valois," she said. "André told me that he murdered Monsignor Valois, my natural father."

"What? Are you certain?"

"Yes," she said, her voice raising an octave. "He's mad! He's inhuman! I watched as he savagely beat the monsignor and then dragged him off. I waited, helpless. When he returned, he was covered in blood, bragging that he'd sent the monsignor back to his maker or something to that effect."

"Calm down, Domenique. Try not to think about it for the time being. Unfortunately, you'll have to relive it all over again when the inspector questions you. For now, let's just be grateful you're safe."

"You're right, Xavier," she said and smiled. "I have much to be grateful for, but at the moment, my head is spinning and my eyes ache. I'm having a difficult time adjusting to the bright light."

"How thoughtless of me," Xavier said, jumping to his feet, drawing back the heavy drapes with a quick tug. "You've been without sunlight for such a long time. Of course your eyes are sensitive. For now, I just want you to lay back and rest. We can talk again once you're feeling better. I have much to tell you."

"Allow me to formerly introduce myself," Piedmont said, entering the room covered in dust and grime. He walked over to the divan and extended his hand. "I'm Inspector Norbert Piedmont and I can't tell you how happy I am to finally make your acquaintance. For a while, I wasn't even sure this day would ever come to fruition. To put it in other words, your outcome looked bleak, but Father Xavier never gave up hope. Even with all the obstacles and distractions, he kept us moving forward, in your direction. I believe the direction was west. You should be proud to have such a brother."

"Thank you, Inspector," she replied, her eyes watery. "But it's all too much to comprehend. Between the kidnapping and everything I've recently learned about my past, I don't know what to think or how to feel." She sat upright and twisted her tortured body to face him. "What about André? He'll come back for me! He'll kill me!"

"Don't worry," Piedmont said. "He won't be hurting anyone anymore. He's dead."

"How did it happen?" Xavier asked.

"I shot him," he said, backing away with a confused expression, his eyes covered in a strange film. "I accidentally killed the bastard! When I thought he was finally cornered, I fired some warning shots, but a stray bullet must have caught him." He paced back and forth across the Oriental rug, scratching his balding head. "It was so dark and he let out such a horrific scream. It sent shivers up my spine."

"Inspector, are you all right?" Xavier asked. "You're mumbling."

"I'll be fine," Piedmont said. "It just happened so fast."

"Where's his body?" Xavier asked.

"I was too late," Piedmont said. "I thought I'd just wounded him, but by the time I reached him, he'd already fallen into a gaping hole. In my estimation, the bastard got off too easy. And my wife wonders why I have no faith in priests. Oh, excuse my vulgar description, Sister."

"Well, I can certainly understand your anger," Xavier said.

"If it's any consolation," Domenique said, rubbing her belly in a circular motion. "I have no faith in priests either. My days in the church are over thanks to André. It seems even though he's gone, he's still in control of my life."

"Don't say that, Domenique," Xavier said. "He's not controlling anything. He's dead. Just lay back and be calm until the ambulance arrives. For the time being, try to forget about him."

"He's right," Piedmont said, walking toward the door. "He's not worth the energy it takes to go to the bathroom."

Before Xavier had the chance to voice his opinion on the subject, Father Beaumont barreled into the room holding his chest, his face flushed.

369

"What's wrong, Father?" Piedmont asked. "Are you ill?"

"Is it true?" Father Beaumont asked, his voice trembling. "Is the monsignor really dead? I overheard Sergeant Major Roget on the telephone. I waited to ask him, but once he'd finished his conversation, he said something about needing to see Reverend Mother and dashed out the front door. Is everything he said about the monsignor true, Inspector?"

"I regret having to tell you this, Father Beaumont," Piedmont said. "But yes, Monsignor Valois was brutally murdered down in those damned tunnels. I found what was left of him in one of the chambers."

"Sweet Jesus!" Father Beaumont cried. "Who could have done such a horrible thing?"

"I'm sure that once forensics is finished with their investigation, they'll find André's signature all over the place."

"Holy heaven," Father Beaumont said, his hands flailing about his neck. "W-w-where is Father André?"

"There is no Father André," Piedmont said in a matter of fact tone.

"What do you mean?" Father Beaumont asked. "I don't understand."

"Father André Jeneau was an alias," Piedmont said. "He wasn't a priest at all. He was a killer. I'm certain Father Xavier will fill you in on all the details, but you should just be thankful that this André character won't be around to harm anyone ever again."

"He's right," Xavier said angrily. "He's the one who kidnapped and tortured Sister Domenique and murdered all those innocent children. The bastard got what he deserved."

"Father Xavier!" Father Beaumont said. "I've never heard you use such language. What is this world coming to?"

"Don't worry, Father," Xavier said with a smile. "I'm certain I'll receive absolution when we meet in the confessional. But for the moment, my sincerest wish is that André spends the rest of eternity in hell!"

"Amen to that," Domenique said, pulling the afghan closer to her neck. "Amen."

CHAPTER 62

In the months that followed, Domenique underwent extensive therapy. It took some time, but she was finally able to push the bad memories to the back of her mind and extinguish most of the nightmares. After much prompting from Father Xavier and Reverend Mother, she opted to keep the child and awaited its birth with a new and positive outlook. It appeared that motherhood was to be her calling in life and she welcomed it with open arms. She believed that her child was an inevitable gift from God. With her family's love, help, and support, all would turn out for the best.

It seemed that God had also ruled in Inspector Piedmont's favor, allowing him to make certain peace with his daughter's premature death and strengthening his belief in the Almighty. However, his faith in the church was gone, never to return. With everything in its proper prospective, he felt meritorious and free to accept the promotion to Superintendent for ridding the world of another serial killer, now known as the Curator of Souls. He promised himself that he'd never fall victim to any man again.

Over time, Grande Cache's inhabitants recovered from the tragedies as well. There was still the occasional car theft and a domestic violence report or two, but overall, the crime level returned to normal. For the first time in a very long time, life felt safe once again. However, even with the placidness, no one could ever forget the horror that had plagued the nation for nearly two years, nor the perpetrator's name, André. Though his body had been swallowed by the earth and he would never face the charges against him, he had gained an infamous reputation with the children.

In sadistic irony, they would skip rope and sing, "Watch your daughters, hold them tight. Let them go, they'll never see the light. He'll take them, break them, and stuff them in a tree. Around their liver, you'll find a rosary. So keep them close and stay around, because the Curator of Souls has never been found."